MY MONGREL PACK

BRIDGET E. BAKER

For Elijah
It's okay if you're different
Our differences make us incomparable
And that's how we're able to change the world

XANDER

On my first day of school, my dad wagged his tail and licked me on the nose. Then he ran off, leaving me to cower in front of three dozen other wolf pups many of whom were much larger than me.

Unlike normie school, where you're taught the alphabet and how to count, the main focus in the first year of were-school is learning your place. You then spend the rest of your formal education learning to excel in it or how to survive, depending on your family background and your strength level.

Something amazing happened on my first day—because of me.

It just didn't happen *to* me.

It usually takes weeks or sometimes even months for a new student to discover what variety of werewolf he or she is: innovator, ranger, nurturer, or shredder. The instructors put the pups through a variety of tasks designed to push our inner selves to the forefront. But for one of the wolves on that first day, all it took was his first scent of a normie.

Unfortunately, that normie was me.

A large black wolf, the normies would call him a grey wolf, turned to sniff my backside. It sounds nasty to normies, but it's a pretty common thing for were-wolves. To be honest, anything that smells really strong smells pretty good to us in wolf form. Fresh-baked cookies, taco meat, and sizzling fajitas are some of my favorites. But a fresh pile of dung, an old puddle of vomit, or the back end of another wolf all smell almost as good.

It took me a while to realize that butt-sniffing wasn't something other supernaturals really *got*.

So when this black wolf sniffed my butt, I just wagged my tail.

But then something strange happened. The fur along his back began to bristle, and a low growl started in his throat. His claws looked like they got *longer* and they dug into the dirt.

And then he attacked me.

Turns out, one of the major things that causes shred-ders to *wolf*, which is what we call leaning into the most primal part of ourselves, is the scent of a normie. They spend most of their training learning to rip other monsters to shreds, and learning *not* to attack people unless it's a strategically good idea. I've always felt it was pretty strange that they work on both attacking better and attacking less.

On that day, Lars discovered he was not only a shifter, but one who could go alpha, and I learned that wolf school isn't a very safe place. It took nearly three more years for me to figure out that I was also a shredder, just like Lars, because I also happen to be the worst, least intuitive shredder known to wolf kind.

If I could just have been born a ranger, a nurturer, or an innovator, I'd have been fine. Innovators come up with new ideas. They organize and manage and teach. Every night, when I finally curled into a ball, covering my face with my tail, I'd secretly pray that I'd turn out to be an innovator. A nurturer wouldn't have been so bad either—they're supposed to care for others, plus they fix problems and make rough things alright. I'd have loved to be a ranger, too. They test things, explore them, and scout new areas. Even as a halfie, I'd probably have been accepted if I were an innovator, a ranger, or a nurturer.

So coming up as a shredder was just really, monumentally bad luck on my part. They're the worst of the lot. They just fight, and as a halfie, I smell strange enough to make almost all the other shredders irritable. It made for a *lot* of fighting, and on my side, a *loooot* of losing.

Funny enough, your average wolf usually wants to be a shredder. They change quickly, they're stronger, and they heal the fastest of any type. They're also the only type of wolf that can be born with the ability to become an alpha. It's rare—maybe one in seventy-five shredders can even become alphas. Only alphas can start packs, of course, but even if I *had* been an alpha, it wouldn't have helped me a bit.

No one would join a pack with a halfie alpha. In fact, in more than twenty years, I've yet to find a pack that will even let me join them. I've wondered from time to time, whether if I'd had those extra three years to learn to kill better and constrain my inner wolf with more strength, I'd have become a better shredder, but I doubt it. My weakness and my skill both suffer from the same thing: I'm a halfie, so my whole heart just isn't in it.

Normies and shredders are just really incompatible. My dad should have known that. I mean, it's not like your type of wolf is always passed on to your pups, but for him it was. He was a shredder, so what was he thinking with my mom?

My life has been like one ongoing cosmic joke.

After Dad realized I was a shredder like him, he did what any smart werewolf dad with a halfie son would do. He called up my mother and asked her to enroll me in normie school.

That's how, at the age of seven, I wound up with a little blue backpack, a pencil box with very sharp, very yellow, very pointy pencils, and a pair of blunt tipped scissors, standing in front of Ridgemont Elementary. I clutched the handle on my Last Airbender lunchbox as tightly as I could and repeated the mantra Mom made me memorize over and over.

"I will not go furry. I will not go furry. No matter what happens, no matter what anyone says, I will not go furry."

Three years at a were-school had taught me enough control for that, I hoped.

Mom was terrified it hadn't.

But Dad told me that compared to were-school, normie school was a piece of cake. I hoped that was true, because I really liked cake. And as long as I didn't get attacked in the first five minutes, it would be better than were-school, right?

Poor little Xander had no idea.

Nothing about my life would bear any resemblance to cake. People like cake. They ask for more. They pay money for it. They write songs about it, or if they don't, they should.

But no one wants more Xander. They don't pay for it —they don't like it.

I'd barely put my Last Airbender lunchbox into the lunch wagon by my teacher's desk when things went awry. It had been more than five minutes—probably closer to thirty—so I guess that was better than my were-school first day.

But that's when I smelled it—someone was bleeding.

Wolves aren't quite as bad as sharks. We don't become mindless when we smell blood, but shredders react strongly to it. When I smelled it that day, the mantra ran through my head.

I will not go furry.

Shredders either shift in times of stress, or they step up and help in other ways. We aren't made to just sit around. I'd had enough training to know that if I didn't want to shift, I needed to find the source of blood and help that person.

"Who's hurt?" I asked.

"Huh?" The girl next to me frowned. "What do you mean?"

"Someone's bleeding," I said.

"You're crazy." She scooted her chair as far from me as she could and glanced at me sideways.

"I'm not." Although, my stress level was rising. "Someone's bleeding."

"Why do you think that?" The kid across from me shoved his glasses up. He looked around. "Everyone looks fine, new kid."

"I can *smell* it," I finally said.

And that's when the teacher walked past, and the

smell washed over me like an ocean wave. . .of acrid copper and tangy rust. It was strong—not just a small cut. "It's you." I turned and grabbed her arm. "Where did you get hurt? Why are you bleeding?"

She yanked her hand away. "I'm not bleeding." Her lip curled.

"You are," I said. "Actually—" That's when it hit me. I'd smelled it before, from other wolves and even from my mother. My teacher was in heat. "Oh." I smiled. "Never mind. You're not hurt. You're in heat."

Her face had turned bright red and her lip curled. She practically snarled, "Shut your mouth, you little brat."

The biggest thing I'd learned in three years at were-school was that you never, ever, ever back down when someone challenges you. If you do, you're sure to be eaten alive. I can't tell you the number of scratches, scrapes, bruises, and full-on lacerations I received because my natural instinct was to apologize. After literally having it beaten into me for three years, I had learned to stand up for myself. I'd still take a beating, but it wouldn't be nearly as bad.

So when she told me to shut up, I got up in her face and gave as good as I got. "No, you shut up, you female dog." Only, I didn't say *female dog*. In my defense, the word I used was a commonly used word at were-school.

Before I knew it, she was marching me and my little blue backpack to the principal's office. He called my mom, and that was my first and last day at that school. That stupid teacher never even gave me my Last Airbender lunchbox back. Of course, now that I'm an adult, I understand why she got so upset. But I was just a kid! I doubt the other first graders had any idea what was going on. Clearly she wasn't someone with a very strong constitution.

Mom actually had to move us in order to enroll me in a new school. I'd have felt worse if she didn't move all the time anyway. She was never very good at her job, and she got fired a lot.

On my first day at the next school, I didn't have a Last Airbender lunchbox. All Mom could find was Sponge Bob, which was so cringey that I held it backward so no one could see the image. That third first day of school, I stuck to my mantra, but I took it a step further. I compiled a *list* of things to make it easier not to go furry.

1. Don't say anything at all unless absolutely required.

2. Never draw attention to yourself.

3. Watch others to see what they're doing before you act.

And above all:

4. Never growl, scowl, or call names.

Thanks to my comprehensive list, and my mother making me watch several hours a day of normie television, I was able to avoid any huge disasters this time around. In fact, I buckled down and worked as hard as I could. I studied, and I paid attention, and I became the best version of a normie child that I could possibly become.

I learned the alphabet, and then I managed to start reading Dr. Seuss. He was my favorite. The rhyming, the silly words, and the bright and cheerful drawings made me smile.

But when my report card came out, sealed in a little brown envelope that I could read, *For Mrs. Binnigas*, I knew that was going to frost her cookies. She and I didn't share the same last name, since she never married Dad. I thought about crossing it out and writing *For Mrs. Haverly*, but I figured she'd notice. My handwriting wasn't the best, yet. I felt proud when I handed it to her, in spite of my concern she'd be mad about the name.

Were-school didn't have grades. They simply had winners and losers, and I was the consummate loser. I figured that had prepared me, just in case my grades were bad. So when Mom opened that envelope, already irritated as I knew she would be about the name, I thought she might actually smile. I imagined she'd hug me for once, and tell me good job or pat me on the head.

Instead, her face fell. Her eyes snapped upward, locking on mine. "Are you kidding me?"

I blinked. "About what?"

"You're failing first grade? How can you fail *first grade?*"

And that's when I learned that normies have winners and losers, too. It's not as obvious, maybe. It's not as savage, but it's not as honest either. When I went home from wolf school as a loser, I was covered in blood. I was limping. I couldn't meet my dad's eye, and I knew why.

But the normies sent me home with a little brown square that looked just like all the other little brown squares that all the kids got. I had no idea that Mom would have the same look on her face that Dad had: disappointment, shame, and disgust. Because I wasn't prepared for it, it hurt worse.

The normies make you think you might be alright. They make you hope that you'll be accepted. And then they yank the rug right out from under you and make you sleep on the wood floor with nothing to eat for dinner. Over time, I was able to bring those grades up a bit, but Mom didn't seem to notice or care by then. To her, as to my dad, as to my entire wolf pack and my normie teachers, I was the same.

A loser.

Not a good normie.

A miserably bad wolf.

There wasn't a place for me anywhere in this world. So I stuck to the shadows around other wolves, hoping I wouldn't be noticed. And with normies, I'd crack as many jokes as I could and hope no one could tell how empty I felt inside.

2

CLARK

My sister never forgot anything in her entire life. She's the most Type-A, organized person I've ever met.

But one day, her junior year of high school—my freshman year of college—she was recovering from a cold, and she slept in, and she accidentally set her book report on the edge of the counter in the kitchen. It slipped off when she grabbed her pile of books, and that meant that when she got to school, she had no report to submit.

I'd already finished my classes and had driven home for the weekend, so I got her panicked message on the machine when I walked in the door.

"Hello! Mom! It's me, Minerva!" As if Mom wouldn't have recognized her panicked voice immediately. Minerva makes Jennifer Lopez seem low key. "I think my book report fell out of the pile of stuff I brought and it's probably on the floor, either in the entry hall, or maybe in the kitchen. Or you could check my room. But I need it. Now!" She pauses, and somehow I can still hear the panic in her breathing. "Please, Mom! I need it!"

I laugh a bit at her complete terror—as if one book report could impact her bulletproof grades—but I scoop the report up off the floor where it's innocently staring up at me, and I head back out to my car. I had no idea that one good deed would change the course of my life forever.

That's the first time I ever clapped eyes on Roxana Goldenscales.

I had no idea what was coming, of course, not when I grabbed a name tag from the front office. Not when I sauntered down the hallway, looking for Mrs. White's history class. And certainly not when I opened the door, completely unwitting. But when my eyes scanned the room, they stopped dead in their tracks.

Roxana was chatting with Minerva, a half-smile on her face, her golden scales gleaming at the edge of her cheek. Her shimmery golden eyes flashed, and her ebony hair shimmered, and my heart went into a-fib.

Okay, not really, but that's what it felt like.

I didn't make the best impression.

I'm not sure how many times Minerva's teacher, Mrs. White, called out to me before I finally stopped staring at Roxana and noticed she was alive.

"Hello? Are you alright, sir?"

"He's not a sir," Minerva said. "He's a Clark." She chucked an eraser at my head. That woke me up. "Hey, dummy. I need that report for next period."

I finally managed to peel my eyes away from Roxana and remembered that I was holding her report. "Right." I crossed the room and set it on Minerva's desk. I knew I should turn around and go, but I didn't know Roxana's name yet, and I couldn't seem to leave without discovering it.

"Thanks." Minerva flicks the top of my hand. "You can go back to researching spells that will make you a fake girlfriend now."

People in the room giggled, and I didn't care. But *she* giggled, and I wanted to die. "Shut up," I said. "I don't need that. I have a real girlfriend."

Minerva's eyebrows shot up like firecrackers. "No, you shut up. You're such a liar."

"I actually have a class to teach, Mr. . . . ?" The teacher looked more amused than anything else, but I knew I couldn't stay there, staring stupidly forever.

"Clark Lucent," I finally said. "And what's your name?" I stared down at Minerva's friend, trying to look dashing.

Judging by the way she frowned, I had succeeded in looking more desperate than dashing. "Roxana."

"Roxana *Goldenscales*," Minerva said. "My best friend. Doy."

That's when I realized that she was the daughter of *the* Santiago Goldenscales, CEO of the Dagobar Group.

"When can we expect you to leave, Mr. Lucent?" In retrospect, Mrs. White was actually pretty patient with me. But at the time, I spent most of my walk back to my car thinking of ways to hex her.

In all the fantasies I had about me and Roxana over the years, and I had a *lot*, I never once faced off against her fiancé, Ragar the Ruthless, the reining dragon prince of Russia. Mostly I focused on kissing Roxana, not roasting her enemies.

So when Lionel Sol, son of the Grand Chancellor of the Illuminae, steps between a livid red Ragar—in dragon form—and Roxana, I'm not exactly jealous. Or, at least, not super jealous.

After all, I doubt I'll be kissing Roxana if I'm a blackened pile of ash.

"You steal my wife?" Ragar asks.

Although, if I'm being honest, I know that's what he asked, but it sounded more like "Voo szdeel my vife?" His Russian accent, combined with the enormous teeth he's sporting in his dragon form, don't make his angry words super clear.

"I'm sorry," Lionel says. "I can't quite understand you. Care to shrink down to your far less impressive but hopefully more comprehensible form?"

"Vat?" Ragar's sides heave, and molten bits of blackish-reddish char spray from his mouth.

"Right. I forget you're monumentally stupid," Lionel says. "Let me use smaller words." He opens his eyes really wide. "You no make sense. Please shrink down." He uses his hands, pressing them together slowly in front of him, to show Ragar that he wants him smaller.

Ragar, clearly understanding that he's being mocked, digs his claws even farther into the concrete, sending cracks running several feet away.

"Hya!" Santiago Goldenscales shouts. "Stop ruining my plaza." In his human form, he's entirely clear, and his irritation actually gives Ragar pause.

The giant red dragon carefully lifts one front leg and reaches for Roxana. "Mine."

That word, at least, is crystal clear.

Lionel's ready, though. His wand, popping into his hand, flicks, and sparks fly, exploding against Ragar's talons. "No. Bad dragon." He smiles devilishly. "She's *mine*."

Ragar rears back, whether as a result of Lionel's attack or to show the vehemence of his claim I'm not sure, and releases the most horrifying, solid stream of liquid fire that I've ever seen.

Again, seemingly unphased, Lionel pulls Roxana closer and spins his wand in tiny circles, the tip pointed upward. It happens so fast that the flames haven't yet reached them when a bright blue bubble snaps into place around them, gleaming.

A *very* high-level protection spell.

But all that fire has to go somewhere. It glances off Lionel's ward and. . .comes careening toward my friends. If I set another ward, it'll merely deflect it into more people who have gathered to watch the showdown. Instead, I dig deep into one of my energy wells and chant. *"Trahunt valorem ad me."*

Please let this work! Because if my spell's not strong enough to withstand however much energy Ragar throws out, or if my extra energy well isn't big enough, it's going to spill over.

And then I'm going to melt into a Clark-flavored puddle of goo.

The fire stops spreading and pulls toward me, funneling just as I ordered it to, more and more and more, and I immediately start to feel the strain of it. The great thing about an absorption spell is that, if the force is strong enough, you recapture more than you spend. It's hard for mages to cast these, but they've always been my highest aptitude.

I've had a knack for stealing energy since I was a kid.

It made Minerva crazy—instead of her spells working on me, I'd often steal them mid-cast, repurposing the energy for something I wanted.

Seeing that his attack isn't working as planned, Ragar finally stops.

Just in time. My wells are now entirely full. If he had kept going for a few more seconds, I'd be dead for sure. As it is, I've never been more powerful. It's a heady feeling, and I need to be careful of it. Mages who have more power than they're used to sometimes do really stupid things.

The blue bubble winks out. "Now that you know that fire tantrums won't work, what else do you have?" Lionel cocks one eyebrow like he's totally unconcerned.

Ragar, shocking us all, shifts. The enormous, fiery red dragon collapses inward, scales rolling over themselves and black smoke rising up. Seconds later, his head lifts above the dark, billowing cover, his ebony hair mussed but still irritatingly shiny. He's wearing a charcoal suit with a crimson shirt and a shimmery black tie.

When wolves shift, they come to as naked as the day they were born, but dragona pack a slightly larger magical punch. I'd heard that the strong ones keep their clothing intact on either end of a shift—I guess it's true. How wonderful to discover that Ragar's as strong as they say.

Lionel still looks confident, cocky even, but there's an edginess in the way he moves, placing himself in front of Roxana slightly, that tells me he knows that even in human form, Ragar's a significant threat.

And then Ragar raises his right arm, waving slightly.

The main entrance into the Dagobar building is large, with massive double doors. Roxana's father and his men occupy that space, keeping most people's attention if they dare to look away from Ragar and Lionel.

So when dozens of men in black suits pour out of the

small, side door, it takes me by surprise. Another half dozen large dragons begin to land around Ragar on all sides—bronze, brown, copper, black, and even off-white. They must have been circling pretty high, or perhaps I was just hugely distracted by the raging crimson dragon in front of me.

Of course he wasn't too nervous to shift.

He's got eighteen other dragons with him who all obey his command, every one of them ready to tear Lionel into magic-imbued mulch.

"Ah, the mob's finally here," Lionel says. "I was wondering when your goons would show up. Are you thinking that my bubble won't work when hit on all sides?"

"Real men do not need bubbles." Ragar's smile is practically wicked. "Real men attack."

"Real men don't have scales," Lionel says. "Real men use their brains, not their brawn."

I've never been impressed by Lionel, whom I knew as Lincoln Sunset. He never got anything done, he was chronically late, and he constantly made jokes at terrible times. But now that I'm seeing him for who he really is, I have to admit that I'm fairly impressed. If I was standing up there facing off against one dragon, much less nineteen, I'd probably wet my pants.

I do wonder what his plan is—given that he seems to have zero backup.

"Hand Roxana over," Ragar says. "Or we'll burn you like faggots."

"That word doesn't really mean what you think it means anymore," Lionel says. "You'll probably want to get a new English tutor."

"Now." Ragar steps toward Roxana, his arm outstretched.

And Lionel mutters, "*Frigidus in glaciem.*"

Not duratus, which would lock him into place. He literally shoots off a spell to ice Ragar over. I'm not sure it'll even work on a creature of fire, but even if it does, it really seems like a very bad call.

Ragar's hand frosts first, and then his body stops moving, and then his entire frame turns blue and ice runs down his legs, sealing him to the pavement he destroyed earlier.

The men behind Ragar reach for weapons—some guns, some swords, and one of them an actual axe. "You attack us, Prinz?" the stockiest one shouts. "Then you die."

"Ah, ah, ah," Lionel says. "If you actually attack me, you'll be declaring war on the Illuminae. You might want to get the approval of your thug-in-chief before you do something like that."

I'm not sure how much of what's going on the dragona understand, but they're speaking Russian to one another at about three thousand miles per hour right now, so I figure it's enough. Finally, the stocky one steps forward. "On behalf of our lord, I challenge you to a personal duel. If you lose, you die."

"And if I win?"

"You live," the stocky man with a thick brown beard and flashing black eyes says.

"How tempting," Lionel says. "But I think I'll have to decline."

"Then we'll attack you and everyone who came with you." They look at Xander, Bevin, Izaak, Minerva, and me.

I stumble back a step.

"Whoa, chief," Xander says. "I didn't even come with him."

"Neither did I," Bevin says. "I don't even know him."

"You were with her earlier." The stocky man points at Roxana, and I remember seeing him in the coffee shop.

How could he possibly remember that?

"You're saying that if I don't agree to fight you in a battle to the death, you'll kill those people I don't know or care about?" Lionel shrugs. "Go ahead."

"Wait," Roxana says. "I care about them."

It's slight, but Lionel shakes his head.

Is he trying to protect us by calling their bluff? Or is he telling her not to bother?

"Alright," the stocky dragona says. "I'll do it, and we'll see how your girlfriend likes you when you let her followers die." He lifts his hand and the dragons all swing their heads our direction, inhaling deeply like they do right before they blow fire.

Why isn't Roxana's dad stepping in? Why isn't *anyone* doing anything?

There's no way my overfull energy wells can take that much heat—so if I try and use the same trick I did before, I'll die a few seconds before all my friends melt. Before I have time to think anything through, the words just burst out.

"I'll fight you," I say. "But if I win, I don't just get to live. Roxana gets to come back home with us. You're right—we're her friends, and she's happier with us than she ever was here."

"And if you lose?" the dragona asks. "Other than your death, what do we get?"

"I'll go home with my mother and father if he loses," Roxana says. "And I'll marry Ragar, but I need your promise that either way, you won't kill my other friends."

She'll marry him if I lose? My anxiety was already through the roof, what with my life being on the line, but it felt like my only play. But now her future rests with me, too?

"Challenges are carried out on the top floor," Santiago Goldenscales says. "It's easier to block them from the humans that way."

And also, all that flying jackal has to do is push me off the edge and I'll lose. Dragona don't have safety rails on their rooftops, or so I hear. Why in the world did I open my big, fat mouth? Lionel probably knew that goon wouldn't follow through with his threat.

That's why he did nothing, right?

The pulsing of energy in my stupid wells reminds me why I spoke up so fast. All the power I inhaled is lying to me. I'm a decent warlock, of course, and my spellcraft is pretty good, but I've never been in a real fight. This guy looks like he's been in dozens. In fact, he has some weird necklace strung with what looks an awful lot like some kind of bones. Does he keep a knuckle bone from everyone he kills or something?

I shudder at the thought of him adding mine.

In movies, this is where it would cut straight to the fight scene—but in real life, it's not like that. You have to suffer through every awkward, off-putting moment that connects the big proclamation to the main event. So I follow Roxana and Lionel into the elevator, and the guy I'm about to fight to the death climbs in right after me. Minerva forces herself into the same elevator, crowding Roxana's parents into the corner.

"Sorry—he's my brother. So, I feel like I can't really leave him to go up alone." Her stupid, dodgy pigeon flutters into the elevator just as the doors are closing and lands on her shoulder, cooing brightly, like we're *en route* to a dinner party.

It's the single most awkward moment of my life. Which is one hundred percent why I toot. I always get gassy when I'm nervous.

Minerva's eyes cut sideways and she tugs her jacket over her mouth and nose.

"Thank you for standing up for me," Roxana says. Clearly she hasn't smelled anything yet.

"Yeah." Minerva drops her jacket. "I'm so proud of you for stepping up back there."

"Proud?" The Russian dragon scowls. And then his right eye blinks rapidly, like something is stuck in it— probably just caught wind of my fart.

Only, he doesn't cough or shake his head, or do anything at all to indicate he's going to stop reacting to it. In fact, if anything, his eye twitch only becomes more pronounced as we travel upward. And it's not like he's blinking or something. His one eye keeps slamming closed over and over, and then his mouth starts to make this clicking sound as his head pulls to the side slightly.

Did I make him sick with my gas? Are dragona super susceptible to bodily smells? I feel like I would have heard this before if that were true. And wouldn't Roxana also be reacting? And her parents?

As we approach the top of the elevator, Roxana finally asks, "Not that I really care, but are you alright?"

Maybe he's suffering from some kind of poison. Did Lionel do something while everyone was distracted? Am I saved?

A quick glance in his direction and a shrug from Lionel, and I realize we're all as lost as can be.

"He suffers from something called Meige Syndrome," Roxana's mother says. "It was on the paperwork we had to process to get their visas. It's a harmless facial twitch that worsens in times of emotional stress."

Like when he's about to kill someone. My toot clearly didn't cause that—too bad. I could do with a superpower right about now, even one like toxic nerve gas farts.

"So you're nervous?" Lionel asks. "That's not very manly."

I doubt my opponent's English is good enough for him to truly understand, judging by his blank look.

Realizing the same thing, I think, Lionel says something in Russian. Which the guy definitely understands, judging by the set of his jaw and the way his hands clench.

"Oh, thanks," I say. "In case he wasn't furious before, rile him up more."

"I got your back," Lionel says.

"It doesn't really feel like you do," I say.

"Oh, I do," Lionel says. "By stepping in, you staved off a war, and even though I might have been happy to finally do something, the more I thought about it, the more I realized that my dad would probably not be pleased. I bet he handsomely awards your family after your death."

I cough. "I think you mean he'll *reward* my family."

Minerva splutters. "As a family member, I can safely say that we don't want an award or a reward—we don't want Clark to die at all."

The stupid dragona definitely understands this whole

interchange. His eye has stopped the repetitive blinking, and his mouth isn't making any sounds at all, but his smile is practically filled with delight. "Yes. Your death."

And with that, the elevator bings and the doors open.

"After you." I gesture for him to get out.

Only, there isn't room. We're so tightly packed inside that I can't just wait for him to get off first. I'm stuck turning my back on the horrifying shifter and walking out onto the very dark patio all by myself.

Luckily Minerva springs out just afterward. I'd feel better about having her here if she wasn't channeling her derpy spirit animal—who is probably about as erratic and unreliable as her spell casting. "Okay, so here's what you do." She yanks a ring off her finger and jams it onto my pinkie. "I only have the one energy well with me, but with that, you should be able to cast—"

I put a hand on her forearm and squeeze. "It's alright," I say, aiming for looking cool in my last moments, at least.

"Clark, you need to do a two-step attack. First block, but set up a—"

"Are you ready to begin?" Santiago Goldenscales asks. And then he begins to ripple—the same dark smoke rising up around him for a split second before the sound of rolling and roaring and ripping surrounds me and a golden mountain rises up in front of us. His head whips up last, his brilliant eyes flashing, smoke rising from his flared nostrils. "You will not touch any bystanders. You will only attack one another." His enormous, savage head swivels from the stocky dragona to me and back again. "Are we clear?"

I'm shocked by how crisp and clean Santiago's speech is while in dragon form. Especially compared to Ragar's butchering of the language earlier. Maybe it's because it's his second language? Although, given his age, English has to be Santiago's second or third language.

Interrupting my thoughts, the stocky man I'm about to fight is also engulfed in the same stupid black smoke and then a smaller mountain—more of a hill—of shiny, ebony scales roll and churn and slide and a head whips upward. How have I never made note of the order of their shift before?

Probably because I've only seen shifts on television until now—never up close. It's just not very common for me to see dragona at all. They're the rarest of the supernatural races, and they're very private. If these weren't my very last moments on Earth, I'd probably be more fascinated by all of it.

"If you harm my daughter," Santiago says—

"Or my sister," I say.

"I'll end you myself." Santiago's mouth opens wide and he bares his fangs. "Are we clear?"

The stocky dragon's head is as long as my thigh. It slowly rises and falls. "Yesh," he says, as if his teeth are too large for his mouth and he can't quite form words with them.

"Then you may begin." And with that very inauspicious little phrase, apparently we're underway.

"Oh." Roxana scampers backward, hiding behind Lionel. So much for hoping something might intervene to save me, like an army of mages, or some kind of scholar with an obscure law. Isn't that what usually happens before the hero is roasted in books and television shows? But for the first time, something occurs to me.

What if I'm not the hero?

I guess everyone *thinks* they're the hero, right up until they die and everyone forgets their name. Clark Lucent, side character extraordinaire. Tried to be a hero and was roasted and eaten by the Russian dragona thugs in Act I.

By Michael's wings, what was I thinking?

I whip out my wand. At least I didn't like, drop it, or break it. What was it Minerva was saying I should do? Cast a shield spell, and then. . .Before I can chant a single thing, a giant taloned claw reaches out and bats me sideways.

And unlike the movies, I'm too shocked to stop it. It sends me sprawling, my shoulder and the left side of my face colliding with the rough concrete of the building. Pain explodes down that side of my body, and before I can even lift to my knees, heat rolls over me.

I snap a protection bubble into place, barely, but I didn't have time for any kind of offensive spell or enchantment. And unlike that time with Ragar, no one's absorbing his heat, so it's starting to melt the frame around me. The metal supports are bright red, and the concrete's heating in a circle around my protection bubble.

I'm literally about to fall through the ground onto the floor below us.

"That's enough," Santiago shouts.

The fire cuts off just before I drop downward like a hamster in a ball. Too bad I can't roll to a less well-done spot. Protection spells don't work like that.

A huge taloned foot slams against my bubble and it

vibrates, pulling more energy from the well Minerva gave me. The second time he slams against me, that well runs out and my protection evaporates.

The heat that slams into me when it pops out of existence feels like an iron to the face. The ends of my hair start to singe. The smell is not inspiring.

I pull on my largest energy well—can't have it blinking out again—and shape the energy into a sharp line. "Hastam en corde!" I shout. The power shoots out of me like a spear, just as I told it to, spitting and turning toward the charcoal dragon's heart, I hope.

He bats it out of the way.

He *bats* it, pure magical energy, and it veers out and over the sky next to our building, hurtling away from me. More than half of my energy reserve is now gone.

"How could he—"

"Dragona are creatures of pure magic," Lionel says. "Direct energy-based attacks can be countered as if they were tangible weapons. You must not have paid much attention in Intraspecies Battle Tactics."

I never even *took* Intraspecies Battle Tactics, because when would a research scientist ever use—another taloned hand slams into my side, this time my already-injured-and-bleeding left side, and flings me off the building. I hang in the air for a millisecond before dropping downward.

Giggles the pigeon is fluttering next to me, squeaking as if she's trying to tell me something.

And I realize that I'm falling slowly—too slowly. Minerva's doing something. If anyone notices she's interfering, she'll be killed. You cannot involve yourself in someone else's duel.

"*Trahunt me ad suror mea.*"

I've never tried to summon myself to someone else who's casting a spell, but to my shock, it works. Only, instead of being dragged to my sister, like I should have been, I seem to be tied to Giggles. As she flies toward the building again, I'm being dragged along with her.

When I run out of energy, the spell snaps, dropping me on the edge of the building inelegantly. Both my arms are broken, I'm pretty sure, and that angry black dragon isn't happy I'm back.

This time, when he inhales in order to roast me, I cast the strongest protection spell I've ever made—and for some reason, it's opaque. Once I'm inside the bubble I've made, pulling energy from my last well, I can't see a thing. I'm stuck like a bug under a cup of my own making.

My energy slowly trickling away.

Wasting the last few seconds of my life alone. Terrified.

As the last of my power funnels into the bubble, I look upward. I have no idea if the akero actually live up high, but they do fly, so I rattle off my final prayer to them, my face upturned. "Please, mighty Michael, powerful Raphael, generous Gabriel, please let the dragona honor their word and let my friends be safe so my sacrifice isn't a complete waste."

As the well drains, I switch to auxiliary power, which is the innate strength all mages are born with. The dragon's flame must be really, really hot, because it doesn't last long before I'm on my last little scraps of strength.

I don't want to die, but it's not the worst way to go—at least being roasted after my spell gives out should be quick. Like an oven that's been pre-heated to a million degrees, I should be incinerated in seconds. A split second, maybe.

And finally, everything goes black, even the ground inside my tiny energy-fueled bug cup.

3

ROXANA

"I can't believe you let him do this," I mutter. "You're the one who started all this."

Lionel quirks an eyebrow at me, looking utterly unconcerned as Clark's batted around like a mouse being played with by a barn cat. "He's the moron who caused all this. That underling wasn't empowered to fight me, and he wouldn't have killed random people in the United States while here on a wedding visa. If he'd tried in earnest, your dad would have destroyed them."

I was pretty sure—from the hours and hours I spent in etiquette classes—that Ragar's lieutenant was bluffing. But Clark clearly didn't know they were safe, and his brave defense of both me and our friends is touching.

And now he's being smashed like recalcitrant steel in a forge, his protection bubble looking perilously weak.

"That's enough," Daddy says.

I'm relieved he seems to care about Clark not actually dying. But then as the irritating coal dragon whams his foot against Clark's bubble, I realize Dad was just worried about the frame of his building not melting and collapsing.

He seems to be enjoying Clark being killed. He's smiling while the stupid dragon whams against Clark's flickering protection bubble. And then, after his protection bubble gives out, Clark totally wastes a large amount of energy by shooting it right at the bully of a dragon.

Who bats it away with a bemused expression on his scaly face.

How could Clark challenge him without knowing the basics about combat with dragona? He looks utterly perplexed. "How could he—"

"Dragona are creatures of pure magic," Lionel hisses. "Direct energy-based attacks can be countered as if they were tangible weapons. You must not have paid much attention in Intraspecies Battle Tactics."

Clark's eyes widen and his hands tremble. He swallows, his Adam's apple bobbing.

And then he gets knocked sideways and disappears. I have no idea what happens, but somehow he ties himself to a bird—wait, is that *Giggles?*—and flies back up to the building.

Only to be roasted.

Again.

Sometimes I hate dragona. I mean, I am one, technically, but I feel like I'm actually just a dragona-incubator. I can't do any of the horrifying and awe-inspiring things they can. I can't protect anyone. I can't even fly.

But as I watch Clark being incinerated slowly, roasted inside some kind of black bubble like slow-cooked pork, I can't stand it anymore. He can't just *die.* Not when my return is what caused all of this. I came back to help my friends, to stop making their lives suck. Not so I could watch them die.

The black bubble around Clark's flickering, just like the bubble did right before it gave out earlier.

I think about how Clark spent hours and hours making potions to hide me. I think about how he turned me blue—but fixed it. About how he helped me find a job. About how he helped me do laundry. And how he followed me here when I left, throwing himself into peril.

All because of me.

I grit my teeth and do something I've never done.

Sprint forward, unconcerned about my own safety, and fling myself in front of the stream of fire that's about to end my friend. As I do it, I realize that I'll probably be the one who dies instead.

But isn't that more fair? Isn't it just?

That's what I'm thinking as I leap in front of the flames spewing from the miserable dragon's mouth.

Dragona love hot things. Saunas, summer days, the desert. But this takes heat to a new level. It feels like my skin is melting from my body, and my arms and legs are exploding.

But when I look down, I'm totally fine.

I mean, I'm naked. My clothing all burned away, but the rest of me is entirely unharmed. And instead of just a few golden scales that show on my cheek, my shoulder, and my upper thighs, my entire body is shining like the sun—a huge mass of glittering golden scales.

My father starts shouting a stream of profanities in Spanish, the likes of which I've never before heard. And then my father roars and snaps the other dragon's neck with his teeth.

I knew my dad was big, but I had no idea he could decapitate a dragon who was breathing flame with a single bite. The large head hits the rooftop with an enormous thud, blood spraying all over me. Ironically, it's far more disgusting and concerning than the flames were.

"What just happened?" My mother sprints toward me, her hand outstretched. But when her fingers touch my skin, they blacken and smoke rises away from them.

"I knew I'd be fine, Mom," I say. "I'm dragona, remember?"

She shakes her head, mute.

"Female dragons aren't immune to flame," Dad says. "Your mother still has a scar from years ago."

Mom turns and tugs her shirt upward, exposing a melted section of skin on her back. "You should be dead right now."

That reminds me. I spin around and check out Clark behind me. He's curled into a fetal ball and he looks very, very pale, but he's definitely alive. Giggles flutters down to land by his side, cooing and clicking and fluffing up around him. Clark's nostrils are flaring slightly, and his chest is rising and falling incrementally. I breathe a heavy sigh of relief.

"What were you thinking?" This time, Dad's voice comes from right beside me, and it's his normal voice.

I turn to face my dad in his human form. He is not pleased.

"Oh, I'm sorry. Are you upset that I didn't let that—" I jab my finger at the grotesque head lying in a pool of black blood. "—kill my friend?" I put my hands on my very naked hips. "Because you certainly didn't do anything about it."

Lionel drapes a jacket around my shoulders. "Nice

work, by the way," he says. Then he whistles. "And you must work out. Bravo."

Before I can even say anything, Dad backhands him, and he goes sprawling across the rooftop. He hops to his feet, spluttering.

"You're going to let that go," I say. "Because your comment was in poor taste."

He rolls his eyes, but he also nods. "It was, you're right. I deserved that."

As I begin cooling off, my golden scales start to disappear, my normal skin taking its place, and I feel more naked than ever. I pull Lionel's much-too-large coat tighter, and I'm grateful it covers me down to my upper thighs, at least.

"I doubt Ragar's going to be pleased when he thaws," Lionel says.

"When do you think that will be?" Dad asks.

Lionel shrugs. "Maybe half an hour or so?"

"You should be gone when he wakes up," Dad says, his expression dark. "I'll deal with him."

"What?" I ask.

"*What?*" Minerva asks. "You'll. . .you'll deal with him?"

Dad nods. "I had no idea you were so opposed to the match, or that you'd fallen in love with someone else." He glares at Lionel. "However stupid."

Before I can correct him, Minerva flies off the handle. "Where was all this fatherly affection before my brother almost got fricasseed? Do non-dragons just not matter to you at all?"

Dad turns toward her slowly, a supremely irritated expression on his face, as if he's being harassed by a member of the paparazzi. "You don't matter to me, no."

His expression is dark—he has a long night ahead of him, dealing with Ragar and the other Russians. He may be powerful, but he's still going to be putting up with a lot of drama and danger because of me.

"Darling." Mom places a hand on his shoulder, her manicured fingers curling around him and squeezing. "She doesn't understand politics. She's a nobody."

"She's my friend," I say. "And she and her brother just did their best to protect me. They've been protecting me for weeks now."

"Then you better get out of my sight, quickly," Dad says. "Before I change my mind."

Minerva's eyes widen, and she whips out her wand.

"Let me," Lionel says. "Your reputation precedes you."

My best friend's eyes narrow. "How could you—"

Lionel walks away as if she wasn't even talking. "*Leva et sequere*," he mutters, and with a twist of his wrist, Clark floats up into the air, moaning slightly, and begins to float along behind him. Lionel wastes no time marching toward the elevator. Another flick of his wand and the button on the elevator for 'down' lights up. "Coming?" He arches that same superior eyebrow again.

I hate how cocky he is. I hate how dismissive. I also can't stand the fact that he instigated this entire thing and then simply stood back and watched as poor Clark, who clearly has less than half his power and none of his training, took all the heat. Literally.

Minerva must be thinking the same thing as me, but we both march across the rooftop and walk into the elevator when the doors open. Because we may not like Lionel much, but he's sort of saving Clark, and there's only one way down.

No one wants to be here when Ragar thaws.

"You are a singularly horrible magical being," Minerva says as the doors close.

"Why, thank you," he says. "Dad raised me to be absolutely savage." He brushes a piece of lint off one sleeve and reaches toward me.

I dance back. "She wasn't paying you a compliment," I say. "She didn't mean that you were being fierce back there."

Lionel, utterly nonplussed, darts toward me, his hand sliding into the pocket of his jacket. He fishes his phone out, and I realize he wasn't trying to touch me. He just wanted to retrieve his belongings.

"Do you really need that right now?" Minerva asks. "She's naked under that coat."

"I didn't take the coat back," he says. "And yes, I do need this." He taps a few things into his phone and swivels it toward us. It's a live feed from SNN, the Supernatural News Network.

The telecaster, a very energetic young witch, is practically shouting. "—hardly believe what just happened. Roxana Goldenscales, who has been missing for weeks now, has reappeared, and her explanation of why she's been in hiding is, well. It's astonishing!" The witch's hair is flying every which way, and her eyes are wild. "Look at the footage we were able to obtain just moments ago!"

The screen cuts to a somewhat grainy image of me. And Lionel. Looking at my dad.

It zooms in on my face as a wad of reporters are pelting me with questions.

"The wedding is not going to happen. I wasn't kidnapped. I ran away." I sound a lot more confident than I felt.

"You what?" Dad's really mad. "You ran away?"

The screen jostles and the whole thing spins around a bit—the camera person is clearly trying to find a better spot. He or she lucks out—the image is nice and crisp when Lionel says, "I'm afraid that the mage's council can't condone Roxana's apology for her departure." Lionel glances at me, our eyes meeting for a long and almost uncomfortable moment. "You see." He turns back to face my dad. "The reason your daughter ran away is that we fell in love." He smiles. "So she most certainly can't say she's sorry and marry Ragar."

I hadn't realized, in that moment, the chaos of the reaction to that proclamation. Lionel pulls me close and murmurs in my ear. I know that for my part, I was freaking out about his false story. But to everyone else, it looks like a lover's embrace, like two star-crossed romantics bracing themselves to finally face the music together.

Lionel slides his phone into his pants pocket. "I'm sure my confrontation with Ragar will also be playing on all channels." He cocks his head to the side. "So while you may detest me." He spreads his arms out as the elevator stops and the doors chime while opening. "Get used to calling me sweetheart." His smile as the cameras start flashing outside is beatific.

"Yes, yes." He waves the reporters back. "Roxana and I are leaving now, to return to our love nest. You'll all have to wait for an official statement."

When they don't part to make way for us, Lionel says, "*Stupefaciunt exteriora.*" The gaggle of reporters crowding us go flying backward, knocking the ones behind them over like bowling pins. "I asked nicely." He waves his wand, threatening to do more.

They scrabble backward so fast that they remind me of crabs fleeing a flock of seagulls.

"Let's go."

To my shock, there's a car waiting for us on the curb. Lionel hails the driver. "Harold, thanks."

A tall vampire wearing a tuxedo opens the door of the car for us and bows.

"You have a vampire driver?" I glance at Minerva.

She shrugs.

"He owes my dad," Lionel says. "It's hard to trust other mages once you reach our level."

The reporters stay a good distance away while Lionel climbs into the car, loading Clark into the front seat.

I can tell Minerva wants to object, and so do I. But one glance at Ragar, who's starting to twitch, and the fight shoots right out of me. "We can deal with him later," I say. "Let's just get out of here."

"Where are Bevin, Izaak, and Xander?" Minerva asks.

"I already took them home," Harold says. "I assume that's where you'd like to go as well?"

"Home?" I ask.

Harold rattles off the address for Minerva's apartment.

"You're surprisingly well informed," Minerva says.

He shrugs. "It's my job."

I refuse to meet Lionel's eyes the entire ride to our apartment. He needs to know that while I may appreciate him helping out, I'm upset about the way he did it.

Clark starts to groan about two minutes from the apartment.

Lionel leans forward, his wand pointed at Clark, and says, "*Restituere salutem.*"

Clark bolts up in the seat, his cheeks flushed, his hair pointing in a lot of strange directions, his wand clutched so tightly in his hand that his knuckles are white. "Where are we?"

"Roxana saved you," Lionel says. "It was absolutely the most spectacular thing I've ever seen."

"We're almost home," Minerva says.

The car stops then, and Minerva whips the door open like she's a racehorse coming out of the chute. "Let's go."

Clark doesn't linger either.

But when I start to open my door, Lionel catches my arm. "Wait."

"I appreciate what you did," I say. "But then you ruined it all—"

"We at least need to work out our story," he says. "We need a plan."

"No," Minerva says from the sidewalk, her eyes flashing. "*We* need to work out a plan, and we'll be in touch. You do what you do best." She kicks the side of his car. "Nothing at all."

I can't help my snort.

"Roxana." Lionel still hasn't released my arm. "I know you're upset right now, but if you'll listen to me—"

Giggles flies into the car, though how she got here as quickly as we did, I may never know, and attacks Lionel's face, her wings beating furiously, her beak darting at his pretty face.

"What the archangel is going on?" He flings his hands up to protect himself.

"Giggles," Minerva shouts. "Stop."

The poor little bird pulls back and lands on my shoulder just in time to avoid being zapped, I think.

"My friends and I will be going." I slide out of the car and stand next to Minerva, who has her hands full keeping Clark on his feet.

This time Lionel doesn't stop me from leaving. But he does glare quite a bit at my feathered defender. "I can't decide whether I love that bird for being so intrepid or hate her for not knowing her place in the world."

"Join the club," I say.

Next to me, Giggles twitters with agitation. And then she poops on my shoulder.

❧ 4 ❧

BEVIN

The world is full of darkness. I know that better than anyone—my dad's a demon. But I firmly believe that we all get to choose what to create, one decision at a time. That means we can choose to bring light into the world, even if it's a single flicker at a time.

We can also reject darkness.

That was always my plan when I decided on my career. I would take things that might otherwise be waste, things that no one cared about, and I would find people who needed them. It felt like a noble purpose, even if there isn't always a huge profit in selling second-hand magical objects.

And even when business was bad, there was always my side job—seances—that helped me pay the bills. I never wanted to live a posh life, so I've always been okay with having enough to eat and a comfortable place to live.

Plenty of people have asked me over the years to contact demons for them. That's the most lucrative form of seance and also the most dangerous. I've always refused that kind of request, both because I wanted nothing to do with interactions like that personally, and also because I think no good can come of more contact with the daimoni.

They've broken enough worlds. The last thing I want is to give them access to Earth, on any level.

Usually, I'm grateful for weeks where I'm fully booked with seances. It means I can go shopping for a new dress or shoes. It means I can go out to eat and not stress about paying my rent.

But ever since I was seen with Roxana. . .

It's been absolutely *insane* since Roxana went back home and the news reporters caught all our faces on television. My phone never stops ringing. I'm booked for the next six months—and I could be booked further, but I flat-out refused to book past that. Now people are offering me double and triple my usual rate to add extra appointments.

There *are* a few things I've had my eye on down at Saks. . . And I've been wanting to start selling ready-made charms and potions for a while, but the startup cost on that is astronomical. So I may have booked a few extra appointments.

Okay, dozens of extras.

I hate that I'm so easily corrupted, but I've always wanted this one red Gucci purse, which, even used, is astronomically expensive. I even *need* a new bag right now. Last week, one of my charmed crickets worked his way loose and escaped through a hole in my inside coin pocket. Charmed crickets work like supernatural mace— their chirp will stun an attacker for long enough that the paranormal affairs officers can come and arrest them.

Only, I didn't realize he'd escaped, and the reaction to their chirp is even a little stronger for humans. Dozens of humans were frozen in place before I realized he'd even gotten loose. I could have gotten in big trouble. Since I have a friend on the force, I called Minerva and she took care of it. It was still embarrassing, for me and for Minerva, but it could have been far worse.

I'm not really accustomed to doing more than one seance, or sometimes in a pinch, two, per day. But a third one really wipes me out. I stagger out my door and into the Grand Central Gloffee Shop. Xander's talking on his phone when I plop down next to him.

Only, he's not.

He's talking. . .to himself?

"You okay?"

He freezes. "Fine. Why?"

"No reason." I mean, I've been known to tell myself some hilarious stories, so who am I to judge?

He's also wearing a weird black bucket hat, pulled down over his face like he's hiding from someone.

"Nice hat."

"Thanks. I'm going fishing later."

"Are you really?" I ask. "Where?"

He rolls his eyes. "I'm not going fishing." He shakes his head like *I'm* the crazy one.

"Okay."

Gavin shows up, depositing a glespresso in front of Xander. The last thing he needs is a double helping of caffeine. Before he can drink it, I reach over and snatch it up. I down it in a single gulp.

I forgot how much I hate glespresso—but this is worse than usual. "Mage flavored? Really? Blech." I cough and make a horrible gagging sound. "I had no idea."

Xander blinks at me.

Gavin does too.

"What?"

"You stole my drink and then you insulted me for ordering it?" Xander's hat may be covering half his face, but his incredulity is coming through loud and clear in spite of that.

"Did you want to order a drink that he might hate?" Gavin asks, his confusion turning to amusement.

"Yes." I nod. "A steamed milk with an infusion of vampire."

"Eww," Xander says. "You know that his vampire is Izaak, don't you?" He gags. "I'm not drinking that. Just another glespresso, mage, stat."

Gavin looks from me to Xander and then walks off, shaking his head as he goes.

"What do you think we'll actually get?" Xander asks.

"Spit," I say. "We're both getting drinks that he spat in for sure."

Xander cringes, but then his face kind of spasms like he's having a seizure. He's always been overly dramatic with his hand gestures and his snark, but this is a new level.

"Maybe you should lay off the glespresso for a while," I say. "You seem to be plenty energetic as it is."

He sighs. "I've been requested for outside security details nonstop since the thing with—"

"Roxana?" I ask. "Tell me about it. I did three seances today. It's good for business—"

"But you're exhausted."

I nod. "Exactly."

"You may not want to listen to this, but basic economic theory dictates what you should do next."

"Huh?" Sometimes Xander really surprises me. "What do you know about economic theory?"

"You may not have realized it," Xander says. "Most people get so distracted by all my delicious muscles and my beautifully cut jawline that they don't notice the huge brain hiding behind the façade."

"Excuse me?"

"I was an economics major who has spent almost a decade watching crazy, fluffy overlords make money, hand over clenched paw."

I slowly scan the room to make sure no other werewolves just heard him call them fluffy.

"Please. There aren't any of them here. I'd smell them."

"I'm not motivated by filthy lucre," I say.

"But you need it sometimes," he says. "That's the point. So when you have a lot of people calling, that means your services are in particular demand. And that means. . ."

"I can book more." I blink. "I have been. But I can't really do more than three seances—"

"You're still missing the point. It means you can *charge* more," he says. "You can work the same as before and make more money, because there's more *demand* for your supply."

"But what about my existing clients?" I ask. "A lot of them are old women on pensions. They can't pay twice as much to talk to their dead husbands."

He shrugs. "Then just charge new clients more. Call the lower rate a loyalty discount or something."

Xander is a genius.

"If I were you, I'd start calling all my newly booked clients and tell them that because *so* many people need my services that I can't possibly take care of them all, I'm doubling or even tripling my rates. Then anyone who's willing to pay? That's your new clientele."

"You should have been a businessman," I say. "You'd have been way better at that—" I can't very well say what he already knows out loud, that he's a terrible wolf. But now I'm not sure how to finish my sentence.

"I'd be better running a business than I am as a wolf in security? Don't I know it." He shakes his head slowly. It looks much funnier than usual, thanks to the dumb bucket hat.

I sink into the cushions of the sofa. "I'm sorry."

He shrugs. "It's fine. It's the truth. It's always been true. Thanks for being honest enough to say it out loud."

"Or almost say it aloud," I say.

He's smiling, at least.

My phone rings. "Probably another new client." I stare at the string of unknown numbers. "I'm booked out for the next six months already."

Xander snatches the phone out of my hands and answers. "Hello, Bevin Bahar's beyond-the-grave outreach program. This is her assistant Xander speaking. How can we improve your day?"

He pauses, making the strangest face at me.

"Well, I do think we could help you get in touch with the. . ." He clears his throat. "The deceased mistress of your brother." He widens his eyes at me and lifts his shoulders.

I nod. "Sure. As long as they're dead, I can reach them."

"The thing is, thanks to her recent popularity, as I'm

sure you can understand, Ms. Bahar has become quite busy."

He pauses again.

"Well, yes, the thing is, her pricing has come up to reflect her limited schedule." He looks my way and presses the phone between his ear and his shoulder, gesturing about something.

I frown.

"What *is her price?*" he asks. "That's a good question." He widens his eyes.

He said to double it. But he probably doesn't know what I charge now.

"One hundred an hour," I say.

"It's three hundred an hour," he says.

I splutter.

"Great. I'll just take a look at her schedule and text you with the soonest available. We require payment in advance, of course. If you fail to show, your slot is forfeit as well as the prepaid fee."

I can barely breathe, but I claw at the phone.

"Alright. We look forward to helping you locate that missing ring. See you soon."

"How could you—" I wheeze.

"How could I?" He hands me the phone. "Text her with a time."

"A hundred an hour *was* the doubled price."

"You charged fifty bucks an hour to speak to *dead* people?" Xander shakes his head. "You were way under-charging."

"My mortgage only costs me a hundred and fifty a day," I say. "Utilities and whatnot are only another twenty-five. If I do a seance a day, more than a quarter of the way there."

"First off," he says, "how is your note that low in New York?"

"This building sat for a long time," I say. "I had to exorcise the spirit of the former owner's dead cat—no one else wanted the building because it wouldn't leave and it hissed and left phantom urine smells all over the place."

Xander's mouth dangles open.

"Was there a second thing?"

He coughs. "You know that people have businesses in order to turn a profit, right? Their goal isn't to cover their building note. It's to make money."

I shrug. "My housing is part of my building note, so if I cover the costs on that, it's also kind of paying me, but that's not my main goal in any case," I say. "I've always wanted to help people, and I like selling people things that they need, used things, things that other people have cast off."

"Be that as it may," he says, "you can't—"

"Be that as it may?" I can't help my smile. "Are you a sixty-year-old woman?"

"Do old women say that?"

"Young guys don't," I say. "But thanks for the help. I still can't believe that if I start demanding it, people will just pay me six times my usual price."

"Then let me do it," Xander says. "For every person I retain, you pay me twenty-five bucks."

I'm smiling broadly when I say, "Deal."

We get our gloffees to go, and two hours later, Xander's walking out my shop's front door, bucket hat finally doffed, smiling. "That was a great afternoon." He waves, and the door jingles, and I'm alone.

I owe him eight hundred dollars, but we agreed I'd

pay him as I earn it, little by little. I still can't believe I'm going to be making so much more money than ever before. Roxana may have caused me a lot of anxiety, but she's also making me rich.

Maybe I should thank her.

Before I can even think about dialing her number, my entire shop shakes like it's secretly a bomb shelter and we're under attack. I've never felt anything like that before—but I have a pretty good guess what's happening.

Someone who means me harm is trying to enter the shop. The shaking's coming from the wards Clark put up. They're keeping me safe, but for how long?

"Bevin Bahar." A giant voice booms. "Grant us entry, or we'll break these wards."

"If you could break them, you'd already have done it," I shout, with more confidence than I feel.

"That was a courtesy knock," the same huge voice says.

I wonder whether the humans up and down the road can hear all this, or whether something as simple as gloffee could keep them in the dark. Mostly, though, I wonder who's threatening me. "Who is it?" I step toward the window and crack the curtain.

The eye that's peering through the glass at me isn't human. It's closer to reptilian than anything else, which answers my question.

Demon-spawn.

"My name is Aquarius Silvertongue," the voice booms again.

It feels like the blood freezes in my veins. Aquarius Silvertongue is the Viceroy of the Demon Council. He's their enforcer. He's registered and stamped—he has five demon marks, and they're powerful ones.

Not a single one of his powers resembles a strong static shock.

Which is my only power. I swallow. "What do you want?"

"We'd like to come inside and talk." When he smiles, his eyes dilate.

It sends a chill up my spine, and I drop the curtain. *We?* I force myself to breathe—passing out would not help this situation. "Talk about what?"

"Are you really going to leave us standing on your front step?" he asks.

"My wards only preclude entry for people who mean me harm," I say. "If you wanted to talk, you wouldn't be stuck, which means I shouldn't let you in."

"Ah." Aquarius chuckles, and when he speaks this time, I can barely hear him, as if he's turned the volume down on his cosmic-boom megaphone. "The one who might take joy in hurting you is leashed, but I think I understand."

There's some kind of murmuring, and then the door opens.

Aquarius Silvertongue is shorter than I would have guessed from the times I've seen him on a television screen. His hair is as silver as his tongue is rumored to be—but it doesn't look like the silver of age. The color's too rich, too. . .varied... too inhuman. It's a silver that shifts as you look at it, changing subtly from silver, to purple, to blue, and then back to silver again. It sparkles in the lighting of my shop, almost as if it's housing some kind of moonbeams. He's still smiling, and his head turns slowly to take in the contents of my shop, his inhumanly silvery, slitted eyes almost inquisitive. Of course he's wearing a tailored three-piece suit and carrying a cane with a snake head at the top.

Behind him, a woman with raven-black hair ducks to enter. She's wearing a minidress made of some kind of dark brown animal skin—so tight that it shows her every curve. She's muscular and simultaneously curvy in a way humans couldn't possibly achieve without silicon, and my throat goes dry immediately.

My eyes dart upward, meeting hers. She's not taking in the shop. She's looking only at me.

Her head tilts, her enormous, violet eyes intent. "Bevin Bahar?"

I nod and swallow, hoping to hydrate the Sahara my mouth has become. It doesn't work.

"I'm Violette Cassiopeia."

She's the Viceroy's partner—they've managed the affairs of the Demon Council for years. I've never seen her in person, and she never appears on television either. Soki, my only reliable source of any information on demon-spawn gossip, is obsessed with her beauty.

But nothing I've heard has ever done it justice.

Her skin is nearly translucent, but not in a way that shows her veins—it looks like stars are suspended inside her body. She sparkles and shimmers like the unfathomable cosmos, and I can't look away.

"Killing animals just to wear their skins is wrong," I say without thinking.

Her very full lips drop open. "Excuse me?"

I force myself to meet her eyes. "You're wearing some kind of leather dress?" I quirk one eyebrow. "You killed a creature to make it. Does that seem right to you?"

She laughs, the sound more mellifluous than it has any right to be. "I've heard you're not normal." She tilts her head.

The prospect that anyone is talking about me is horrifying enough. But why would Violette Cassiopeia have heard about me?

"I thought the whole do-gooderly thing was an act, or perhaps a gimmick." She glances around the room and sighs. "But could you really believe it?"

I use her musing to study her more closely. She should have at least one visible demon mark, but she looks more like the akero than anyone I've ever seen.

"You've piqued Violette's interest. That's a feat in and of itself."

"I can't tell you how delighted I am to hear it." I fold my arms. "What do you want?" I frown. "And is your leashed beast outside going to harm anyone while you're chitchatting in here with me?"

Aquarius laughs. "You're much funnier than I expected." He glances over his shoulder. "Horatius won't do a single thing without our permission. All the stupid, powerless humans parading past your shop are safe, I assure you."

"As to what we want." Violette's voice reminds me of the soft ringing of bells. "You received your first demon mark, and then you never petitioned to join the Demon Guild."

"Surely it's optional," I say. "You can't force anyone to join."

Aquarius quirks one eyebrow. "Yes, the human officials have written that into the accords."

"You say that as if it doesn't matter," I say. "But the last thing we want is war with the humans."

He shrugs. "I'm not sure I'd list that as the *last* thing we want. But I think it's safe to say that our agenda and theirs differ. Substantially." He glances at his hand and then begins to clean under his sharp, shiny black nails. "Let me make a friendly suggestion."

Somehow, I doubt it will be friendly. You don't have to say that a friendly suggestion is friendly. It just *is* a nice thought. "What's that?"

He drops his hands and takes a step closer. "Join the Guild, or you might find things become. . .uncomfortable for you. We provide a tremendous amount of support for new demons, for one thing."

"I'm not a new demon," I say. "I'm a *demon-spawn* who has no desire to descend a single speck farther than I have."

"You're the most famous demon-spawn in the world right now," Violette says. "Your last name is almost certainly evidence that you're a daughter of Rahab, who is really hot right now. And your twin has done great things already. We've been eager for you to join us for quite some time."

"Don't make the mistake of shunning your own people." Aquarius glances around at my shop again. "It's quite a darling little place you've made for yourself here. It would be a terrible shame if something happened to it."

He bobs his head at me and ducks through the door.

Violette pauses for a single moment. "You really have no idea what you're turning down." She steps closer, much closer. Her breath washes over me, and it's a spring breeze, and it's moonlight on violets, and it's the cool press of sweet tea against my brow, all at the same time.

My brain short circuits and I *long* for. . .for what?

"I'd be delighted to show you exactly what you've been missing. All you need to do is join us and *ask*." Before I can move, before I can even think to stop her, she presses a kiss against my forehead, and then she's gone.

It takes me fifteen minutes to be able to form coherent words again, but the second I can, I call Clark. "The good news," I say, "is that business has really picked up since you almost died trying to save us."

"Good to hear from you too," Clark says. "And thanks. Work is going well enough for me, I guess."

"Yeah, yeah," I say. "Chit and chat and all that."

"What's going on?"

"I need a favor," I say. "And this time I can afford to pay you for it."

"A favor?"

"How strong do wards need to be to keep out greater demon-spawn?"

He swears.

I'm guessing that's not exactly promising.

❦ 5 ❦

IZAAK

One of the first questions I usually get when I meet a new vampire is, "How on earth did you get into acting?"

It's not a common job for our kind. The whole *terrifying people naturally* is one impediment, obviously, but so is the whole, *I want to drink your blood* thing. The acting gig kind of requires you to maintain close proximity to humans, unless you can land a solo gig where you're shooting scenes with a volleyball, I guess. But all my attempts to get producers to remake that movie have been rebuffed.

Thanks for nothing, Tom Hanks.

My introduction to acting was actually a complete fluke. During the single semester I spent in normie school, the only elective that had extra room in the class was theater. I was stuck in with a bunch of freshmen, since that time slot fit my schedule. Having no interest in acting, they stuck me on lights and sound. That was fine with me. Climbing up to change lightbulbs and filters wasn't scary to me like it was to humans, and I almost never had to interact with other kids.

Plus, my one friend was in there with me—D. And he was a great actor. In fact, he landed the coolest role in the play we were doing, *Romeo and Juliet*. He was Mercutio. He's really the only person who added humor to the whole thing. I enjoyed my time in the sound booth, listening to them practice their lines over and over so that I could change the lights or adjust the sound at the right time.

Only, the day before the first performance, D's grandmother passed away.

He and his grandma were tight, and he was wrecked. There was no way he was going to be able to perform. When the teacher asked if *anyone* could fill in for him, D turned his sad eyes on me.

I couldn't really argue that I didn't know the lines. I'd heard them seven hundred times. It really could have been a train wreck, but it wasn't. And on that stage, with the lights in my eyes, I couldn't even see all the people in the audience.

But when I said, "If love be rough with you, be rough with love," and everyone laughed?

It was like crack is rumored to be for humans.

I couldn't give it up.

After I dropped out of school the second time, I joined community theater, to my mother's great dismay. One time I played Scar in *The Lion King*—one single villain role—and afterward I vowed never to do that again. If I wanted to scare people, I could work a job that paid more and was much easier.

It's always been a challenge to find roles I want, and

I've rarely gotten any that are as fulfilling as Mercutio was.

But after the fiasco with Roxana, it's now impossible.

I'm not kidding, sadly. I had no idea how much of the entertainment world is bankrolled by the dragona and their deep pockets. And none of them want to support one of Roxana's friends right now. Sure, most non-dragona magical people would love to watch a movie with one of her friends in it, but they're a fraction of the people who pay for movie tickets. Most movie goers have no idea that some of the actors are mages, werewolves, or demon-spawn.

Which means the marketing team can't overcome the irritation of the people writing the checks. They're understandably angry that we created such chaos by supporting Roxana in leaving her dad and defying the Russian dragona.

"I'm sorry, Izaak," my agent says. "I still got nothing."

"You can't even find me an audition?" I press. "What about cold calls?"

"Are you really willing to go back to that?" she asks.

It doesn't seem like I have much choice.

"I don't have any auditions you'd be willing to consider."

Xander's at work, but he left a pile of mail on the counter. I flip through it absently.

Every single letter is a bill.

Rent.

Electric.

Gas.

Internet.

Trash. *We have to pay for people for our trash? We're the*

ones who haul it to the chute. And can't they, like, recycle it and turn it into stuff they can sell?

It's not fair to Xander that I never pay. I absolutely have to find something and soon. "What do you mean, *willing to consider?*" Even as I ask, I realize what she's saying.

"If you were willing to lift your moratorium on playing *bad guys*, I've got a friend who specifically called about you. The project's a relatively small one, but I think it's going to do really well at Sundance, and it has a decent budget for an indie film—that tech guy, Pollack James, is behind it."

I grit my teeth and force the words out. "What kind of bad guy are they looking for?"

Stella makes a choking sound. "A serial killer."

I close my eyes, tightening my hand on my cell phone. "I—"

"Izaak? You know, lots of women write letters to serial killers in prisons. There are plenty of people who really like that kind of character." Disgusting weirdos. She must be almost as desperate as I am.

I clear my throat. "I said—"

"You said?"

It's harder to say the words than I expected it would be, but I force them out, finally. "I'll do it," I say. "The audition, I mean."

"You will?" She whoops. "That's great news. I figured one day you'd come around and—"

"This isn't my new thing," I say. "I'm not going to start doing roles like this all the time."

"You're a vampire," Stella practically coos. "I mean, it's not a bad thing to lean into your strengths."

I want to take it back. I want to shout at her, hang

up, and never consider it again. But she's right. I *am* a vampire.

And we are the bad guys.

Before I have much time to wallow, Xander breezes through the door.

I can't help but notice the time. "You're home early."

"And you're up early," he jokes. "I guess it's a day of small miracles all around."

"Hey," I say. "I'm not up that early."

Xander lifts his eyebrows. "Four-thirty p.m. is pretty early for you." He glances at the window in the family room. "I mean, the sun's still out. You'd usually be snoring like a woodcutter in the other room right now."

"I know I haven't paid rent in a while," I say. A while. Or like, once in the last six months.

Xander shrugs. "Rent's not exactly my biggest concern right now." He cringes. "Although, it *is* a pack apartment. So if something were to happen to my job. . ."

"I thought they loved you over there. Aren't you their most requested security hire?"

He sighs. "That's why I'm off today. I have to work all weekend, so they're letting me go early today and tomorrow."

"That sucks," I say. "Really? You get off an hour or two early and have to work two extra *days*?"

Xander shrugs. "I don't get a lot of chances to be a team player, so when I get them, I take them."

My phone bings. It's a message from Stella. AUDITION IN ONE HOUR. YOU NEED A MONOLOGUE.

For a villain. I barely suppress the groan that tries to escape.

"What kind of sound was that?" Xander asks.

I guess I didn't suppress it after all. "I need to go down and give blood for Gavin." I can't tell him I've got an audition, or he'll get all excited and ask what it's for. If I confess it's for a serial killer, he'll never let me go. He has enough going on in his life right now—pulling all the financial slack for both of us too isn't fair.

"But you gave yesterday." He frowns. "Is that safe?" He whips out his phone.

"It's not like there's an internet search for how often vampires can give blood," I say.

"Is he selling it to other gloffee shops? Why does he even need more?"

"Lay off, fam. Geez. It's not like I'm unhealthy, right?"

The hurt look on his face almost changes my mind. If I just tell him. . .but he'll stop me. And sometimes we have to do things we don't want to do to keep from slacking.

"Fine," he says. "Hey, you know what? I'll come with you. I could use a little pick-me-up today. A glespresso may be just the thing."

By the angel. "Okay, look."

Xander pauses, but then his eyes widen. "Do you smell that?"

Vampires and werewolves both have a keen sense of smell. Usually we notice the same things at the same time. "Smell what?" I inhale carefully through my nose, searching for anything out of the ordinary. "Did you fart, because if so, just say. I can always smell your brand."

Xander rolls his eyes. "No, not that. It's the smell of something strange—fear? Can fear have a smell?"

What is he talking about?

He's still sniffing the air, looking around in confusion.

I can't help think of the werewolf waiter downstairs. The one who's always smelling and batting at things that aren't there. "Maybe you should stay here while I go grab you a gloffee."

Xander should argue with me. He should twist my arm until I confess what I'm really doing. That's how he is—he'd then mock me mercilessly and insist that I cancel the audition. He'd remind me that in order to succeed, I can't cave when there's resistance. If I take one professional villain role, my bright line will be gone and it's all I'll ever get.

But he doesn't fight back. His shoulders slump, and he takes a few steps into our small family room and sinks into a chair. "Fine. Whatever."

Even more than sniffing the air, that's my sign. Something is not right with Xander, and I'm terribly worried that I know what it is.

The fray.

I've worried about it since the day I signed the lease. I'd never even heard about it before then, but the strange clause he insisted we include made me look into it.

Whereupon tenant discovers lessor is acting strangely, and whereupon tenant believes such odd behavior might be signs of the "fray," as defined in the introductory clauses, tenant has an absolute obligation to immediately notify Pack leadership of the same.

. . .

I didn't realize until later that the pack must have insisted I include that, as part of finding him the apartment and subsidizing the rent. I have absolutely no intention of reporting him. But his behavior makes me nervous. Should I point it out to Xander? Should I talk to our friends? Maybe Minerva will have an idea. She always knows what to do.

That's it.

I'll ask Minerva tonight, and maybe she or Clark will know how to handle it.

"You don't have to worry," Xander says.

I can't help startling. "Worry?"

"You don't need to report me, either." I've never heard him sound so dejected in my entire life.

It makes my blood run cold.

"I know I'm fraying." His voice is entirely flat. "I think Bevin knows, too. I'm sure the pack has noticed. They're ignoring it because I'm making them a lot of money right now. But as soon as that dries up, they'll take action. I need to address it before then."

"Take action?" That sounded vague.

"Frays are put down."

I don't remember crossing the room, but somehow I did, and I'm crouching in front of Xander, grabbing his arm. "No. Absolutely not."

"No, what?" he looks as tired as he sounds.

"No, you're not going to go and report yourself. You're not going to 'handle' it, either."

Xander blinks. "It's a werewolf thing," he says. "There's nothing you can do about it, and you shouldn't even try. In early stages, wolves who are fraying are confused, lost, and disoriented. But as it progresses, they become violent, unpredictable, and dangerous. They either have to join a pack, or they have to be put down."

"What if they still won't let you join their pack?" I don't say this out loud, but I can't help wondering what it will mean for us if they *do* let him join. He'll have to move over to live on their property, for one thing.

Which means we'll never see him.

I've known as long as I've been friends with Xander —for almost four years—that our time was limited. As soon as he joined the pack for real, he'd become an old acquaintance. There are a lot of reasons why vampires and werewolves aren't friends, and most of them aren't faults on the vampire side. But the biggest one is that packs kind of control your entire life. They have to, from what I understand. It's a bond akin to the one vampires only share with a blood-and-sex bonded human.

It's pretty hard for a buddy to compete with that connection.

Not that I'd even try.

But a deep sense of sadness fills me, causing something very rare to happen. A tear rolls down my cheek. "I don't want you to leave."

Xander looks just as sad as I do when he says, "Me either, buddy."

After a moment, it gets a little weird, so I pop to my feet. "I'll just run get that glespresso."

"And maybe a few pounds of meat?"

"Brisket, right? Raw and thin cut?"

Xander's smile tells me he's still into that.

"You know me," he says. But it sounds like he's getting ready to say goodbye, and I hate it.

"I'll be back as quickly as I can," I say.

And then I duck out to do my audition. Now more than ever, I can't be mooching off him. I need to get my crap together so I can come up with a solution. As sad as I'll be if he joins that stupid pack, it would be so much worse if they decided to kill him. I can't let that happen.

Money isn't a cure-all, but it sure does make hard things easier.

So when I show up for the audition, I don't approach it half-heartedly. I give it my all. I curl my lip when I voice the threats. I let the evil glint in my eyes fly when I'm glaring at my intended victim.

And I don't do a thing to suppress the natural reaction humans feel to vampires when I meet the director, the producer, and the casting director.

"You are—you blew my mind," the casting director says. She shivers. "I mean, that was amazing."

"When you first walked in," the tall, rangy producer says, "I dismissed you as just another pretty face. Most Americans don't want a good-looking serial killer, but for our movie now, it's a must."

"But wow." The director shakes his head. "I think we can let the others waiting out there go home." He glances back at the other two.

They nod.

"You're our Orson."

I hate how grateful I am for something I never wanted. And I also really, really hope that it will make a difference.

❦ *6* ❧

MINERVA

The higher the stakes, the lower my magical ability sinks. It's always been that way.

If I'm in the middle of an arrest and the perp goes haywire, I can assume my magic will backfire too.

If a crazed werewolf comes at me, fangs bared, I'm sure to draw a blank.

If a vampire's about to bite my neck, my stun spell will misfire and turn him into an ice cube.

It's just the way my life goes.

When I'm doing something low key? If I'm casting a spell that's way off the beaten path? Then I'm usually totally fine. For some reason, those oddball things are where I shine.

And now I finally know why.

It's been really hard to force myself to report for work since I found out the truth. After all, the people of New York City deserve a strong and powerful PA officer. My partner Amber should have someone she can trust at her back. The only person I'm fit to partner with is here with me, scratching around in the dirt at my feet.

"Giggles," I say.

She turns, her head cocked, for all the world listening as if she knows her name. Which is apparently possible with a pigeon, but only if you're practicing teaching her several times a day, which I never have. I guess I'm lucky that if a flying rat has to be my familiar, at least she's a smart flying rat.

"Come here." I pat the spot beside me.

She flutters up onto the park bench. She coos and her head bumps my hand. It shouldn't make me feel better, but for some reason, it does. She's just further evidence that I'm really not fit to be a cop. I mean, what kind of self-respecting witch bonds a *pigeon*? What kind of person almost *likes* having a pigeon that won't leave her side? I sigh, but I don't stop petting her back while she coos and fluffs next to me.

And then she takes a huge dump. I think about cleaning it up, but it's easier to just move to a new bench. It's not like the park is really hopping at four-thirty on a Thursday. If I were actually going to work, I'd just be waking up right now—preparing for another day of sucking at basic paranormal affairs officer work.

Amber deserves better than a partner who's a half-human flunkie. I only got the job because my dad hid the truth about who I am. Come to think of it, I've probably only kept my job through my monumental mishaps because my dad was close friends with his replacement, the new paranormal affairs chief, before he died.

I wish I'd never looked into my past.

At least wondering why I was a screw-up left the

possibility that I might be able to fix things. But you can't fix *who you are*. And who I am is not only not who I thought I was. . . it's someone no one wants to be.

Probably the only person who can really understand how I feel is Xander. Without even thinking about it, I text him and ask him to meet me here. Shockingly, he shows up ten minutes later.

"Shouldn't you be getting ready for work right now?" He frowns, his eyes way less bright than usual. "Because Izaak's about to bring me some glespresso, and uh, I'm not there."

"Thanks for coming." I pat the seat next to me. "Sitting on a bench in Central Park feels less pathetic when I'm not doing it alone."

Giggles coos and burbles when he sits down, but eventually she rearranges herself on the other side of me.

"What exactly are you doing out here?" he asks. "I mean, not that Central Park isn't great." He's staring pointedly at a man who has just unbuttoned his pants and is about to urinate on a tree.

Just like a dog, only way nastier. A week ago, I'd be over there, badge in hand, telling him not to do that. A week ago, I cared about things like right and wrong. I thought I could make a difference in the world.

I was a moron.

"Did you notice what that guy's doing?" Xander's lip's curled in disgust. "I'm someone who would actually *do* that in my other form, and I still think it's gross."

Better to answer his earlier question than dive into why I don't care anymore. "I come sit here whenever things are hard for me. Usually it helps."

"Sitting in the park makes you feel better about your life?" He's tilted his head now, and I follow his gaze—to a woman who's rifling through a big metal trash can. "Really? I mean, I guess I can see it. Things can always get worse."

The woman pauses when she pulls out half a sandwich, and I brace myself to watch her eat it. But she chucks it over her shoulder in favor of a melted ice cream sandwich. Who buys ice cream sandwiches in November?

"It's not always the most sanitary place," I admit. "And some of the people are. . ."

"Disgusting?" Xander's eyes are awfully wide.

"But there are also always people who need a little more luck in their lives," I say. "And I may never be an excellent witch, but I've always been good at helping people find luck."

"What does that mean?" he asks. "You can't just *find* luck. It's not like it's lying around. Life isn't a video game where you waltz around finding weapons and money."

"It might be easier if I show you," I say. "I just need to. . ." I scan the people again. Other than the trash digger, who is moving along in pursuit of more fruitful trash bins, and the urinator, who has more trees to mark, presumably, there are still dozens of other people. I just need to find one who's more worthy and whose needs are clearly apparent.

That's when I see it. A mother and her small child. He's pointing at balloons. She shakes her head. Then he points at the hot dog stand. He's whining and bouncing. He's clearly hungry and wants one. He looks thin. She looks tired. She's pointing at the price, which is admittedly a little high for mystery meat in a dried-out bread wrapper.

"Watch," I say. Then I slide my wand into my sleeve

so it's not quite so obvious. "This always works, when I *feel* what they need and make up my own spell."

Xander grabs my arm. "Maybe we don't make up spells on families with kids."

I shake him off. They clearly need a little extra dough —that kid looks practically bony. And his mother could probably use something happy, too. Before he can grab me again, I whip my wand tip their way and whisper, "*Non multum habent. Da illis plura. Plena sit bursa eorum.*"

"Wow, that was a long spell. What did you say? Bless them with hot dogs and balloons and no tree-peeing men?"

I roll my eyes. "Just watch."

At first, nothing happens. That's usually how it works. When I make up my own spells, ignoring everything they taught me at school and leaning in to what makes sense to my half-human brain, it takes a bit for it to take hold. "Watch her purse. That's where the magic should happen this time."

Xander's Adam's apple bobs as he swallows, and he looks pained. "What exactly did you say? They don't really teach Latin at were-school. Or human school, actually."

"Too busy learning mailbox marking and the finer points of toilet bowl drinking?" I kill myself.

But then the woman gasps. "What in the—" Dollar bills are rolling out of her purse and blowing away from her. Her tiny son goes bounding after them like a golden retriever chasing a tennis ball.

"Cuz I caught it, can I get a hotdog now?" he asks, his eyes bright.

The mother looks baffled, like someone just handed her a winning lottery ticket. "I. . . well." She glances around as if to see whether she's being punked. She goes back to unfolding dollar bills from her purse. "I suppose so."

"Hold the phone," Xander says. "I thought witches and wizards can't make money. Isn't that a basic rule?"

"I mean, technically we can't," I say. "But I didn't say that. I merely cast a spell that her purse would be full. I didn't even specify what, though I knew money was what she needed."

"You could have filled her purse with bugs," he says. "Or with lead. Or with water. Isn't it a little irresponsible to cast a spell like that? Couldn't it do way more harm than good?"

"I think the money thing is because they never go well when we do them for our own personal gain." I shrug. "But it never works out badly when I'm out here just helping. I started it when I was a teen who could barely cast normal spells at all—before anyone told me not to do stuff like this. In fact, Mom didn't believe I could."

"Do another one." He's grinning ear to ear. "This is better than Christmas."

"You hate Christmas," I say.

"Do you blame me? Every year at Christmas, my parents would argue over who had to take me. And my stocking was always full of MilkBones because they're cheaper than human candy."

If I'd found him in a park as a kid, I'd definitely have cast a spell for him, which makes me sad. "Alright, let's find another good candidate."

"You should find a job where you can do this kind of magic," Xander says. "Instead of the high-pressure kind that always makes your spells backfire."

"Right?" I sigh. "Too bad there's not a lot of demand for a 'sleight-of-hand do-gooder.'"

"What about that lady?" Xander points.

"The one with the yappy dog?"

"Nah," he says. "She seems like she has everything she wants. I mean that one." He points around her, at a little woman with knobby knees covered in bagging stockings. She's pulled her cap off her head and she's muttering something to herself while she tries to smooth her hair down.

"*Audi quietem*." I whisper.

And suddenly her muttering is clear. "—can't believe she said that. I have plenty of hair. I just wear these hats because it's cold outside. Her hair looks worse than mine —she should have cut it years ago."

In spite of her muttered defenses, her hair is clearly quite thin. There are noticeable bald patches on the side, and even on the top, I can see scalp.

"Is that the kind of thing you can help with?" Xander asks.

I've never tried, but I get a kind of tingling feeling, and that's always how I know. I nod my head up and down slowly and think carefully about how to phrase it. "*Ubi parum est, satis sit*." When I whip the tip of my wand toward her, I can almost feel the spell zing outward from it.

"What did you say?" he asks, his eyes bright.

"I'm not sure it matters that much," I say.

"Huh?" He turns almost entirely sideways, his eyes spearing me. "I thought the words are all that matters—don't they guide the energy? Because that poor woman does *not* need to be, I don't know, made worse. It really doesn't matter what you say?"

I shrug. "I was always taught that we have to say the right thing in the right way with the right movements. But probably because I'm not a real witch—"

"Stop." Xander wraps an arm around my shoulders. "You're a real witch."

"You know what I mean." The whole reason I asked him to come is that I figure he'll get it. "I'm not quite right—not quite whole."

He flinches, but doesn't move his arm. "You're exactly who you're meant to be."

I realize that he's right. I am who I am, and maybe learning *why* I'm different is also the reason I can better accept that my magic just works differently than it should.

I'm not like Clark.

I'm not like my teachers.

I'm different.

And maybe that's okay.

"But their method of casting spells doesn't work for me. Maybe I can't quite get the intonation right. Maybe I whip my hands wrong. Either way, when I cast spells like *this*, it's about the feeling. The words I used were 'where there is little, let there be enough,' but it has more to do with the feeling I infuse into my spell than anything else. I want her not to be embarrassed anymore. Maybe that means more hair, or maybe it changes her heart. I'm not sure."

"So it's possible that *nothing* will happen that we can see?" Xander raises one eyebrow. "Seriously? Because that's depressing."

"Maybe." I shrug.

"Then how do you know it worked?"

"Sometimes I don't. Sometimes it's about faith."

Only, that's not what happens today.

Maybe my magic knows that I need a visible win. Because in that very moment, the woman's hat falls off, landing in the dirt on the side of the walkway. She cries out, bending over to retrieve it. But her free hand lifts up toward her hair, which is now much longer, much fuller, and a bright, orangey-red.

"Holy fang," Xander says. "You saved a redhead. No wonder she was muttering so fervently."

"I hope she likes it," I say.

The woman has forgotten all about the hat, and now both her hands are stroking her new, full head of hair. "Lawdy, it feels like a wig. What in the good Lawd's name just happened?" When she moves away from us, she's skipping. I think that's evidence that she's pleased.

"Who's next?" Xander asks.

We sit there for almost two hours together, and I find three more people who need a little extra help. Each one heals something in my battered heart.

We'd probably have found more, but someone unexpected turns up.

"Minerva?" The voice is husky, deep, and confident. "What are you doing out here?"

When I turn to my left, my eyes can hardly believe it. Ricky's here, in full uniform. The guardian I've had a crush on for almost two years.

"What are you doing here?" I ask.

"I could ask you the same thing. The Chief says you're an hour late for your shift already, and that you've called in sick for three days. In all the time he's known you, you've never once called in sick."

"You've never called in sick?" Xander blinks. "That's weird, isn't it?"

I shrug. "I'm pretty healthy."

"I guess," Xander says.

"What's going on?" Ricky asks. "You don't *look* sick. A little pale, maybe, but not sick."

My shoulders slump.

"You know what? I'm gonna head back." Xander stands. "I bet Izaak's freaking out." He's gone faster than a popsicle in July.

Surprisingly, Giggles is my more valiant friend. When Ricky walks toward me, she hops onto my knee and flaps her wings, a strange clicking sound coming from her beak, like she's gnashing her pigeon teeth.

"What's this?" he asks. "She's become an attack pigeon?"

I want to die a little bit. "I'm quitting my job." As soon as I say the words, I realize they're true. I hadn't even admitted it to myself yet, but I can't keep working there. Not anymore.

Not now that I know who I am.

And what I'm not.

Ricky practically splutters, which is quite unexpected. He's always so *confident*, so *muscular*, and so *put together.* Seeing his eyes bug and watching him cast around for something to say is oddly satisfying. I may not ever be a great officer, but I can at least cause the excellent ones to be at a loss for words.

"I found out some stuff," I say. "Now that I know, I don't think I'm suitable for police work."

He takes a seat on the end of the bench, side-eying Giggles warily. "I have no idea what you could have discovered, but I've watched you enough to know that you're an excellent paranormal affairs officer. One of the best, in fact."

"Not good enough to be a guardian," I say. "But excellent?" I can't help snorting.

"I voted for you every time," he says. "Some others had their qualms, but even they were coming around."

"They were?" I can hardly believe what he's saying.

"If it hadn't been for your chief," he says, "it would have happened a long time ago."

If it hadn't been for the Chief? What does that mean?

Ricky slaps his forehead. "Pretend I didn't say that. It's classified."

I slide over, dislodging Giggles from my leg with my shoving hand by accident. "You're going to have to explain, now that you've said that much."

He swallows slowly.

"Come on, Ricky." The more I think about what he said, the more I need him to interpret it for me. "Because it almost sounded like my chief is the reason I *didn't* get the job."

He sighs. "He is."

Suddenly, nothing makes sense. Dad's friend is the only one who believes in me. He's got my back, because of his faith in Dad's legacy.

Right?

"We've never hired a guardian who couldn't get a recommendation from their own Chief, but we were strongly considering it in spite of that. You just never wavered—you never gave up, and that's a very impressive trait." He touches my hand and then backs off. "Look, I don't know what you discovered, but how bad can it be? You're so close."

I still can't believe the Chief didn't recommend me. How could that be? "I saw his recommendation letter," I say. "He showed it to me."

Ricky shrugs. "I'm not sure what he showed you, but I've read the same letter from him a dozen times. He says that while you're a bright and capable person, your spellcraft is simply not up to level, and you'd be a danger to both yourself and others if we were to bring you onto the guardian force."

It feels like someone hit me on the nose. "But if he thinks that, why do I still have a job at all?"

"That's what we all wanted to know." Ricky's broad shoulders slump a bit, and he focuses on Giggles, who flew right back up on the bench. She is for sure glaring at me, though. "Is she really your familiar?"

"It's a long story," I say. "But yes."

"That's strange, but somehow, it fits."

As I watch my janky and still-fat pigeon hop down and strut around me to peck at the plastic lid to a soda and the discarded shells from peanuts, I am profoundly depressed. The man I thought was in my corner has been stabbing me in the back. My attempt to wow my co-workers resulted in me bonding a flying rat familiar.

More than ever, I realize that I actually should quit my job.

"I know you don't want to share, but I'm a safe person to talk to," he says. "If you want to get feedback from someone, I'll keep your secret safe."

"My secret?"

"You said you found out something that makes you think you're not suitable for police work. In my experience, the number one thing that makes someone suitable for police work, other than intelligence, which you clearly don't lack, is bravery and the will to serve. You certainly have always had those attributes in spades."

"I did, anyway."

"I can't really think of anything that would render you unsuitable." He shrugs. "So don't feel pressured. But if you're planning to walk away, what do you have to lose by telling me?"

When he puts it that way, I realize he's right. What *do* I have to lose? "I'm half-human." The words are flat, falling like boulders into a stream with a heavy plonk.

And even though he said he couldn't think of anything, I can tell by the look on his face that Ricky does see why that's a problem. "It explains the need for remedial magic classes. Most half-humans are magical duds." He inhales sharply then, as if just realizing it's not a very nice term to use around someone who is very close to that.

All my hopes that he might somehow cast new light on my situation evaporate. He simply stares straight ahead, his brow furrowed. "That is hard," he finally says.

It's all I can do to keep from bawling on the bench in the middle of the herd of humans now milling around us. Central Park has gotten busier and busier as I've moped. No matter how many cheer-me-up do-gooder spells I cast, I'll never really be able to change who I am.

And I'm unsuitable for my chosen profession. Even Ricky doesn't disagree now that he knows.

As if she can sense my severe depression, Giggles flutters up to my shoulder and rubs her face against my cheek. It would be a more touching movement if she hadn't just been eating a cold and dirty French fry off the ground.

But even so, it makes my heart a bit lighter.

"The one good thing about it is that, if you really are giving up on becoming a guardian," Ricky says, "there's something I can finally do." When he turns toward me, his eyes are sparkling. "Something I've wanted to do for a really long time."

My heart skips a beat. "What's that?"

"Since you wanted to come work with us, I had to keep things professional. And I know this isn't the best time for you." He ducks his head a bit, which is about the cutest thing I've ever seen. "But I've had a crush on you for a while. Would you go on a date with me?"

I may not be fit to be Amber's partner. I'll definitely never make guardian. But the fact that Ricky knows the truth. . .and still wants to take me out? That means something.

"Okay," I say. "I'd like that."

❧ 7 ☙

XANDER

Wolves like rooms without windows. It's probably some kind of connection to our home world, which was purportedly dark, or maybe it's because it makes our homes feel more like dens with a single entrance and exit.

Either way, the first day of college for me was already a hard one. The dorm room they assigned me at NYU had *two* windows.

Even more ominous was the fact that there were two beds.

"Excuse me," I said as loudly as I could muster.

The resident hall assistant didn't even turn back.

I walked closer and waved my letter in his periphery. "I'm supposed to have a single room. I think they put me in the wrong place."

He didn't even glance at my paper. "All single rooms became doubles."

"I'm sorry?" My hands clenched at my sides. My nostrils widened. I needed to calm down, or I was going to get furry right here. "I *need* a single."

"You sound just like him." The resident hall assistant shook his head and walked off, apparently unconcerned that my life was now in jeopardy.

Without anyone here to even yell at, I didn't really know what to do.

It was my mom's brilliant idea that I enroll in a normie college—I had become reasonably proficient in controlling my inner wolf, and she was tired of me being mauled, attacked, and beaten to a pulp. Daily. I agreed with her. The idea of masquerading among the much less vicious, much more friendly normies was an appealing one. Dad argued at first, but not for long. He just shrugged and said that it wouldn't work out, and told me to call him when I failed.

Now that I was standing there, in the middle of a normie-occupied dorm room, I was thinking how annoying it would be to tell him that he was right. I would have to slink back to the advanced pack training coordinator and beg for whatever spots they could spare. I schlepped my way back to my room as calmly as I could, preparing myself to call my dad and tell him the words I really didn't want to say. If I was suitably humble, maybe he could come pick me up before my roommate showed.

I glanced at the depressing mattress on the second bed, just as saggy and squashed as the one on mine. I ran through my options. At least once a week, I had to shift. If I didn't, I would shift involuntarily, and there was no way to know when that would happen.

Most roommates were worried about finding a decent time to poop without their roomie getting pissed about it. Not me. I was worried about him catching me in the middle of looking like a giant dog. The more I thought about it, the less workable it sounded. Reluctantly, I picked up my phone.

And the door swung open.

The widening of his eyes behind his dark-rimmed glasses, the quick inhalation of breath, and the slight scent of spiked perspiration told me he was as surprised as me at the presence of another person. He glanced down at a paper in his hand. "I'm sorry," he said. "I must be in the wrong place."

"You had a single room too?" My tone was flat.

His brow furrowed. "Or maybe you're in the wrong place."

"Apparently they had too many students," I said. "Singles all became doubles."

He shook his head. "Oh, no. That can't be. I need a single."

"You have irritable bowel, too?" I asked.

"Huh?"

"Nevermind." I waved. "I'm Xander. I make jokes when I'm nervous. But don't worry. There's no way I can do a double either. I'm calling my dad right now."

"Oh good," he said.

Only, my dad didn't answer. An hour later, none of our parents had picked up when we called. And I'd discovered that this Clark guy was actually pretty funny. "I can't believe that they thought having a single room would make up for you having to come to NYU instead of Columbia."

"Mom was mad," Clark said, "but I felt like I was just lucky to have a scholarship here at all. If I hadn't, I might be learning to plunge toilets right now."

"I might yet be doing that," I said. "But what exactly did your dad do with your college fund?"

"You wouldn't believe me if I told you," he said.

"I'm a pretty gullible guy."

"Since you're not planning to stay," he said, "why not?" He glanced left and right, as if he needed to make sure no one else could hear him. "He spent it on a wand."

I blinked. A *normie* spent money on a *wand?* I must have misheard him.

"You know, like the Harry Potter variety."

A collectible wand? What kind of collectible costs enough to put someone through Columbia? "You're kidding."

He shrugged. "It had a pretty fancy core."

"Don't tell me," I said. "Akero feather."

His jaw dropped. And that's when I realized my mistake. I hadn't spent enough time around normies. The Harry Potter stuff had phoenix and dragon and some other kind of feather or something. But normies don't know about the akero. I cleared my throat. "I meant phoenix. Isn't that the best?"

Clark stood up, his eyes laser-focused on mine. "You said akero."

I swallowed. I didn't remember what the punishment was for disclosing secret information, but I was pretty sure accidentally using a word didn't count. "Aki-what?" I forced a laugh. "I don't even know what I was saying. I definitely meant phoenix."

He tilted his head, his eyes scanning my face, then my body, then my bags. "You wanted a single room, too. In fact, you said you'd go home without one."

I stood up. "Good reminder. I should call my dad again."

"If I said I *wasn't* supposed to be going to Columbia,

if I said I was going to the New York Institute. . . would that mean anything to you?"

The New York Institute. . .of Magic? It was on the tip of my tongue to ask, but I couldn't quite bring myself to do it. Could he be supernatural? Wolves keep to themselves. We don't go out and meet others, and I could clearly smell that he wasn't a were.

But what about a wizard? His dad spent a fortune on a *wand*. It would almost make *more* sense if it was a real wand and not some quack pot normie collectible inspired by a movie franchise. I wanted to say more, but I just swallowed and sat back down.

"Do you *want* to stay here? Or are you happy to call your dad and go home?"

I squirmed a bit. "I mean, he told me I'd end up calling him and coming home, but I figured I'd at least make it a week or two first."

He frowned again. "Why'd he think you'd come home?" He scanned me again, as if looking for clues.

"What kind of institute were you going to? To study what?" I asked.

He circled toward the window. "Were you happy to have two windows in here?" He tossed his head behind him.

That seemed like an easy enough question to answer. "No."

"Because you wanted privacy?"

"I don't like there being other places people can come through to get inside," I said.

"You have a lot of bags," he said. "More than I do."

I noticed he was right.

"Are you big on fashion?" As he asked, his lip curled,

taking in my cheaply made jeans and t-shirt. "Doesn't look like it."

"I'm pretty hard on clothes," I said.

"I knew it." He made a fist and pumped it. "You're a wolf, right?" The gleam in his eye, like he'd solved a puzzle, was what did it. I should have denied, called my dad, and gone home.

He was clearly *not* a wolf, and one thing no wolves did was make friends with non-wolves. My dad had destroyed my life by violating that with a normie.

I knew better.

But he wasn't a normie either.

Wolves especially didn't make friends with other supernaturals, but this guy was funny. He was different. For the first time in my life, I didn't feel like I was a piece made for a puzzle that didn't exist.

I felt like he might be a *friend*. Something I'd never had.

"I am," I said. And I didn't look away.

The brilliant smile on his face told me I'd made the right call. "Maybe a double wouldn't be the worst thing," he said. "I'm a wizard."

"I kinda figured," I said. "You didn't smell like a dragon, and your dad bought a wand."

He chuckled. "An akero feather wand—you nailed that one. Only, we don't have cores to our wands. They mostly just focus our energy, and sometimes they store it up. The akero feather ones, though, they can boost us. Dad shouldn't have bought it, but they're so rare, I don't even fault him. He said I can have it when he dies." He cringed then. "Not that I'm, like, eager for that day."

"Of course not."

"So what do you say?" He stuck out his hand. "All

wizards who want jobs that require interface with humans have to do a year at a human institution. I figured I might as well do it before I get used to college. If I have to be here, I may as well do it with someone I like."

Someone he liked. The words were casual. To someone else, they might have been meaningless. But it was the first time in my life anyone had ever said that to me.

My mom hated that I was a wolf.

My dad hated that I was a normie.

The wolves couldn't accept my weakness.

The normies couldn't accept my otherness.

But this wizard, after barely an hour, *liked me.*

I wouldn't have called my dad again if someone had a gun pressed to my temple.

"Hey, how about we make a deal?" Clark asked. "I need about an hour a day to practice spells, and I'm sure there's something you need, too."

I nodded. "I have to shift at least once a week."

"Great," he said. "We can block the windows however you want. And if you'll cover for me when I make a strange sound or when I'm practicing, I'll cover for you, too."

"I can shift to a wolf and back in five minutes. The most important thing you can do for me is watch for something," I said.

"For what?"

"The worst thing that can happen to a wolf who's away from a pack is that he can fray."

He bobbed his head. "I heard of that, but I don't know what to watch for." His eyebrows shot up. "Wait, you go crazy, right? You attack people?"

I shook my head. "Nah, first you start kind of spacing out, and then you get super jumpy, and then you start to rage out. If you're doing that, you're already in real danger."

Clark had crossed the room then, and clapped a hand on my shoulder. "No problem. The first time you start losing your keys, I'll organize an intervention and sew up the raw edges."

"Sew up?"

He rolls his eyes. "Fraying?"

I laughed. At the time, the idea of the fray was actually funny to me. That year at NYU, a lot of things went wrong. We had so many near misses, I should have run home, not walked. I was almost exposed as a wolf a dozen times. Clark had trouble with two guys who hated him for no reason. Normie classes were hard, and the food was almost inedible.

And it was the best year of my entire life to that point.

True to his word, Clark watched me for signs, but there weren't any. I was as solid as I'd ever been. He made a lot of jokes about me fraying, and they were funny.

But I've noticed he doesn't joke about it any more. Gavin brings me the check, and I realize I don't have my wallet. Again. "Uh—"

"I got it," Clark says.

"I've got money upstairs," I say. "I've been working so much overtime that I have tons of money. It's just that I'm tired and so I—"

Clark claps his hand on my shoulder. "No big deal, man."

"Are you guys leaving?" Roxana's voice startles me and I practically leap out of my chair.

"Whoa, easy there tiger," Clark says.

"Tiger." Roxana laughs. "Because he's a wolf. Good one."

Clark's jokes and pet names are never very funny. I wonder if it means something, that she's laughing at them. The two of them have been acting weird ever since he fought that dragon on the roof. I keep meaning to ask Clark about what exactly happened, but I only think about it when Roxana's around. That's precisely when I can't ask.

"I've got to go soon," I say. "Duty calls."

"Did your boss say anything?" Roxana asks, the note of hope in her voice awfully close to desperation.

"Er, well, actually—"

"You didn't ask?" She sighs melodramatically as she sinks into the corner of the couch and drops her head into her hands. "I need a job, Xan."

"Trust me when I say, you do not want to work with a wolf pack," Clark says.

"They're working Xander to the bone," she says. "I figure maybe they could use some help with *something*. Plus, it's his connection to me that makes him so attractive to clients."

"Why don't you just ask Lionel to help you find a job?" I ask. "It seems like—"

"He's the last person she should ask," Clark says. "The less ties to him, the better. When they fake their breakup soon—"

"Do you even want to do that?" I ask. "I mean, he's handsome, he's funny, he's smart, he's powerful, and he's *loaded*, right?"

Roxana frowns. "He's officious, he's arrogant, and most importantly, he's got his own agenda." She folds her arms. "I need to find a job with no connection to him, pronto. And if I'm surrounded by a pack of wolves all day, even better."

I don't have the heart to tell her that my boss, while happy making a profit off the notoriety of my connection to her, has no intention of wading into the risk she drags along with her. "I did mention it," I say. "But I don't think there's a lot you could do there."

Her sigh is so deep that her shoulders droop. "Oh, fine." But then she perks up. "Maybe if I went in with you today, they might change their mind." She smiles slowly, and then she bites her lip.

My heart races. My eyes can't seem to look at anything but her. What she's saying makes sense. "I mean, it can't hurt."

"Roxie," Clark says. "Reel it back in. Geez."

The words penetrate the fog around my brain, and I glance around. Almost every person in the room is looking at Roxana, all of them with glazed eyes.

Her charm.

"Are you kidding?" The irritation I feel shoves it back a bit. "You're charming me?"

She rolls her eyes. "Can you blame me? If you can get me in the door, I think I can convince your boss to find me something to do."

Before I can object, she sticks her lower lip out, and my gut clenches. Then she bats her eyes, and I swallow. "I mean, I guess it's fine. It's not like you pose a threat."

She stands up and moves toward me, almost like a cat. "Thank you so much, Xander. You're such a good friend."

Clark stands and grabs her wrist.

I want to rip his throat out.

Before I can do anything to defend her, Roxana frees herself, twisting out of his grasp. "Now Clark, we all use the weapons at our disposal."

"I think he should take her." Izaak darts around the corner of the sofa and sits down. "And I know you need to leave for work soon, but we need to talk."

Something about his tone snaps me out of it.

Roxana and Clark are staring at him, too, open mouthed. She looks so distracted that maybe it was just that Roxana released me. Who knows?

"Can you guys sit?" he asks.

I glance at my watch.

"I'll be fast." Izaak never looks this serious.

Reluctantly, I sit back down.

Roxana perches on the arm of my chair, which is really distracting. Clark sits, too, but he's glaring at both of us.

"I wanted to get Minerva and Bevin here too, but I think it's more important that we address it quickly than all together." He glances around the room. "Clark?"

Clark blinks, and then whips out his wand. "You want a ring of silence?"

Izaak nods. Watching him like this is freaking me out.

I have a sinking feeling in my stomach that tells me I might know what he wants to say. My hands ball into fists at my side. I can feel the set of my jaw tightening.

Once Clark is done, Izaak sighs. "You know I'm not great with all the pretty words."

"Or even the ugly ones," I say.

"I'll just say it. I think you may be fraying." Izaak's

eyes are sad, but he doesn't drop them. "You've been forgetting things. You've been spacing out. And you're always shocked or worried about things."

I think about how much Roxana startled me when she walked in. Did Clark react the same way?

"I know you haven't been raging out on anyone, but isn't that the last stage?"

"Sure," I say. "But—"

Someone bumps into the edge of Clark's bubble and we all feel the reverberation as he passes on through.

I'm not the only one who turns.

It's another mage. He should have sensed the resistance.

"Do you mind?" Clark asks. "Private conversation here."

"Do you mind?" the guy asks. "Public shop." He points at the sign. "Lots of people here need gloffee, and that's the closest route to the counter." He gestures right in front of Clark and me.

"You look like you could benefit from the few extra steps," Izaak says. "Didn't your mama teach you manners?"

The stocky man's lip curls and he glances down at a ring on his hand. It flashes red. Then he looks at me. It flashes yellow. "A vampire and a wolf?" He strides forward, kicking Clark as he passes.

Intentionally.

"You should think about who you want to be seen with." His sneer stops cold when his eyes reach Roxana. And he freezes. "Oh."

"Dragona," she says. "You don't even need to waste energy on that ring to name my race. I'll tell you for free."

"I know who you are," he says. "But I don't know why you're with these losers."

Clark can protect himself. So can Izaak, mostly. But Roxana can't. When the mage reaches for her, I don't even think. I've been trained my entire life to protect, but fighting for what's mine, that's an instinct.

I kick the man's ankle as I stand, my hands shifting into claws, my jaw and mouth changing shape. Before I realize what I've done, I'm snapping at the man's exposed throat, my clawed hand pressed against his throat.

"Whoa," Clark says. "Easy tiger."

"Pretty sure no one here thinks he's a tiger," Izaak says.

"Does this mean he's showing signs of rage?" Roxana whispers.

But I hear her loud and clear.

And I'm worried that she's right.

8

XANDER

I can't believe that I listened to Izaak. I know she wants a job, and Izaak wanted a witness present when I tell my boss that I may be fraying, but bringing Roxana along was a terrible idea.

Every single wolf in the Manhattan pack, male and female, tracks our movement from the first step we take inside the pack's compound. In the past few years, I've essentially entered and departed like a ghost. No one hails me. No one waves goodbye. I was never part of the pack, and for some of the wolves, I was barely tolerated. Okay, for most of them.

I'd walk through the wide double doors of the pack and through the courtyard with my head down, my eyes focused on the cobblestones under my feet. I'd dodge and scoot and leap out of the way whenever necessary to keep from being a nuisance. I'd usually duck into the security door immediately and keep to that small set of rooms whenever I was inside. In fact, I've only been to the alpha's apartment—in the dead center of the pack complex—one time before.

But today, as we walk directly toward Lo Ren Fang's apartments, passing suite after suite of doors—benefits coordinator, the clinic, tech, pest control, installation— the resident wolves start lining up along the path. The murmurs were initially quiet enough that only I could hear them, but even Roxana is starting to react at this point.

"—dragon shifter from the tele?"

"So he is friends with her?"

"—wasn't a lie?"

"She's even prettier than she looked on the screen."

"I thought they'd used computer enhancements."

"—boobs are for sure fake."

"What about her lips? Think she gets filler?"

"—are useless. She can't even shift. Her only job is to make eggs."

Roxana stiffens when she hears that, and for some reason, I start itching to shift. Fur sprouts along my arms, and my incisors start to lengthen.

"Easy, Xan." Roxana takes my hand casually, like we often stroll along holding hands. "I'm sorry for the extra attention, but at least management will know people are watching."

I gulp. If someone had told me, the day I met Roxana for the first time, that we might walk through my pack—er, the pack I want to join—hand-in-hand? I'd have called them crazy. But I can't really enjoy it, not while I'm wondering if I may be put down soon.

Because at the end of the day, if I really *am* fraying, the only solution is to kill me. That's the reason for Roxana tagging along. If I came here alone and Lo Ren decided I *was* fraying, I'd never walk back out again. No investigation, no hearing, no second opinions, just *done*.

I can't even blame him. That's an alpha's job, and a truly frayed wolf is a menace. But some wolves start to fray and just sort of. . . stay a little loopy, but never dangerous. They can stay like that for years, or so I've heard.

"Everything's going to be fine." Roxana sounds like she believes it. I suppose that's the difference between us. She was raised being told that the world will generally be okay. People will take care of her, and she's destined for greatness.

Not me. I've spent my life with my face shoved into the dirt, and I have every reason to believe things will only get worse from there.

So when we near the alpha's front door, and he's standing there ready to greet us with his mate at his side, a wide smile spread across his face, I have *no* idea what to expect.

"Roxana Goldenscales." Lo Ren Fang's smile looks genuine, but since he's never smiled at me, I can't be sure. "What a welcome surprise." I never pay attention to what he looks like—he's been a fixture in my life for years—but with Roxana beside me, I think about what she must be seeing. He's taller than I am, broader too, and he has an edge to him that is hard to explain. It's something about being an alpha. His jaw is squarer, his teeth shinier, and something about him is feral in a way that no one else you meet is.

"You must be Lo Ren Fang," she says. "The Manhattan Pack Alpha."

"Xander has said good things, I hope," he says.

"Actually, he never talks about the pack at all," Roxana says, her lips twisting. "I was under the impression that he's not allowed to. The things I've learned about you all came from my studies back home."

"I should have expected that your mother would provide a broad education for her daughter." Lo Ren Fang backs up and gestures toward the open doorway. "And do we line up with what you were taught?"

Roxana inhales and exhales slowly, as if she's preparing to pronounce judgment. I suppose, in a way, she is. Everyone in the pack lined up to watch her enter. She's essentially royalty from the dragona world. There are far, far more wolves than dragona, mostly because of what she represents. Only a few females are born, and they can have a limited number of children—almost all of whom are more males.

But dragona live twenty times as long as we do, and one male dragona could probably kill a dozen of us, if not more. They're bigger, scarier, and more powerful. Having her here is kind of like having an ambassador whom every dragona in America would listen to—her opinion on the Manhattan pack could literally impact Lo Ren's life in the future. It's strange to be walking alongside someone who matters so very much more than I do. I'd never even thought about her that way, because she never acted like that.

It makes me like Roxana more.

The wolves who lined up alongside the path start to collapse inward, coalescing behind us, all of them wanting to hear and see a little more of her.

"I think everything looks very organized and tidy," she says. "And the alpha certainly looks every bit the powerful, savage leader I was told he would be." Her smile is forced, but I doubt anyone other than me will be able to tell. I've seen too many genuine smiles from her to believe this lie.

"Please, come inside and we can talk more," Rylan

says. She's much, much smaller than Lo Ren in her human form, but her wolf form is close to the same as his. I wonder if it bothers her to meet people in human form and be seen as so petite and small.

Wolves don't like to feel weak—ever.

"Thank you so much for the invite," Roxana says. "We do have some things to discuss."

"Excellent," Rylan says. "I've always thought we'd be friends if we met in real life." Her smile isn't fake—or at least, it doesn't seem fake. She hates me, so I've never seen anything even pleasant-adjacent from her in the past.

"Today I'm just here for moral support," she says. Then she spins around and eyes all the wolves behind us. "My dear friend Xander needs to talk to the alpha. It may be hard for him to do that without a little privacy."

"Of course." Rylan, Lo Ren's mate, tosses her long shock of black hair behind her shoulders and squares up to face the crowd. "Do none of you have work to do?" Her eyes flash, and the wolves freeze.

"Get to it," Lo Ren barks, reinforcing his command with a pulse that I can barely feel. My connection to the pack is even more muted than usual, a bare echo of his former power. I hope that's not further evidence that our fears are justified.

"Come inside," Lo Ren says. "Tell us the reason Xander needs support from you."

He may have sent most of the wolves away, but an alpha is rarely alone, especially when outsiders are present. His favorite shredder, Cliff, stands near the window, leaning against the frame to make it look like he's not on guard. Harlan, Rylan's brother, is sitting down at the front of the long table in the dining room, probably just finishing up his report. He's the chief ranger in the pack, and he provides a summary of the day's surveillance and intel every morning.

Once the door closes, blocking the remaining wolves from listening in on our conversation, I get right to the point. No one here wants to catch up on my life, no matter how friendly they may be acting in front of Roxana.

"I think I may be fraying."

Rylan's hand flies to her mouth, but I still hear her gasp loud and clear.

Lo Ren, conversely, freezes. His eyes harden and narrow.

"I'm sure there's a test you can do, or something like that?" Roxana hasn't released my hand, and she tightens her fingers. I didn't tell her beforehand that if I *am* fraying and they can confirm that it's progressed to a dangerous point, they'll kill me. Right here. Right now. And they'll be right to do it.

For the first time, I'm struck with guilt. If they kill me in front of her, how traumatic will that be for poor Roxana? I should come up with a reason for her to leave, but I just can't seem to think of what to say.

"You brought your friend with you to make sure that we're cautious in our judgment?" Rylan cocks one eyebrow.

"Judgment?" Roxana asks, shifting closer to me.

"A werewolf who frays must be eliminated." Lo Ren's voice is practically glacial. "They're a risk to everyone around them."

"You say it like it's black and white," Roxana says. "We've barely seen anything with Xander, but he doesn't have a pack that's watching his back." She purses her lips and scowls, making her opinion on that clear. "Consequently, he has to be doubly careful."

"Wolves with packs don't fray," Rylan says.

Roxana drops my hand and steps toward her. "So you knew that leaving Xander out of your little club put him at risk of this thing that could require you to *kill* him, and still, you left him out?"

Rylan's nostrils flare. "You're not a werewolf so you don't understand."

"I understand bigotry whenever I see it," Roxana says. "I recognize small-mindedness, too. Believe me, dragona are *excellent* at doing the same thing. But I refuse to stand around while someone like that harms my friend." She crosses her arms.

Lo Ren steps closer, deceptively calm. The menace is practically rolling off him. "You're a female dragona. Correct me if I'm wrong, but you can't shift. Am I right?"

"I can't shift into a dragon," Roxana says. "But everyone knows who I am, and my people take my well-being very seriously. I was caught by no less than four cameras on my way into your compound. If I don't leave this compound in one piece, my father will send dozens of male dragona here to deal with it." She doesn't look the least bit intimidated. "Is that something you think you're equipped to handle? Fighting my father?" She quirks one eyebrow.

"Calm down," Rylan says. "He was just asking."

"You may both think I'm a joke, and I may personally pose you no threat at all, but that's the exact reason why I'm the perfect friend to come with Xander. I can't hurt you, but you can't hurt him without consequences either." This time, it's her nostrils that flare. "Think long and hard about what you do today to Xander. If you don't handle this well, it won't be swept under a rug. It'll be lit on fire."

"He's a halfie," Rylan says. "We don't even need to sweep anything under a rug. He's under our purview, and he has no value."

"That's what's wrong with the entire supernatural world," Roxana says. "You all think that people's value comes from how strong they are."

"It does." Lo Ren steps closer still, his eyes focused entirely on Roxana. "If you're really so naive that you think value comes from anything but power, then I pity you."

Roxana, instead of backing down, steps closer to him, her index finger out. "You may think he has no power, but he's got powerful friends. And you are the most—"

I jump forward and grab her arm, because this doesn't seem to be going anywhere good. "I think what she means to ask is, can you check whether I'm fraying, and if I may be heading that way, is there anything you can recommend?" I glare at Roxana out of the side of my eyes. Did she forget that we're here to ask for help?

Her entire face falls, and she makes apologetic eyes at me. "Right." She nods. "That's what I meant to say."

"The only way to tell whether a wolf is fraying is for me to check your power conduit. If it's closed off. . ."

I swallow.

"What's a power conduit?" Roxana asks.

"Wolves have a connection in their brains," I explain. "The alpha can sense all of us through it, and he can discipline us, too."

"It's more than that," Lo Ren says. "I can share

energy—taking, or giving—that speeds healing, increases strength, and also boosts speed. I can also send punishments or pleasure. It's the core of what makes a werewolf a pack animal instead of a solitary individual. Wolves who don't experience this shared connection will eventually start to close off, and once they're no longer able to connect, they start to unravel."

"Then test it," Roxana says. "Tell us already."

My connection to him has never been strong—it was never formally established. I was never offered a permanent line, nor did I ever have a chance to accept one. I knew my connection was muted when we walked in, so I'm dreading the pulse of energy he'll use to test me. I brace myself for it, and then it comes.

A zap. Small. Barely there. I flinch, but it's nothing to what I should have done. That ought to have sent me writhing in pain.

"He's fraying," Lo Ren says. He cocks his head. "Now, Miss Goldenscales, what exactly are you proposing we do about it?"

"Can't you just bring him into your pack? Won't that fix it?"

Rylan's laugh is bitter. "Not now that it's begun."

"You think something about this is funny?" Roxana's eyes are flashing again, and she looks ready to strike Rylan. "Someone's life is at stake, and it's *your fault* and now you're laughing?"

"How is it our fault?" Rylan asks.

I'm guessing they won't come out of this as besties.

"Xander has always been a liability." Harlan almost never speaks, so I'm surprised when he does. "I voted against letting him work with us at all."

"And who are you, to be saying such rude things?" Roxana asks.

"I'm Rylan's brother," Harlan says. His hair is just as dark as his sister's, but his eyes are a startling blue. He stands and walks toward her. "And I wasn't being rude—only honest. You seem to value that. Halfies don't have the control, and they don't have the connection capacity of a full-blooded wolf to begin with. They're always at risk of fray, much more so than a usual wolf. And a wolf that's mid-fray can send others spiraling. It's like a virus." He stalks closer to Roxana, his eyes intent. "It must be contained."

Without even thinking about it, I step in between Harlan and Roxana. "No."

"No?" His cerulean eyes sparkle. "You think you could stop me from harming her, if I chose to do it?"

It happens again, an involuntary shift. This time, hair ripples down my spine, and my legs start to bend inward.

"Enough," Lo Ren says. "The reason I allowed you to join us to begin with is that I hoped you might find a mate. The one thing that can stabilize a halfie is a true mate—it will strengthen your conduit and reinforce your connection. Any children you had would be nearly full-blooded. You've been here for years, and as far as I can tell, you've made no efforts to even seek—"

"Don't you believe that mates are written in the stars?" Roxana asks. "So if he didn't have a mate within your pack, how would he ever have found one?"

Lo Ren blinks. "What?"

"Did you send him on assignments where he'd visit other places?" She puts one hand on her hip. "Did you bring other packs here?"

"Well, no," Lo Ren says. "But—"

"Then do it now," Roxana says. "Introduce him to other packs. Let him try and find his mate, so that he can stabilize or whatever. And if he does, then bring him in as a member of your pack." She takes my hand again. "You said it's *starting*, but you didn't say he's frayed. He still has a somewhat open connection, so let him look with purpose at the very least."

Lo Ren's brow furrows. "I suppose—"

"One week," Rylan says. "We'll send you to see every pack within an easy distance of ours, and you'll take your little girlfriend with you."

"My little girlfriend?" I ask. "Do you mean Roxana? Why should she—"

"With the amount of charm that pumps out of her naturally," Rylan says, "if you are at all attracted to a woman in the other packs, you'll know she's your mate."

"Charm?" Roxana asks. "I haven't used a speck of charm since walking in here."

"And yet, every single male who was gathering was experiencing feelings of lust, along with most of the females," Lo Ren says. "As the alpha, I can feel that. Intentional or not, you bring that out of everyone around you."

"Fine," she says. Clearly she already knew some of that. "I'll go with him. And within a week, we'll be back here with his mate. I want your promise that you'll bring him into your pack when we are."

Rylan snorts. "If he returns with a bonded mate, sure. We'll let him in."

"Great," Roxana says. "Then give us a list of packs."

And that's how I wind up renting a car the next morning and driving out toward New Haven, Connecticut. "You know we can't possibly see all those packs in a week."

She's flipping through page after page. The printout that Rylan gave us had a hundred and forty one packs listed that are all within a three-hour drive, and she seems determined to visit them all. Judging by the enormous suitcase she threw into the trunk of this tiny car, she's prepared to be gone for a while.

"Your mate could be at any of these places," she says.

"Or at none of them," I say. "Just being pragmatic, I may not even have a mate. Or if I do, my only hope at finding her might be at an all-wolf meet."

"Ooh, yes, let's do that."

"They're once a year, during the summer, in Montana."

"Well that's inconvenient," she says.

"You can only go if you're sent by your pack," I say. "So I was never eligible."

"Wait." She drops the papers in her lap. "You're saying that you need a mate so you can join their pack, but you can't find a mate, because you can't go to the mate-finding conference without already having a pack?"

"You've just summed up the gist of my entire life."

"The whole deck was stacked against you."

"Always."

"Well, I still have faith," she says. "One of these places—"

"Roxana, don't take this the wrong way," I say. "I really appreciate your excitement and your willingness to just drop everything and help, but—"

She starts laughing.

"What?"

"Drop everything." She's still laughing.

"I have no job. What I do have is a fake boyfriend who promptly disappeared after essentially causing a horrible ruckus on the roof of my daddy's building. Then there's Clark, who I'm pretty sure has had a crush on me since high school. He's always coming over and kind of mooning over me. And then there's every single person I meet in New York City who says, 'Whoa, you're Roxana Goldenscales! Holy Angel. Can I take a photo?' and then they try and grope me or kiss me or get my phone number. Trust me when I say, I had nothing going on that I didn't want to escape."

"You do need to find a job, though," I say.

She shrugs. "I don't feel like it's going to happen right now, at ground zero. So don't feel bad about taking me away from all that. Honestly, it feels nice to be someone who might possibly help you find your mate. For once in my life, I'd be doing something helpful."

"I just don't want you to blame yourself when I don't find someone," I say. "That's just how my life goes." As I say the words, I realize what they mean. If I can't find some kind of fated mate in the next week—a woman who will be doomed to be tied to a half-human for the rest of her life—then I'll be going back home. . .to die.

"It's how your life *went*," she says. "But you're not alone anymore. You have friends, and we're not going to just let that idiotic pack eliminate you. If we don't find your mate, you don't go back there. We'll have met dozens of other packs, and surely one of them will be run by good people who will care about helping you."

Poor Roxana. She knows nothing about werewolves.

But by the time we've met with our third pack, she's starting to get the idea.

"They were as bad as Lo Ren."

Worse, actually, but I don't say that out loud. She already knows.

"I'm sure this one will be better," I lie.

"It's not like Fishkill, New York is a really auspicious name," she says. "But maybe the people there are really nice."

When we approach with the tonic that Rylan wanted us to deliver to the alpha's mate as an excuse for visiting, a contingent of wolves runs out to meet us. It happened at the second place as well, so at least Roxana's not caught off guard.

I explain why we're here and ask to be taken to see the alpha and his mate. All the wolves' heads swivel toward Roxana, but no one asks why she's with me. So far, no one has. She's not quite as recognizable out here, but most people still figure out who she is quickly. It helps that wolves can smell dragona and she's clearly female. Now that she's not using Clark's elixir to hide her scales, people can put the gold scales and the dragona smell together pretty fast.

I hate to admit it, but her charm isn't hurting us either. The thoughts the wolves are thinking—I'd kick them if I wasn't here to try and meet most of the females in their pack.

"I'd be happy to meet the pack and pose for photos," Roxana says. It was her idea—no matter how miserable it seems like the task would be. It has been an effective way to get most of the wolves to gather. "I am Roxana Goldenscales, and I just *had* to escape the overcrowded city. I'm so lucky my dear friend Xander invited me along. She half-drapes herself across my shoulders, and I have to block out the stream of filth from the shredder guards.

"Maybe tone it down a bit," I whisper.

"Why?" she asks. "Isn't it the best way to get them to gather, and also for you to meet everyone?"

"Trust me," I say. "The male wolves don't need any encouragement."

"But if they're all frenzied, the females come along, don't they?"

I can't really argue with that, but the problem is that when she turns on the charm, I can't seem to ignore it either. Having her arms wrapped around me definitely isn't helping me keep control. The closer the other wolves come, the more I want to rip them limb from limb.

Mine! keeps pulsing through my brain, when other wolves circle round, panting and pacing. At least that means Rylan was right about one thing. If I notice a wolf through the haze that Roxana keeps creating, it'll be memorable for sure.

This time, when we're escorted inside, the wolves are already gathered. "Welcome," a blonde woman says, falling in step beside us. When she reaches us, the wolves stop guarding me and fall back to trail Roxana.

"We brought a tonic that Rylan said Harriet wanted."

"I did want it," the blonde—clearly Harriet herself— says. "But you've arrived in the middle of a pack meeting. We're reorganizing pack assignments and some of the wolves aren't too happy about the changes."

"Should we come back another time?" Roxana asks.

Harriet stops walking and turns to stare. "Why would you come back?" She holds out her hand. "Give me the tonic, and you can be on your way."

Duh. It's not like we can say that we'd sure like to meet a lot more wolves.

I can tell Roxana's trying to come up with an excuse because her mouth is compressed and her eyes are practically frowny. "But usually when—"

"You like to have people show you attention," Harriet says. "I can tell." Her smile is not friendly. "But you're not welcome here, dragona."

Something about the way she says it, the underlying menace, or the derision, rubs me the wrong way. "She has a name," I say. "What's more, I imagine you know it."

Harriet's nose scrunches, and her lip curls. "I don't care about her name, and I don't want any of you here in our compound."

So much for hoping they'd be nicer farther from the big city.

"Let's go," I say.

"Why are you in such a terrible mood?" Roxana asks. "We came with a gift, and we drove quite a way to deliver it. The least you could do is offer to let us use your restroom or grab a glass of water."

"Would that be enough?" Harriet asks. "If I give you water, will you leave?"

"Do you hate the dragona that much?" Roxana asks.

Harriet steps closer, baring her fangs in Roxana's face. "I don't have feelings about dragona one way or another, but I hate any female who comes into *my pack* and makes everyone want her."

"Oh." Roxana smiles. "That, I understand. How about this? I can go back to the car and wait. Xander's the one who needed to use the bathroom."

Harriet scowls, but she nods. I'm actually impressed with how well Roxana defused that situation. Unlike a wolf, she's capable of stepping down and backing off at will, seemingly.

But when Roxana turns to leave, the wolves following us trot after her.

"No," Harriet says. "Stay."

"Me?" Roxana turns.

"You, go."

Roxana is clearly confused, but she turns to leave again. Only, the wolves don't listen to their alpha's mate. They trot after Roxana again. Harriet's hand clenches at her side. That's the only warning I have before she shifts and lunges at Roxana.

Instinct takes over—Roxana's a friend, and she's being threatened. I shift on the fly, faster than I ever have before, and leap after Harriet. I snap at her, miraculously managing to grab the end of her tail and pull her up short before she can maul my friend.

But then Harriet turns, and the wolves who were following Roxana realize there's a fight—between their alpha's mate and another wolf.

I realize that I'm about to die right here. I release the tail immediately and loop around, coming up between the seven wolves that are close and Roxana, but I sense that more are coming. Many more.

We're about to be attacked by a *lot* of snapping teeth and bunched-up muscle.

"Everyone needs to stand down." Roxana holds up her hands. "Your alpha's mate is a real *female dog*, but that doesn't mean you have to make such a huge mistake."

The wolves were moving toward her steadily, but they stop, clearly still rational enough to listen to her words. "Harriet didn't like me, and that's fine, but I'm

Roxana Goldenscales, and I've been checking in with my daddy regularly, and he knows I'm here."

As far as I know, that's a lie.

"If you attack me, if you so much as harm a hair on my head, he'll bring his entire group of dragona here to roast this place to ash. And if you think you can fight them, think again. They won't even land. They'll melt your entire compound to the ground from the air."

A huge man walks through large double doors and into the clearing. "That may be the case," he says. "But Harriet tells me that your friend is that grey wolf right there, and I'm pretty sure your daddy won't care what we do with him." His grin is practically feral.

"But *I* will care." She stupidly steps in front of me, her arms spread.

"You can't do anything," the man says. "I've done my research. You're a female dragona, and they can't shift."

"I'm not entirely without power." Sparks fly from Roxana's hands, setting two of the closest wolves on fire.

I had no idea she could do that—it's pretty cool.

"Once you're done with your parlor tricks, I'd advise that you move aside," he says. "A little fire won't dissuade us, and my mate is so angry, she's not going to be able to just let you both go. He did attack her, on our pack territory, and that's not excusable."

"He attacked her to defend me," Roxana says, still not backing down. "If you can't let it go, then neither can I. She was in the wrong, no matter what ground we're standing on."

He shrugs. "Right and wrong don't mean much with wolves."

"I can see why all the wolves here like me so much," Roxana says, staring right at the blonde wolf Harriet shifted to become. "You're so ugly, they didn't know what beauty was until I showed up."

Harriet's lips curl up, and she lunges again.

Only this time, Roxana shoves me behind her. "Run," she shouts. "Now. Get to the car."

And as the wolves close in, following the lead of their alpha's mate, I know I should listen to her. The alpha won't let them hurt her—I'm virtually sure.

But I can't do it.

Instead, I brace myself for the fight of my life— probably the last fight of my life. Because I'd rather die than let them hurt her.

Only, when they're a foot away, something happens. Something I don't really understand. Something I'm not sure Roxana understands either.

A ball of fire explodes from her—I can't tell from where or how. But it takes out all the wolves in front of me. They aren't even burning. The fire is so hot and so huge that. . .

They're already piles of ash. The ground in front of them is blackened, and the tree behind them is practically burned almost to the ground.

"*Now* will you run?" she asks.

And I do.

We barely reach the car in time to get away. And I don't take my foot off the gas for quite some time.

9

XANDER

"We should probably head home," I say, realizing that we're nearly to the next pack on the list.

"Please. They aren't following us," Roxana says. "They're afraid of me."

"They might have called the neighboring packs and warned them about us."

"I doubt they'll start calling around and telling people that a lone woman and a solo wolf took out their alpha and six other wolves."

She's probably right about that—wolves fear looking weak above all else. But I still think we should head back. "We may have more to do this week than finding my mate. Don't you think you ought to get checked out?" Because I'm pretty sure that's not a normal thing for female dragona to do.

Her hand should frighten me. I think a fireball just erupted from it. But when she rests it on my forearm, it doesn't scare me at all. It calms me.

"Let's visit one more pack today, and then we can go home."

"You want to see another pack after that?"

"How likely is it that we'll run into another Harriet?"

I don't answer. It's not like she wants to hear that most wolves are Harriets. "Well."

"With as fast as you were driving, we're nearly to Waterbury. It would be a waste to turn around without even talking to anyone."

"Fine, one more pack, and we go home."

"Deal," she says.

I should have pushed harder. We nearly got killed, and then she flambéed half a dozen wolves at the last stop. I mean, they were trying to kill her, but still. "Are you sure you're alright?" I pull over on the side of the road. "You just did something back there, and while you don't seem to want to talk about it, I feel like we should." I mean, the first time I killed someone in a fight that was forced on me, I puked for an hour. I kept right on hurling, even after everything in my stomach was gone.

"It was awesome, right?" Now that I'm looking at her, I realize that she's not freaking out about having killed anyone. She looks practically giddy.

"Uh, sure. It was. . . awesome."

When she turns toward me, her eyes are open wide, and they're full of wonder. "I've never been able to do anything. I've always been. . .helpless. Useless. A waste of space. An egg incubator."

"That might be a little—"

She shakes her head. "No, it's true. No one has ever been afraid of me. Afraid of my dad? Sure. His men? Ragar? Yes. But not me. Never me."

"You want people to be afraid of you?" I'm beginning to wonder who Roxana really is.

"No." She freezes then, as if someone socked her in the jaw. "Of course I don't." Her shoulders slump and she pulls inward, like a cat curling into a ball. "I mean, I never wanted to hurt anyone either." She drops her face in her hands then, and suddenly she's crying.

I've been picked on my entire life, ganged up on, beat up, mauled, but I've never been totally helpless. How much worse would my life have been if I had been undervalued and pushed around without even a way to defend myself?

Oh, no. Why didn't I let her be happy? What did I do?

I broke her.

"I can't believe I. . ." She drags in great heaving breaths. "I killed six people! Or, Harriet was right there at the front. Probably *seven*."

"Yeah." I'm not sure what else to say, so I just sit there. Eventually, as her crying kind of starts to ebb, I drop a hand on her back and pat, slowly. "It's okay, though. They were going to kill us, so. . ."

Her bawling turns into hiccups and she swipes at her cheeks. "They were." She bobs her head up and down a little too forcefully. "They would have killed us. That yellow wolf was bonkers."

"She was."

"And they didn't even care that my dad would have—"

"Done what you did?" The second I say the words, I realize they weren't prudent.

But it's too late. We're off to the races again, sobbing and hyperventilating.

By the time she finally calms down, I realize that even with as amazing as she looked, she hadn't been wearing a speck of makeup. Most girls would be a mess right now—tears spreading mascara down their cheeks, lipstick smeared on their teeth, and puffy eyes. But Roxana looks just like she always does, with lips that are perhaps a bit more swollen than usual.

It feels like I'm living in some kind of alternate world where I'm brave and strong and not a total loser who's about to completely lose it and be put down like a mutt in a pound. "You're really beautiful, even when you're distressed. I can see why people want to make you smaller than you are."

"What?" Her voice is less sure than I've ever heard it.

"You've been amazing today," I say. "You shouted at my alpha and his mate. You threatened them and pulled it off. Then you've been with me, helping me meet wolves and make progress all day long. You've been brave and polite and. . .perfect. I still have no idea how we wound up as friends, but I'm grateful." And hopefully she won't realize what a miserable sod I am right now. It would be pretty Xander of me to point out to the stunning creature who's been helping me that I'm not worthy and lose her aid.

"You don't know how we became friends?" She tilts her lovely head. "You have two best guy friends whom you've supported for years in anything they did. Your next door neighbor is also your friend Clark's sister, and you make her laugh all the time. You pay for everything for Izaak as he spends his time doing. . . well, most people would say he's wasting his time, trying to make people smile. He is a vampire, after all. But you support him. And Bevin's a demon-spawn who wants to do the opposite of what demon-spawn have been raised to believe they must do."

"It's not like I—"

She shakes her head. "No, don't make yourself smaller than you are, either. You could have handed me in to your bosses at any time, and you'd have been given a lot if you had. Anyone else I've ever met would have done it." She looks down at her hands. "They'd have let you join the pack, and then you wouldn't be in this mess. If you think about it, the fact that you're fraying, well, it's kind of my fault."

Does she really think that? Is that why she's here? She's trying to fix her mistake? "Roxana, it's not your fault. None of this is."

She swallows slowly.

"I mean that." I reach for her chin, turning her face toward mine. "It's my biggest regret, that I even considered turning you in to get a place in that pack. How pathetic must I be to even consider betraying someone else to benefit myself?"

"I endangered your entire circle of friends, a group of people who welcomed me in kindly. I caused Bevin to descend, which she never wanted, and I wrecked all Clark's mornings for weeks."

"I think he forgave you for that."

"Yeah, people always forgive me—because I'm pretty. Because of my charm." She sighs. "I want to do something to help my friends, and I want to bring something to the table that I'm able to do. Not just my face."

"You need to know that, if we can't find my mate, and I think it's likely we won't, that it's not your fault. In fact, I'm pretty sure that I don't *have* a mate. I'm not sure how it works with halfies, but I doubt we really get one. I mean, what kind of crap draw would it be for some poor wolf to be doomed to be stuck with me forever?"

"Xander." Roxana takes my hand. "You're a kind man. You're good looking—hot, even. You have stunning eyes and great hair. But more than that, you're strong. You're brave. You're funny. Any wolf would be lucky to have you."

Every thought in my brain has disappeared, like a fart in a tornado, gone in the avalanche of emotions she just churned up.

As if she has no idea what I'm feeling, she keeps talking. "And stop saying halfies. I swear, the next time someone says that, I'm going to melt them."

The thought of her melting every single wolf we meet from now on breaks through all that overwrought emotion and lust, and I laugh. "That's just what I am."

"I hate that word, though. It makes it sound like you're not complete, and that's just not true. You're a whole person, and a whole wolf, and you're *more* than they are, because you have the perspective to think about other people and you do more than just growl and order people around."

"Yeah, perspective and empathy aren't things that are really considered strengths for a werewolf."

She releases my hand and her index finger draws a line over my thumb and up toward my wrist. My entire being focuses in on that small connection. "They should be."

I can't speak. I can't even move.

"Dragona don't care about that stuff either, and I've always thought that if the females could shift that maybe. . ."

My words come out strangled, but I get them out. "Maybe what?"

She glances up at me, her eyes concerned. "Are you alright?"

"You might want to scale back the charm." I can feel the heat in my cheeks, but I can't seem to look away.

"Oh." She blinks. "But I'm not using any charm."

I swallow.

"Let's drive," she says. "The best thing to do when I'm too much is get to a new place and get out of the car and move around."

Right. Focus on something else, Xander. Focus on sandwiches. On the road. On the pack we're about to meet. *Not* on the stunning woman who is so amazing that I can't even imagine ever liking anyone else. It would be like admiring a candle after staring at the *surface of the sun.*

"Aren't we just one exit away?" She points. "Let's get there."

"Right. One exit." It's one of the hardest things I've ever done, to focus enough on the road to put the car back into drive and make it that one exit and then follow her directions until we're turning onto the back-road that leads to the Waterbury pack.

"Now, remember. Nothing bad happened today. We're just here to drop off. . .what are we here to do?"

I pull into the first parking space I see and remind myself that I *do not* love Roxana. It's merely the dragona charm, and she can't help herself. Everyone feels it around her, and I'm not going to turn into a lunatic because of it.

Once I've gotten myself back under control, I force myself to look around. The pack compound in front of us is not impressive. In fact, it looks terrible. All the packs I've ever seen have a large compound with a main central building, surrounded by smaller buildings. The wolves usually live onsite, strengthening the alpha with their presence. The young pups learn from the entire pack, and the older wolves are kept safe in the center.

The largest outbuilding is almost always occupied by the pack alpha, and the others take residence according to their strength and importance, with the smallest buildings for the weakest members. No matter how large the pack, the parking lot's always kept immaculate, and the buildings are well kept.

That's certainly not the case here.

Clumps of grass and weeds are growing all over, and vines cover the fence around the compound. A section of the roof in the center building looks like it's about to collapse. And there is most definitely a bird's nest in the chimney of the closest outbuilding.

It looks like we've reached the sticks.

And they're rotten.

Roxana's nose scrunches as we climb out. "We don't even have an excuse this time?"

I shrug. "Doesn't look like it. Wanna just head back?"

She squares her shoulders and shakes her head. "We're here already. May as well go see if we can meet some of them. You never know."

Plus, I really need some fresh air. Even now that I'm out of the car, all I want to do is grab Roxana by the shoulders and kiss her. And then I want to run my hand—

"Do you want to or should I?"

My mouth goes dry. "Should you what?"

Roxana frowns. "Are you okay?"

My gaze gets stuck on her lips. They're so full. They're parted, just a bit. If I could just—

"Xander."

My eyes snap up to her face. "You don't look so great. How about I introduce us?"

"Oh." That's what she meant. Should I introduce us, or should she? Duh. "Yeah, that's probably a good idea."

Her eyes fill with concern. "Is it the fray?"

I don't dare tell her that spending all day with her has been harder than thinking about whether I'm going crazy. "Uh, maybe."

She reaches for my hand again, but I snap back, almost falling over the front of the rental car. "Let's just go." The last thing I need is more physical contact. I already can't stop thinking of ways I could touch her.

"Alright." She shoots me a sideways glance, but I ignore it.

"Who are you?" A rangy man in overalls and no shirt —I wish I was kidding—jogs through the open front gate and spears us with a glare. "What do you want?" He still has some of his teeth, so that's a surprise.

"I'm Roxana Goldenscales, and—"

In all my life, I've never been able to use the word guffaw.

Until today.

That man guffaws loudly, and then he slaps his thighs. "And I'm Dwight Yoakam. Who you really? You from the bank?"

Oh for the love. The bank?

"I really am Rox—"

"This is probably a waste of time," I say. "Let's just go."

"You're a wolf." The man's sniffing the air, and for the

first time in my life, I want to make a dog joke. He looks, for all the world, like a dog who has just smelled bacon.

"I am," I say. "But—"

"Are you a shredder?" His eyes light up.

"Uh, well, yes, but—"

"Oh, mama, Jewel's gonna be so excited to meet you."

Jewel? I turn toward Roxana and meet her equally perplexed gaze.

"You don't happen to be. . .Know what? Nevermind. Let's go."

Roxana has been the one who was the most optimistic from the start, but even she's starting to have second thoughts. "I'm not sure—"

"Who is it, Hawthorn?" a woman's voice asks. A split second later, her head appears around the corner. "Oh."

"He's a shredder," the man—presumably Hawthorne—says. Then he sticks a piece of straw—honest-to-goodness straw—in his mouth and grins.

"Is he?" The woman's not very pretty, but when she smiles, dimples pop out on both sides. They almost make up for the large gap between her front teeth. "I bet you're the one we've been waiting for."

"Waiting for?" Roxana mouths the words, her eyes alight with hope.

"Come inside." The woman gestures.

"Um, okay," I say. "But only for a few minutes. And we are not buying anything."

I push past Roxana, walking slowly toward Hawthorn and the woman who may or may not be Jewel.

"Are you getting Hansel and Gretel vibes?" Roxana whispers, "Because I am."

I can barely suppress my snort. "Get those fireballs ready."

"Can she wait in the car?" The woman glares at me.

"She?" I turn around slowly and realize that for the second time in the same day, someone wants me to come, but doesn't want Roxana to come nearer. Wolf females are strange. "This is Roxana and she and I are close friends. If she can't come inside, then I won't—"

"Fine, fine." The woman waves a bony arm at me, clearly telling us both to hurry up. "And I'm Jewel, by the way. Sometimes when I get excited, I get ahead of myself."

"Xander," I say.

"I love that name." She beams at me as if I've told her one of the secrets to the universe and then sets back off again, heading to the interior of the pack compound.

Sometimes things look shabby from afar, but up close they're better.

This is most certainly not the case with the Waterbury compound. The closer we get, the worse things look. A birds' nest is not the only indication that pests are living here. I smell rat feces, which means every wolf here does too. . .and yet, they seem to be doing nothing about it.

The paint is peeling on every building, except the few that appear to have only had a primer coat. Several of the buildings have rotten siding. There's a large trash pile that really needs to be hauled away or burned in the center of the courtyard, and I'm pretty sure that's a five-year-old kid, buck naked, popping a squat next to the wall.

He's not even in wolf form.

"As you can see, we are not the most well-run pack in the area." Jewel's watching me closely.

"I noticed," I say.

"We're lacking something important," she says.

"Money?" Roxana asks softly.

Jewel shakes her head. "Nah, although we ain't rich. But that's not our biggest problem."

Oh, no. What else could be wrong? It does seem likely that, if I have a mate, this is the kind of place where I'd find her. "What, then?" Please let her have teeth. And be able to read and write.

Jewel leans closer to me than I'm comfortable having her. Then she sniffs deeply, very like Hawthorn did moments ago. "Ah." She closes her eyes and moans in a very unsettling way.

"Are you ill?" Roxana asks. "And is there a chance we could have caught it?"

"Ill?" Jewel snorts. "You mean sick? No way."

"Why are you sniffing him like that?" Roxana asks.

"Had to confirm it," Jewel says.

"Confirm what?" Roxana asks.

"That you're an alpha," Jewel says. "I smelt it the second I saw ya, but I had ta make sure."

"That I'm—what?" I ask.

"You're an alpha," Jewel says again. "And that's just what we need."

10

ROXANA

My life is complicated right now. I have an ex-fiancé, which is frankly exciting because of the ex part. He was a real disaster. I also have a boyfriend, but it's not one whom I picked. His dad and my dad don't get along, and in fact, I haven't seen him since he announced to the world that we were dating. (Which we weren't.)

I'm starting to wonder whether his dad locked him in a cage to keep him away from me or something.

The absolute last thing I need to add to the mix is a crush.

Especially on a half-werewolf who is, apparently, an alpha. Although, there's no real way to know whether this woman is a total crackpot or whether she's right. I mean, she *looks* like a lunatic who would be a full-length feature on the Maury Povich Show.

Do I only find him hot because he's an alpha? I've kind of been attracted to him all day, so it's hard to blame it on that revelation.

"I'm not an alpha," Xander says. "Trust me on this. I think I'd know."

"Have you ever been hungry?" The strange light in the woman's eyes tells me that she has. "So hungry that all you can think about is food? Steak, hamburgers, pulled pork." She sighs and moans again.

I swear, her moan is the most disconcerting sound I've ever heard. Every time she makes that noise while looking at Xander, I want to punch her in her gap-toothed mouth.

"When you're that hungry, do you think there's even a chance you'd mix up the smell of food and the smell of garbage?"

Xander looks absolutely adorable when he tilts his head and says, "Would you *normally* mix up the smell of food and garbage?"

"The point is that I've been waiting for you for a long time," she says. "I'm guessing your alpha never told you what you were because it made you easier to control."

"But I don't have—"

Her eyes widen. "You're not in a pack?" She's a kid on Christmas morning, her hands shaking with equal parts greed and joy. She turns her eyes skyward. "Thank the angel. Thank them all."

"But I think you're mistaken," Xander says. "I'm actually here looking for my *mate*, because I've begun to fray."

I expect her to freak out. From what I've seen today, she should get angry. Fraying wolves are dangerous, and the other wolves didn't seem to appreciate the prospect of having them around at all. I prepare myself to spread my hands wide and try and make another fireball. Not that I really think I can—I'm not even sure how I did it the last time.

"Fray?" she asks. And then she laughs.

Heartily.

For a long time.

An uncomfortable amount of time.

I didn't expect her to laugh, and neither did Xander, judging by the confusion on his face.

"You're not fraying." She finally winds down and wipes at her eyes. "What would make you think that?"

"I've forgotten some things lately," he says, his voice dropping. "And then I almost attacked someone this morning."

"Someone who was threatening a person you care about?" Her eyebrows rise.

Xander swallows.

Who was that guy threatening?

Oh, right. It was me. I can feel heat rising in my cheeks. Hopefully they're too busy talking to notice.

"That's a natural alpha instinct. You must have felt like whoever got threatened was a part of your pack."

Xander frowns. "It wasn't a wolf."

Jewel sighs. "Who taught you about pack bonds?" She blows her bangs out of her face. "Because they sucked at it." She starts walking again. "Come with me. I'll get you two something to eat, and I'll explain whatever you don't already know."

"Don't eat anything," Xander whispers. "You'll get salmonella."

"Do you think maybe she's right?" I ask. "Maybe you're not fraying at all?"

He shrugs. I bet it's hard for him not to hope too much.

"You coming?" Jewel's trying to pretend she's not desperate, but she can't hide it. Not now. It's far too late.

The inside of the main building isn't much better than the outside. At least it's free of rats.

I think.

My sense of smell isn't as keen as a wolf's, but I can smell most things. The double doors Jewel walked through open into a huge open meeting room, but she doesn't stop there. We almost have to trot to catch up to her, but we do reach her by the time we near the far wall. Wolves line the path, which means she's somehow told them we're coming. They're all standing at attention as if they always do this, but they're wearing anything from overalls to Daisy Duke shorts, so I'm guessing this isn't a normal contingent. When Jewel finally reaches the far wall, she ducks into a room with a very tall door.

We follow after her, Xander entering first. It's been set up to accommodate thirty or so people with a long, large table in the center. The place smells like lemon oil, which is a far cry better than the refuse and sadness combo from the courtyard. I'm guessing they sent someone in here to wipe it down just before we came, from the strength of the odor. If you don't look too closely, you can hardly see the dings and scratches in the well-worn table.

Although, when it's used by a wolf pack, I doubt any boardroom tables stay in pristine condition for very long. From what Xander was saying in the car today, brawls will often break out between shredders unpredictably, and the alpha usually sort of lets them work those out.

Jewel takes a seat at the far end and gestures for us to

join her. "What do you already know about the wolf pack structure and the alpha bond?"

Xander shrugs. "The basics. There's an alpha. He controls everyone else, and they get a sense of security from it. When he wants to share energy, he can. He can also take from the pack without permission—all part of the bargain. He can send pain or pleasure, and he can communicate, and allow communication between pack members much farther than wolves can do intuitively."

Xander explained to me earlier that all wolves can hear most thoughts of other wolves. It takes effort and control to shield your thoughts from weres who are near. But when you're in a pack, you can send messages from farther than you could hear physically. It takes effort, but you could send a cry for help from farther away, for example, through the pack bond.

"Were you picked on as a pup?" she asks.

Xander's face shutters, which is as good as saying yes. I wonder how bad it was. He's so good looking and funny—why would they pick on him? Was it just because he's a half-human?

"I'm a nurturer," Jewel says. "It's safe around me. That's why we all decided that if we had a chance to bring in an alpha, I'd be the one to talk to him or her."

"Look, I suspect you're confusing something about me that is different than what you're used to with being an alpha," Xander says. "It's probably time that I explain so I don't waste more of your time."

Jewel sits back, a small smile on her lips. "Go ahead, then. Tell me what you need to say."

"I smell different to you because. . . I'm not really a werewolf."

She purses her lips, clearly unconvinced. "Oh?"

"I'm half-human." Xander's words are forceful, confident—in just the way they would be if he was bracing himself to take a beating. Maybe I've finally known him long enough to see it.

Jewel doesn't even blink. "So?"

Xander frowns. "Did you understand me? My mother's a normie."

She shrugs. "That doesn't mean a thing. You can shift, right?"

He nods.

"That's enough—everything else should work the same. In fact, it's *more* impressive that you can block your conduit off the way you have, given that you're half-human. You are one strong alpha."

"Wait," I say. "The alpha of the Manhattan pack told us that his power conduit, or whatever, was closing off as a result of the fray."

Jewel blinks. "He said *what*?"

Xander looks angry. "Is that not true?"

"Wolves who fray start trying to attach to anyone and everyone. One of the things that makes them so dangerous is they'll attach to non-alphas and start draining their power, because they're so needy. Their power conduits are *wide* open. There's no way that alpha didn't know you were an alpha too. *Everyone* who has been training you for the past decade or more should have known."

I shake my head. "Why wouldn't his current alpha tell him?"

"I thought you said you weren't part of a pack," Jewel says, ignoring me.

I'm kind of sick of her addressing him like I'm not even here. "He's an independent contractor." I lean toward her, bracing my hands on the table. "He can join the pack for real, but only if he can find his mate first."

Jewel laughs. "That alpha must have been nervous—for him to bring you into his pack, there would have to be a fight for domination. If he couldn't easily link with you, you might have won."

"He's a much better fighter than I am," Xander says. "I had no intention of challenging him."

"You don't get to choose," Jewel says. "Did no one really explain this to you?"

"I was too busy getting the crap kicked out of me during were-school to get much out of my lessons, and I'm not exactly invited to the guys' nights in the Manhattan Pack."

She swears under her breath. "The alpha who's been stringing you along is Lo Ren Fang?" She shakes her head. "I'm surprised he hasn't killed you. No one on this side of the Mississippi is stronger." Her smile grows. "Except maybe you."

Xander's shaking his head. "No way."

She shrugs. "If I were you, nothing anyone said could force me back to that pack. He knows you're not fraying—there's a smell to that too, you know, like molding cheese—and he's playing you. He's worried that in a straight-up fight, you'd take him. He needs you to surrender."

"But what should he do?" I ask. "He's never going to be accepted there."

"No pack with an alpha is going to take you," Jewel says. "But it just so happens that our alpha got himself into a fight he couldn't handle last year, and we haven't found a new leader yet."

"What a shock," I say. "Because this place is niiiice." Something crawls over my foot, and I leap to my feet.

"Just a cockroach," Jewel says. "She scares easy, huh?" She laughs.

I feel plenty angry—maybe I could summon another fireball. I force myself to calm down, and as I'm doing that, something occurs to me. "If he became the alpha here," I say, "he'd have to live here."

Jewel looks at me like I've got drool running down my chin. "Uh, yes. He would, princess."

I swallow. "But he wants to stay in New York."

But Xander doesn't say anything. He's staring off into space, probably reliving his past experiences or interactions with Lo Ren, or who knows what?

It's a lot of information to process in a five-minute period.

"Right, Xander?" I sit down again. "You don't want to move, do you?"

His head snaps up. "Of course not, but I may not have much choice."

This time, I'm the one who's dazed. We came here looking for a mate to save his life. I should be delighted to hear he's not fraying.

Instead, I'm trying to deal with my disappointment that my favorite wolf is probably moving to a crap shack in the middle of the sticks.

"Listen, I'd love to introduce you to our pack here, but I don't want to make you feel any more pressure. Just know that we're ready to welcome you whenever you want." She stands. "And we don't care whether your mother was furry or not."

Xander looks poleaxed.

Actually, I'm not sure exactly how to use that word,

but I read it in a book once, and my mother said it was something that hillbillies would say about someone being shocked. It feels appropriate, given our location.

Jewel tosses her head and two wolves enter with plates of food. It's all fried, but it doesn't look that bad. "Feel free to eat if you're hungry, and stay as long or as short a time as you'd like."

Then she just. . . disappears.

"I had no idea how hungry I was." Xander stares at the food, like it's the thing causing all the raw emotion I see playing across his face.

"They don't care whether you're half-wolf." I may be a dragona, but I understand the significance. For someone who's been told his whole life that he's not good enough, for a guy who has been enduring abuse every single day at work, and as a kid who was picked on for something outside of his control, I imagine they're the words he's always longed to hear. "And you're not fraying."

"I'm not even sure I believe it," he whispers.

"We should eat." I can't quite bring myself to take the first bite—it *looks* good enough for fried chicken strips, but you never know. Plus, Jewel hasn't been overly fond of me.

Xander shoves to his feet, not taking so much as a single bite. "Let's go."

I can barely keep up as he strides for the exit, but once we reach the car, I manage to wheeze out a few words. "You didn't eat anything? Isn't that rude?"

"Accepting food has importance for wolves," he says. "I never eat at work, for instance. I'm not part of their pack." He shudders. "She seemed very upfront, but I think they need an alpha quite badly.

Badly enough they're willing to resort to shameless tricks."

"You need a pack almost as badly, don't you?" I'm not pleased by the situation, but it's much better than it was this morning. "At least it's not the fray. Right?"

Xander's eyes meet mine. "I think I might have preferred that."

I want to press him about what that means, but I'm not sure I can handle the answer. So when he plays music the whole way home, I don't argue. He has a lot on his mind, and I don't know what I want. But after surrendering the rental car and hopping on the subway back to the apartment building, I realize how strange it is that we live across the hall from one another.

A wolf and a dragona. A witch and a vampire. How did we all become friends in a world where everyone sticks to their own kind?

We climb off the subway and walk the half a block to our building.

Xander stops at the base of the stairs. "Did you want gloffee?"

I shake my head. "Had some this morning, so I'm fine."

"Oh, right. I was with you. Duh." Xander's looking at his hands, for some reason.

For a split second, I wonder whether maybe he felt something around me, too. Is there a chance that he. . .

"Can you do me a favor?" He finally meets my eyes. His shining golden ones look. . .nervous.

"What?" My heart's racing. What kind of favor could I possibly *do* for him? So many inappropriate things occur to me that my mouth goes dry.

"Don't tell anyone about the other pack? I don't want them to freak out until I know what to do."

I'm such an idiot.

I'm worried about whether I have a crush on him, and he's literally facing the biggest decision of his life. Of course he's not thinking about whether he's attracted to the dragon shifter who lives across the hall.

"Oh. Okay." I should probably have thought it through, but that's not really my thing, I'm discovering. I'm more about bold gestures and fireballs out of nowhere. Speaking of... "Can you keep the fireball thing quiet, too? My mom would freak out if she found out, and well. . .everyone would, really."

As if she's somehow listening to my conversation, my phone rings at that moment, and it's my mom.

"I better take this."

"I'll head up." Xander's gone a moment later, bounding up two stairs at a time.

"Hello?"

Mom's voice is light and full of mirth, which is uncommon for her. "You are never going to believe what happened today."

That's never good.

"Some mangy wolfpack filed a claim for damages against us claiming, get this, that *you incinerated* seven of their wolves." She's laughing now. "The wolves have always been ridiculous, but this is a new low. Everyone knows female dragona can't shift, and at best they can spray sparks."

"Right. Everyone knows that," I say calmly. But inside, I'm panicking. What do I tell her? What does it mean that they filed a claim? Can they. . .put me in jail?

"Are you still there?"

"Yeah, Mom, I'm here."

"You don't think that's funny?"

"What happens with claims like that?" I ask. "Like, say if it was about something else?"

"Well, usually they have to go through a whole arbitration and then formal proceeding, but in this case, I'm sure the judge will just dismiss it."

Because it's that ridiculous. "But if it was true?"

"You're a hoot today."

"Right." A wave of exhaustion rolls through me. "Did you need anything else, Mom?"

"You're irritable."

"I've had a long day, what with killing seven wolves and all." The weight of that sinks into my bones, and I really do just want to sit down and cry. However horrible Harriet was, I didn't want to kill her.

But my intentions don't matter.

I did it.

"Your father's badgering me. He wants to have a sit down with you and this Lionel."

"*This* Lionel?" Like he's someone she neither knows nor approves of? "When I reached the tower, he was just leaving a meeting with Dad. I'm sure you've sat together before."

"This is different and you know it."

I sigh.

"I could call his parents, I suppose."

"No," I practically shout. "I'll set something up."

"Do it soon," Mom says. "In the next week."

I don't even know whether Lionel's in the country. "Sure." Lying gets easier the more you do it, apparently.

"I'll follow up," Mom says. "Don't forget."

I know she means it, but I wish I could forget all

about it. I wait on the elevator for a few minutes before giving up. I'm trudging up the stairs slowly when I hear some commotion up there.

"—almost died."

Judging from her tone, Minerva's sure upset about something. I pick up the pace and reach the top of the stairs just as a man comes rocketing out the front door of our place. He slams into the door on the guys' apartment seconds before it opens.

It's Lionel. He should look angry, but he only seems bemused.

Xander's head pokes around the corner, his eyes meeting mine. "Everything alright?"

"Minerva and I have some trust issues to work through," Lionel says. "But it's fine. We have plenty of time." He straightens and brushes his jacket off. It doesn't look like he really needed to—he looks as polished as ever. I bet he has anti-stain spells on all his clothing. That seems like the kind of thing a posh wizard like him would have.

"I came by to see if you wanted to set up a time to meet my parents. They're chomping at the bit, so to speak."

"Mine are asking too," I admit.

Minerva's leaning against her doorframe, arms crossed, glaring.

Xander's stepped out entirely and is clenching his fists and scowling.

My friends certainly haven't rolled out the welcome mat for my would-be-boyfriend. I don't really blame Minerva. He didn't exactly have Clark's back.

"How about tomorrow?" he asks.

"I barely know you," I say. "If we meet one another's

parents tomorrow, they're bound to find out this is fake. Wouldn't it be simpler if we just break up?"

"Oh, I don't think so," Lionel says. "It would make us look capricious at best and downright dishonest at worst."

I sigh. "What do you recommend?"

"We can only delay our parents so long," he says.

"That's rich coming from Mr. Absent," I say.

"I had a situation," he says. "But I'm here now, and I've missed my girlfriend."

"Oh, have you?" I ask. "You could have fooled me."

He grins, and I hate that it kind of sways me. His perfect teeth and penetrating eyes all brighten when he smiles. "I would never try to fool you."

"It'll have to be this weekend. You may have time suddenly, but I'm too busy right now."

He narrows his eyes and tilts his head. Then he shrugs. "Fine. I'll take it." He steps a bit closer. "Good enough for the time being."

A low growling sound is coming from Xander.

"Sorry," I say. "My good friend Xander's fraying, it seems. You'll want to keep your distance."

Lionel looks so alarmed, I worry that he won't leave. "You need to look into that right away." He turns toward Minerva. "Isn't that your job—dealing with that kind of thing?"

"*That kind of thing*?" I want to kick him.

If Xander really were fraying, it would mean he might die. Should Lionel be making jokes about it? That's a little hypocritical, I guess, since I just made a joke. But I know he's fine, so my joke was benign. Lionel knew no such thing.

"I'll pick you up around eight?"

I shrug. "Fine."

He starts moving toward the elevator, but at the last possible moment, he darts toward me and lowers his head toward mine. Then, before I can slap him, he freezes. "I'm really looking forward to it."

I was interested in him too, a little bit, before. . . But something about spending the day with Xander has muddled my feelings up enough that I don't know what I want.

But I'm pretty sure it's not Lionel.

MINERVA

I shouldn't have made it on the Paranormal Affairs force in the first place.

Like the NYPD, entrance to the NYPAD requires that candidates have completed either four semesters of college-level training or two years of active military service, as well as passing an entrance exam. I was never going to get into any magical college with my terrible grades, and unlike Clark, I wasn't sure I would survive at a non-magical school in person.

He got really lucky being paired up with Xander.

But I knew I was smart enough to take online classes with ease. Which I did. After which, I had to ace the Paranormal Affairs Entrance Exam. Dad helped me there—he was still alive and kicking at that point. He ran me through drills over and over and over. I was as ready as I could be.

The written portion was a breeze. I've always been really smart. But no matter how many times I practiced for the practical exam, I biffed it up one hundred percent of the time when there was any pressure applied.

What killed me is that not every NYPAD officer has to be able to cast perfect spells. It's always felt a little unfair that the different paranormal applicants take different tests. I mean, I get that they pair up spell casters with non-casters, and that system has worked for hundreds of years. But even so, why do I have to pass a test that half the force can't pass?

Witches cast spells to deal with aggressive magical creatures.

Warlocks, same.

But vampires and werewolves have their own barrage of tasks to complete, many of which include astonishing feats of athleticism or things that are magical in their own way.

I suppose it doesn't really matter. It's not like I could bite through a steel lock to compensate for my abysmal casting. I couldn't charm a recalcitrant perp into changing his or her tune, either.

Being able to take their test wouldn't really help me, but I still felt like we should all have to do the same things or that there should be more latitude for those of us who couldn't cast every spell with total precision. After all, true police work is about dealing with the unknown, the shocking, and the unexpected.

I stink at casting spells when I'm under pressure, and the test discovered that right away. I'm pretty sure I flunked it, start to finish. But while I was waiting for my results, I noticed a vampire who was having trouble. She couldn't quite bite through the lock she was supposed to destroy. No one else was watching, so I pulled out my wand and. . . *"Omnen viam."*

I felt the tingling sensation that told me it would work. My spell zoomed its way through the open window, spiraling and twisting, and hit the gorgeous young vampire from the side. Unlike humans, vampires usually feel the spells being cast around them. Her head snapped up, and our eyes met, and I realized I should have stayed out of it. Her lip curled back and she snapped right through that lock.

And then she beamed at me and threw me a thumbs up.

Sometimes I still wonder what I was thinking.

I should have kept my butt right where it was, feigned innocence, and prepared myself to go home. But I couldn't quite help it. I jogged around the partition to watch her complete the next part. I was vested now, and I wanted her to get in, even if I knew I wouldn't.

But it looked like luck wasn't with her either. The werewolf in front of her was a bit nasty—and clearly not very honest. He was pouring something out of his water bottle as he went over the obstacles. As the gorgeous vampire with the long, dark hair followed him over, she slipped and slid all over the place. And afterward, there was a little puff of purplish smoke.

Spelled slippery oil.

I'd seen it before, on obstacle courses at school. It made it practically impossible for the person behind you to complete the course with a decent time. The lowest two scores to complete the course were automatically failed, and clearly this guy was worried he'd be near the bottom. It looks like he felt that slowing someone down a bit more than they would have been might be enough to keep him as a contender.

That kind of poor sportsmanship really rubbed me the wrong way, even if, as he poured out the end of his bottle, I realized there was no way for me to make him pay for it. The evidence was literally going up in smoke.

But as I saw that poor vampire girl I'd helped biff another big fence because of him, I couldn't do nothing. The tingling was so strong, it practically made my entire arm warm. I whipped out my wand, made sure no one else was watching, and chanted, *"Pedes sicut alis,"* and with a twist of my wrist, again the spell flew sideways and crashed into the beauty queen.

She didn't stop slipping or sliding, but her feet really did look like they had wings on them. She practically flew as she ran, floating lighter, jumping higher, and sailing more intensely over each slippery and unfair obstacle.

The oil did its job. . .and it didn't matter. She was just that phenomenal, passing the slimy werewolf.

At the end of the course, I realized that she'd probably have been eliminated if it wasn't for me. It felt good knowing that someone who was trying their best would get in.

I did *not* expect the gorgeous vampire to come introduce herself while we were waiting for results. "Hey." She folded her arms under her chest, shoving her already fabulous assets even higher. "I'm Amber Crimson."

"Oh." I swallowed. "Minerva Lucent."

"A witch. I knew it."

I had to make sure she knew not to tell anyone about my spells, or I not only wouldn't get in. I'd get kicked out of the test, and that would embarrass Dad even more.

But before I could think up an excuse, she said, "Thanks." Her smile was beatific.

"For what?" I shook my head. "I didn't do anything."

"You're the most gifted witch I've ever seen."

I snorted. "Hardly. I failed the entrance exam."

She frowned. "How could that be possible? I'm sure it was you who helped me. See, I had a magical crown put on yesterday—too much sugary blood—and they messed it up. My left incisor where they did the crown is killing me. I didn't think I'd be able to do it, and then. . ." She shrugged. "You saved me. I know it."

"Sh," I said. My brain was usually my greatest asset, but it totally failed me in my moment of need.

"Oh, I'm not going to tell another soul." Her sideways grin made her look even more gorgeous. "I really want this job."

I looked down at my feet. "Me too." I sighed. "But good luck to you."

"Wait, you failed the written part?" she asked. "Or the performance one?"

"Not the written one," I said. "Please."

She smiled. "So, the performance one."

I blinked.

And she jogged away.

When they announced our scores, my written was posted—a perfect score—but the space for my performance one didn't have a score. It simply had the word, "Pass."

"What happened?" I asked my dad later.

He shrugged. "No idea. When we went to total everything up, your performance test card was nowhere to be found. The instructor said you hadn't done very well, but he couldn't remember any details after testing so many applicants, so we decided to just let the decision rest on the score we did have."

And that's how I got in.

"How did you do it?" I asked Amber at orientation.

She shimmied, her considerable assets jiggling. "The warlock who administers the test is disgusting. I distracted him, and from there it was easy to bump your test into the trash can."

I was floored. Why would she take that risk for me?

"I wasn't sure it would work."

I lowered my voice to the barest of whispers. "What if you'd been caught?"

She smiled. "I need a really great partner, and I want it to be you."

I opened my mouth to object.

"But before you say no, I swear that my teeth are fine now."

"It's not for myself that I'd say no," I said. "I'm really not great—"

She rolled her eyes. "I saw you in action. I can't think of another witch I'd rather work with." She crossed her heart. "Hope to die."

And now, years later, I'm worried that if she keeps working with me, she really will. But I have to go in to the precinct and face her in person. I owe her that much.

After skipping four shifts, it feels strange to walk through the doors. Like I'm a teenager who faked having the flu, or a toddler who's finally confessing to finger-painting the bathroom walls. With my own poop. I'm not someone who misses work, and I'm definitely not someone who quits stuff. But I can't keep doing a job where I endanger people I care about.

"You're here!" Her expression changes when Amber eyes my plainclothes. "Did all your uniforms shrink? Or did someone steal them?" She straightens. "Or, did you cut a deal to do nothing but scut after missing a few days?"

I shrug. "Nothing like that. I need to talk to the chief, but can we chat first?"

Her expression's even more troubled than before, but she nods.

We grab some of the nastiest gloffee known to man from the pot in the corner of the break room and shuffle across to the wobbly, scuffed plastic table. I carefully avoid the collapsing stool. This time of night, no one's really sitting around. It's the beginning of our shift, so they all have active tasks they need to perform.

"Why have you really been gone?" Amber has never been one for small talk. It's one of the things I've always loved about her.

I can't look at her, though, so I focus on my disgusting gloffee. "Why they insist on combining all the different gloffee flavors, I will never understand," I say. "I mean, they can't afford dragona-flavored glaffour plants? Fine. There aren't any demon-spawn on the force —they could make it all demon-flavored."

Amber opens her mouth.

But I cut her off with my rambling. "No one likes demon-spawn, I know. I mean, they won't admit it, even if they do. Why do they all hate demon-spawn so much? They aren't all criminals, and I've seen several people on the force down at my friend Bevin's shop, getting seances."

"Minerva."

My head snaps up, and our eyes meet. "I found something out a while ago." Has it really been less than two weeks? "I—"

"You're half human." Her voice isn't flat. It's not even concerned. It's casual, like she's telling me that her mom's birthday is next week.

I inhale sharply, my fingers curling around the mug in front of me. "How did you—"

She shrugs. "I figured it had to be something like that."

I blink.

"I mean, you don't cast like anyone else I've ever met. You're brilliant with helping people, with off-the-cuff magic. I'm not a witch, and I didn't know many before joining, but the more I've seen, the more I've worked with—you're different. I've known that from the start."

"Different." I sigh.

"But I have to ask—why do you even care?"

"Excuse me?"

"Why does it matter?" She leans toward me, her hands braced against the table. "You've been doing this job with more grace and intelligence than anyone else on the force for seven years. Why do you *care* that you were adopted, or that your mom was human, or that you secretly have pink hair."

"My hair isn't pink," I say.

She laughs. "But the other two are apparently true. And they matter just as little as your hair color, as far as I'm concerned."

"Amber, be reasonable. I shouldn't be here. You should have a partner who can actually cast spells when you need them. Then you won't be in danger all the time."

"I've never been in any real danger with you. Your spells are fine—they're creative. They're unpredictable, but they never misfire when the situation can't be handled another way."

"Excuse me?"

"I picked you, right from the start," she says. "I've always wanted you as my partner, and I've never regretted it for a second." She pauses. "Okay, maybe for a second or two, like when I was standing frozen in the —you know what? Doesn't matter."

"Yes," I say. "Those times. There are too many to count—times where I screwed up and you paid the price."

"But what about all the times I screwed up and *you* paid the price?" She shrugs. "That's what being a partner means. And you fix things more often than you mess them up. That's the important part of the ledger. None of that changes just because you've finally figured out what made you different."

"I just skipped almost a week of work," I say. "There's no way the Chief—"

"You just don't want to tell him and you think quitting would be easier." She tilts her head. "But do you really think he didn't already know?"

"Huh?" I think about what Ricky said, how the Chief disrecommended me to the guardians. And then I start to wonder. Does he already know?

"Just like me, he knows who you are, and he knows our precinct is better because you're part of it."

Giggles slams into the tiny window at the top of the break room. Then there's a big popping sound, and the window slides open.

"Also," Amber's voice drops to a whisper. "I think your familiar's magical. Can that happen?"

"My pigeon?" I cringe.

"She's the coolest pigeon I've ever seen."

Giggles flutters down to the table and lands, sliding into Amber's arm. Amber lifts her hand and runs two fingers down Giggles' back.

"If she was magical, she'd be smart enough to stop pooping all over."

"I think she does it on purpose," Amber says. "Whenever she's displeased by something?" She makes a tooting sound. "Not a coincidence."

"You have got to be kidding. You think she's weaponized the function of her bowels?"

Giggles is staring right at me when she fluffs up, squats, and takes a huge dump next to my gloffee cup. Then she flies up to the top of the fridge and sits down.

"See?" Amber shrugs. "She's as strange as you, and I love her for it."

Could Amber be right? Is Giggles actually pooping to show she disagrees with me or something else? She coos, fluffs up, and I swear, I know it sounds crazy, but it sure looks like she rolls her eyes.

"I never thought I'd say this, but I think your fluffy, flying pet is kind of an undercover bad-a." Amber stands up. "Now please tell me you brought a uniform so we can get back to work."

"They're in my car," I say absently. "I figured I'd be surrendering them."

"Great. I'll grab those, and you go tell the Chief you're back, effective today." She smiles. "Ooh, and maybe tell him it was the Tasmanian flu and you were too sick to even pick up the phone. I hear that's been going around."

"That's the cover for when people have been drinking too much," I say.

She shrugs. "Perfect."

As if she's my mother and I'm just obeying whatever she tells me, I march into the Chief's office. But once I'm there, and his head pops up, and he stares at me with those fatherly eyes, I lose my purpose. I don't want to tell him I'm back. I don't want to lie and say I've been drinking or that I'm recovering from being sick.

Now that I'm looking at him, all I can think about are those letters he showed me where he gave me a glowing recommendation. And the fact that Ricky said he wrote letter after letter saying I'd be ill-suited.

All I can think about is that he *lied* to my face.

I can't yell at my dad for keeping me in the dark, and I can't shout at him for hiding the truth about who I am from me for my entire life, but the Chief is alive and well. I can yell at him.

And I'm pissed enough to do it.

"You knew." My hands clench. Hot saliva pours into my mouth. My muscles flood with adrenaline. "You *knew* I was adopted, and you *knew* I was half human, and you not only never told me, you actively worked to keep me from ever reaching my dreams." Wow, I am really on a roll.

He sets his bifocals on the desk, upside down, and he sighs. "I loved your father, you know. He was as close to me as a brother would have been—closer, maybe. He never gave me wedgies or shoved my head in a toilet. We never had to compete for our parents' affection."

I don't want to hear about my dad. I'm mad at *him*, too.

But before I can shout more, he continues. "I'm not sure I would have been selected as Chief without your dad's recommendation."

"And now you withhold yours for me? Why? Because you think I'm a disaster? That people would laugh at his memory if they saw me trying and failing?"

"Child." With a flick of his wrist, his door slams shut. "I withheld my recommendation as your dad asked me to do." He sighs. "Entirely because we both wanted to keep you safe."

"*Safe?*" No matter what Amber says, if my dad didn't want me to make guardian, he knew I was deficient, too.

"Your dad loved you as much as if you were really his child, you know. Maybe more."

As if I were really his child.

Because, of course, I'm not. I'm just some random child he was trying to make a point with. A broken child. A hazard to herself and others. "I'm quitting," I say.

"That would be a mistake," he says. "Doing that would draw attention to your file. You might even be outed."

Outed.

Like what Xander has dealt with his entire life. Prejudice for being a halfie. Prejudice that he's weaker, less-than, and not good enough. His dad made sure everyone knew.

My dad went the opposite direction and hid it.

Both options suck.

Because the problem isn't really with us. It's with a world that says we aren't good enough because we aren't who they think we should be. The Ambers of the world see that we bring special attributes to the table, but there aren't many Ambers out there.

Not nearly enough.

My eyes have welled up with tears. "So people may find out. So what?"

"You're also good at your job," he says. "I may have promised your dad I would do my best to make sure you never made guardian, and I may have watched as you handled things in—" He clears his throat. "Unorthodox ways." He straightens. "But you're a fine PA officer, and our force would miss you if you quit. Your partner has been in here throwing fits every single day that I've assigned her to work with someone else. So if you quit, I'm transferring her skinny butt right out of here."

"You *want* to keep me?" I don't understand.

"Badly," he says. "In fact, I could see you becoming the best possible Chief some day. I'd recommend you for this job all day, every day."

I was not expecting that.

"But I swore to your father that I would keep his daughter as far from the most horrifying dangers of this world as I could keep her, and I'll do that until the day I die."

Guardians protect the world from demon-spawn who are hoping to Descend—to become daimoni themselves. Sometimes it's easy to feel like all they do is record descents and deal with demon-spawn who have gone too far. But it's more than that. They're the trained warriors who will be on the front lines if something goes really bad. They're out there, risking their necks every single day. Dad knew that better than anyone.

He'd been a guardian himself.

And he knew I wanted that for myself.

But he wanted to keep me safe, and he put that first.

"You'll never recommend me as guardian?"

The Chief shakes his head.

"Then I'd like to request a transfer." I jut my jaw out and refuse to meet his eye.

"Minerva."

"No, I'm requesting a transfer, and that form doesn't go through you at all, so I don't need your approval."

12

CLARK

I've always enjoyed my job. Sure, it's mostly solitary, but it's rarely boring.

Okay, other people would find it boring, compiling different varieties of the same spell to test efficacy and potency. But there's an element of excitement about trying things that no one has done yet. And what I do dramatically impacts the lives of humans—not that they know I'm the one doing it.

But spell research has given them migraine medicine, diet treatments, and fertility advancements, to name a few. Magical life may not always be a smooth path, but at least we can even out some of the bumps for the everyman.

Of course, nothing is perfect. When other employees call in sick, I get stuck pulling double duty, and when I nearly die dueling a dragona—but ultimately win? Yeah, that kind of thing means nothing here.

Actually, the extra media attention has probably hurt me at work. I'm badgered by reporters on the way in and out of the office every day. The phones still ring far too often with people asking our beleaguered office staff whether they can speak to me. My time in the sun will probably be quite short, but I'm just holding my breath that it will end soon, and praying that my job will last that long. All the attention was neat for a day or two, but my boss has gotten more irritated with it every day.

"The humans aren't supposed to know that we're here," Simon gripes. "But with a steady stream of reporters, even the humans are trying to figure out what's going on in this building."

"I'll reinforce the diversion spell on my way out tonight," I say. "Sorry again."

He casts his eyes toward the ceiling and sighs. "It's not your fault—I know. You're the hero—the brave defender of your friends. I'm impressed and all that, but we still have to hit our quotas and keep the shareholders happy."

"I do know," I say. "I think it's starting to taper off."

Simon arches one eyebrow. "Let's hope so." He spins on one shiny black shoe heel and marches out of the lab. "Oh." He glances over his shoulder. "Chad is gone today, so I need you to approve the deliveries."

I don't groan. I don't huff. And I don't grumble. I'm proud of that. Since I'm currently the most annoying employee in the office, Simon's been pushing all the scut my direction lately, and I can't say I love it, but I also don't have much room to complain. I've made everyone's life harder, so I can't really whine about doing a few extra tasks.

"I hope he's alright."

"He says it's the Tasmanian flu, but I think he just drank too much again."

Awesome. My co-workers are out partying, and I'm

being punished for defending my friends. If I were dating Roxana, I'd be fine with the attention. Actually, if we were dating, it would likely be much worse, and long term. But at least I'd have something to ratchet up my joy. As it is, I have to watch her date Lionel up close and personal while dealing with the fallout of being close to a magical celebrity.

"Hey, is your friend really dating Lionel Sol?" Almost eight days in a row he's asked me now. I'll give this to Simon Summers, he's persistent. I kind of hoped they'd announce that it was all a hoax, and so I've put off answering the question. But seeing as they now have a date set up, per Minerva. . .

I grit my teeth and force the words out. "She is."

"Wow." He blinks. "Why the secrecy before?" Without giving me time to answer, he plows ahead. "I still can't believe he was working here—I mean, if you think about it, they met because of us. If you hadn't asked me to get your friend a job, or if I had refused, or if you hadn't gone for that interview and asked him to be the substitute delivery driver that day, they wouldn't even know each other, right? Or is it really true that she left because she already loved him? Did he approach you and ask *you* to get her a job?" He's practically hyperventilating now. "Wait, are you really good friends with him? How long have you known him?"

"Hold the hysteria," I say. "I didn't know he was Lionel Sol. I didn't know him at all, and neither did she."

"What?"

"She's an old friend of my sister's, and yes, they met through this job—the job you helped her find."

He claps. "We are amazing matchmakers."

I'd actually never even thought about how their acquaintance is entirely my own stupid fault.

"We could have become best friends." Simon shakes his head wistfully. "Think where I could be right now, if only I'd realized who he was."

It's bizarre to me that he thinks that, if only he'd made friends with Lionel, he'd somehow land some amazing promotion. The world doesn't work that way—or it shouldn't. Friends don't *owe* you favors. And you shouldn't make friends just so that they can help you in some way. That's not a friend. That's a connection.

Of course, I'm only a researcher for a magical spell lab, so it's not like I'm exactly burning my way up the corporate ladder. I turned down the professor job I wanted because I worried it might endanger Roxana, too. Clearly I'm not great at doing what it takes to improve my career. Maybe I should be taking notes instead of throwing shade.

"Ooh." Simon's still standing in the doorway. "Looks like things are heating up with your friend and her famous beau."

What does that even mean? Before I can ask, he finally leaves. Of course my idiot boss would leave right after saying something that I actually want to hear more about. Or more specifically, that I *don't* want to hear any more about, but that I now can't stop thinking about.

I should search it on my phone.

That would be stupid. The last thing I need to do is get my news from some kind of gossip site. I resist the urge to whip my phone out and start searching. Besides. It's probably all sensationalized and doctored scenes.

Right?

Minerva said that last night, Roxana set up a fake date with Lionel. That's it. Boring. Simple. Not sensational in the slightest.

"Can you review the deliveries?" Hannah asks. "They're all ready to go."

I duck into the warehouse and snatch the clipboard off the hook. Reviewing deliveries is the most boring task in the world, and I've been stuck with it a *lot* lately. It seems like Chad is always gone. If there was a 'most unreliable employee of the year' award, he'd win it, hands down.

I check truck after truck after truck, waving them off as I finish my review. I know this job has importance, but honestly? The inventory sheets on the clipboard keep turning into lines of numbers and words.

Because I keep thinking about what Simon said.

Things are heating up with your friend.

What does that mean, heating up? What could the media possibly know that I don't? Minerva told me last night that Roxana spent the whole day with Xander and that Lionel came by for the first time since the dragona incident for like five minutes.

I still can't believe that Roxana saved me that day— Minerva insists it's true, but I just can't envision it. She may not be able to shift into a dragon, but being able to withstand fire is still pretty amazing. I've gone by Minerva's to see her a half dozen times, but she's always either out or busy. I haven't found a decent time to talk to her about any of it.

"So?" the driver asks. "Am I good?"

'Heating up' implies something romantic, right? Something racy? I can't ignore it any more. I need to figure out what Simon was talking about. I start tapping into the search bar, "Lionel Sol and Roxana—"

Lionel Sol and Roxana Goldenscales' Hot Night Together? pops up as the top search on the magi-web. I think I'm going to puke.

"Can I go, or what?"

I wave the guy off, and click on the hyperlink with a terrible sense of foreboding.

And it's a video clip that's clearly taken in the hallway outside Minerva's apartment. Roxana's standing utterly still, her hair a bit mussed, her cheeks pink. She looks as gorgeous as ever, and it's not faked, unfortunately. That's her, alright.

The video's not even grainy. Those security cameras must be nicer than I thought.

"Oh, have you?" Roxana asks. "You could have fooled me."

He smiles at her with the cocky, rich guy smile I've always hated. "I would never try to fool you."

What a liar.

"It'll have to be this weekend," Roxana says. "You may have time suddenly, but I'm too busy right now."

He looks annoyed, which is rich, given what he was doing over the last few days. "Fine, I'll take it." He steps into view of the camera, and I realize he's dressed to impress her. He means business—in dark slacks and a bright blue shirt that practically screams *Look at me!* Then he angles his head toward her. "Good enough for the time being."

By the angel, they sound like they're flirting. She's actually talking about having a fake date, but to anyone else listening, they'd hear her response as banter, mocking him for using the phrase, 'real date.'

Then there's some kind of interchange I can't make out—it's too garbled and quiet, or maybe the video glitches, and then Lionel says, "I'll pick you up around eight?"

Roxana's face is blocked, but I can hear her say, "Fine."

So far, though, it feels like clickbait. Nothing hot has happened. Then Lionel starts to leave, moving toward the elevator. At the last minute, he cuts back, leaning over her and invading her personal space egregiously. His voice is husky when he says, "I'm looking forward to it."

And then, it's hard to tell for sure from this angle, but it sure looks like they kiss.

The video goes black.

I almost throw my phone against the wall, but unlike a spell or a potion, I can't remake this. I'd have to buy a new one. That's a hassle *and* a waste of money. Instead, I force myself back to work.

"It could have been way worse," I tell myself.

Not that I really believe it. I can't believe Minerva said this was nothing. I force myself to keep checking over all the dumb inventory checklists and then I drag myself back to the lab. I have deadlines to meet, after all. But I'm definitely not doing my best work, not today.

At least, unlike Chad, I showed up.

"Clark Lucent!" Simon's voice sounds very, very upset.

"I'm in here." Did he think I left early? "I'm finishing up this batch of—"

He storms through the doorway, his hands gesturing wildly. "Do you think I care about some stupid experiment?"

I blink. "I mean, it's your job to care about mine, isn't it?"

"Correct me if I'm wrong, but your job today was to check over the deliveries. And the reason one of us checks them is that we have a bunch of minimum wage employees who deliver the stuff we pack up. And it's minimum wage employees who load up the trucks to begin with. I always need at least one intelligent brain looking over these things."

"Okay."

"That brain was yours today, or it was supposed to be."

I'm still so confused. "Did something happen?"

"There was a very large, very full box of recalled spells that was supposed to go back to headquarters last week. It got put in the wrong place, and it was being sent back today."

"Okay."

"But they didn't *go back*. Someone got confused and sent them to a pharmacy—recalled spells that turn humans' skin bright purple. Like a red seedless grape."

I swallow.

"That box was delivered and orders were filled, Clark. And whose signature do you think approved that delivery?"

I close my eyes. "I'm so sorry. I'll grab my wand and personally—"

"No," he says. "You most certainly will not."

He doesn't want me to fix it? I can't help frowning. "But—"

"You won't be casting clean-up spells, because only our employees can do that, and you're *fired*."

Over signing off on the wrong delivery? That feels. .

.dramatically disproportionate for an oversight. But no matter how long I argue, no matter how much I plead, Simon doesn't budge. Eventually I give up. . .and gather my things and walk out the door.

Not just unemployed.

Fired.

It feels so much worse, somehow.

Last year, Yolina stole a case of Devrom, which is a spell that literally makes your poo not stink. She didn't get fired. She just had to work with the janitorial staff for free for six hours a week for two months. She stole it and she got a slap on the wrist and scut work.

Last month, Nolan fell asleep in the middle of an experiment and set the lab on fire. They charged him the cost of repairs—that's it. He's been promoted, and now he's handling mid-level admin.

Last week, Chad called in sick three times, and again today, which is why I was doing his job. But he's not going to be fired.

Just me.

I've never felt so wronged in my entire life.

So a few humans turned purple. So what? Most of them are paying tons of money to dye their hair that color. Why should they care if their skin matches for a few hours until I can fix it and wipe their memory?

I'm wracking my brain to try and think of who Simon's boss's boss is so I can appeal when I notice that someone in dark clothing and a dark hat exited at the same metro exit I did. And he's following me around the corner. I duck into a shop—and he does the same.

I think I'm being tailed.

It's not easy, but I've always been good at modifying spells under pressure, and I cast an illusion spell that makes a second Clark. Then I make him keep walking while I duck into an alley.

And when the dark hat, dark clothing guy walks past me, I reach out and snatch his arm. "Who are you?" I ask. "And why are you following me?"

He drops his wand.

I kick it.

He swears under his breath.

"I've had a long, hard day," I say. "I thought about going into law enforcement, and I'm pretty good at personal defense spells. I'd recommend you just come clean."

The man shakes his head and his hat falls to the ground.

And I'm staring at Orion Sol, the Grand Chancellor of the Illuminae. I can barely believe my eyes. For some reason, even though I know Lionel is his son, these two don't feel connected.

His hat must have housed a pretty powerful illusion spell. He was formerly a nondescript, slight young man with pale hands and a hooked nose.

Now he's tall, broad-shouldered, and decently handsome, for an old guy. It actually feels remarkably unfair that such an important and powerful person should still be handsome and strong. When does he have time to work out?

"You're Clark Lucent."

I can hardly believe he knows who I am, but I nod dumbly.

"You know my son?"

I shrug.

"And you know this Roxana person, too?"

I nod.

"You lost your job today."

How could he know that? "Yes."

"You can speak. Good. I was beginning to wonder if you were a halfwit."

"A halfwit?" I splutter. "I graduated at the top—"

He waves his hand and his wand flies back to it. "I don't care. Look, the point is that I'm here to make you an offer."

"What kind of offer? Why?"

"Doesn't matter why," he says. "But the offer is this. If you do a small favor for me, I'll find you a new job—a much better job than the one you just lost."

"How did you know I lost my job?"

His smile is eerie. "My dear boy, did you think it was a coincidence?"

"Wait. Are you saying you *cost me* my job?"

"With one phone call."

It's all making so much more sense. I wonder how involved Simon was. Was he looking for a reason to fire me? Is that why he gave me the delivery with the recalled spells? Did he set me up? "I can't believe—"

"You're focusing on the wrong things. Who cares whether you lost that boring, low-paying job?"

"Me," I say. "I care."

He waves his hand again, and then he looks me dead in the eyes. "I'm here to offer you something so much better. Three times as much money, full benefits, prestige."

"Why?"

"If you'll agree to help me break up Roxana and Lionel, then I'll create a position for you within the Illuminae. You can come up with your own title, even. Think how much it could change your life."

I'm tired, and I think that's why it takes me so long to process what he's saying. "You don't want your son dating *her*? Why not?"

Orion Sol draws up to his full height, his shoulders squaring. "It's none of your business what I want or don't want. Just do what I say, and you'll be rewarded."

Is he kidding? He wants me to do what I've already wanted to do every day for more than a week? And for that, he'll compensate me? It's a no-brainer. Getting angry at him for having me fired is a total waste of time. People like him do things like that as easily as breathing. "Fine. But I'm not sure I can." I'm certainly not going to tell him the whole thing is fake. Clearly his own son didn't share that information for a reason.

"I'll make it easy on you." He hands me a manila envelope. "You plant these somewhere your friend will find them, and the rest should take care of itself."

"And the job?"

"I'll be in touch. Once I hear word that you've delivered the information, you'll get an email from my legal team. Then just sign the employment agreement—two-year term—and we're in business. Literally."

For a split second, I wonder whether this might be a little disloyal. Should I refuse him? Am I making a mistake?

As if he can read my mind, he leans a little closer. "You're helping your friend out, you know. This isn't a good thing for her, either. And beyond all of that, it's doomed to fail. We're just speeding things along."

He's right about all of that. I'm not even sure Roxana really likes Lionel. She may already have dumped him, for all I know. And knowing her is what cost me my job in the first place. The least I should do is take the opportunity to make up for that loss. I didn't seek him out. This good luck just came to me.

"Alright," I say. "You have a deal."

He doesn't shake, but I don't much care. I have a feeling I'm holding a smoking gun in my hand, and I can't wait to watch this phony relationship give up the ghost.

13

BEVIN

I'm not going to lie, although now I finally can. I was pretty worried for a while. I paid Clark a lot of money for some spells he assured me would help with the 'rival secondhand magic shop owner who had a vendetta against me.' I just didn't think they'd work against the Demon Council.

I had to make up some kind of story about why I needed Clark's help after I decided to hide the truth.

For one thing, knowing what was going on would make Roxana feel even worse. She already apologizes about once a day for causing me to descend and for drawing so much attention to all of us. If she found out that thanks to my recent descent, I was being threatened by the Demon Council because I don't want to join their guild?

Her apologies would become incessant. And really, it's not her fault. She didn't force my mother to consort with a demon.

I've managed to avoid my own nature for a very long time, but it couldn't last forever. Demon-spawn have been known to live for as long as a thousand years, so it was almost inevitable that at some point, I'd be forced to do something I shouldn't. And because of who I am, the results were always fixed.

Even so, I don't want to join their little club and get updates and tips on how to be more evil.

I got the distinct impression that if I didn't join, I'd be *forced* to do it. Only, it's been several days, and other than a single call each day around dinnertime, from a very polite woman named Linda asking whether I've changed my mind, no one else has come by, and nothing has happened. Maybe they're like your average pyramid scheme—they push really hard at first, but if you hold the line, they eventually give up. I'm still a little jumpy, but less so every day.

After I finish my last seance, and after I wrap up the sink gremlins—they work so much better than a garbage disposal, and they never grind up things they shouldn't— for an older lady who has been waiting for weeks for them to come in, I release Henrietta (my charmed chicken) from her station by the door, put her in her pen in the back with her dinner, and close up shop. For the first time since Aquarius and Violette came by, I don't feel a sense of foreboding or fear when I walk away from my cute little shop. I worked for years to earn enough to open it. And now that I have it, it's been everything I wanted it to be.

My own little corner of the world.

A safe place for me to work hard helping people with strange things. A spot where I never feel out of my element, or ostracized, or othered. Even now that I have a tail, no one looks at me sideways for it.

I've mostly been avoiding my friends since Aquarius

Silvertongue told me he'd make things 'uncomfortable' for me if I refused their offer. The last thing I want to do is make them into targets. But days without a single threat has calmed me down. What would they really do? There's an Angel Council for just this reason—the akero won't let the demon-spawn harass and attack other magical people for not joining their club. Right?

Right.

I push into the gloffee shop with forced confidence, my eyes already scanning for anyone I know. Thankfully, Clark's there. Strangely, he's holding a cup of gloffee like it's a whiskey, nursing it with tiny sips and long sighs.

On second thought, maybe I'd better head back to the shop. . .

"Where are you backing up to?" Izaak asks from behind me.

Clark's head whips around like a rattlesnake, ready to bite.

Dang. Stupid Izaak. "Um, I just remembered that I forgot—"

"Come have a cup of gloffee," Clark says. "I never see any of you anymore."

"I was here yesterday," Izaak says. "I'm stuck drinking double shots just so I won't fall asleep during filming."

"But it's four o'clock," I say. "It's hardly midday."

Izaak shrugs. "It would be like you waking up at four in the morning." He yawns. "It's a rough start time."

"You're lucky they let you film mostly in the afternoon." Clark scootches over on the sofa and I realize I'm going to get stuck sitting right by him. Clearly something's wrong, and we're going to have to hear all about every single boring detail of it.

"Are you alright?" I force the words out as I sit. With anyone else, I'd genuinely be concerned, but Clark's always been the kind of person who turns a molehill into an avalanche. And with the least bit of encouragement, he'll start downright bawling.

"Oh, I'm fine," he says.

I can tell he doesn't mean it, but I'm definitely not about to press. "How's the filming coming?"

"It's okay, I guess." Izaak drops into the armchair. "Usually I'd have a few weeks to, you know, read over the script. Work with the director. That sort of thing. But after Antony Starr backed out, they were scrambling for someone—I'm lucky to have the role. It's just already underway. I hate feeling like I'm already way behind."

"Antony Starr?" I ask. "Really? I loved him in *The Boys*. Do you think I could get an autograph?"

"Did you hear the part where Izaak replaced him?" Clark asks. "They may not be on great terms."

"Maybe Antony is grateful that he saved him," I say. "You don't know."

"Bev, I've never even talked to him," Izaak says. "Sorry, but I can't get his autograph."

"Is there anyone else famous in this?" I can't help asking. I mean, if you can't use your friends for stuff like this, who can you use?

"What about *him*?" Clark asks. "He's in this."

I don't laugh, but I can't help a little snort. "Right. Like I need Izaak's autograph."

Clark and Izaak are just staring at me. I hate when they do that.

Minerva breezes through the door, thankfully, which distracts them. "Hey, lady," I say. "You look happy."

"I have a first date in just two more days."

Clark frowns. "Didn't he ask you, like, days and days ago?"

"We're officers of the *law*," she says. "We have busy schedules."

"That's hot," I say. "I mean, talk about losing the heat—'Um, excuse me. When might you be free?'" For some reason that came out in a British accent. "'I'm not quite sure. How about half past three next Tuesday?'"

"I've never said 'half past' in my life." Minerva squishes in between Clark and me.

Gavin appears right then, taking our orders rotely, until he gets to Izaak. "And what can I bring for our A-list celebrity?"

Izaak rolls his eyes, but I can tell he loves it. "It's really not a big deal—and it's a villain role."

"Villains can be super hot." Gavin wiggles his eyebrows. "And in this case, he really is."

Izaak is actually blushing. Since I know he's not into Gavin, he must be embarrassed that he's finally taken a villain role. I know he's refused for a long time, and I'm not sure why he accepted this time.

"At least you're getting paid well," Minerva says. "I mean, I know it's not what you wanted, but the notoriety can't really hurt."

"You've been back at work for a few days, now," Izaak says. "How's that going?"

Minerva swallows slowly. "Fine."

"Wait, back at work?" Clark quirks an eyebrow. "Were you *not* at work for some reason?"

"Well, it's not like—"

Someone opens the door and smoke pours through it. The sound of sirens follows right behind. I stand up, and Minerva, Clark, and Izaak all do the same. "Smoke?" I ask.

"Something's definitely on fire," Clark says. "It smells like it's close."

But we're not the only ones rushing toward the door. Dozens of people are in front of us, but it's clearly happening somewhere to the right of Grand Central Gloffee.

The same direction as my shop.

I'm being paranoid, obviously. I'm sure nothing is wrong. I have wards, and I have state of the art fire protection that was installed before I moved in—overhead sprinklers. I'm sure it's not my shop. But I can't help worrying anyway.

When no one will shift even an inch to let me past, I throw my hands out and shock them.

"Ow," the vampire on my right says. "What was that?"

"By the angel's earlobe," the mage in front of me says. "Watch where you're zapping."

"Then move over," I hiss.

And by some miracle, they actually do. I force my way to the door and push right on through, no longer paying attention to anything going on around me.

Because flames are licking upward almost a hundred feet—and the shop they're consuming like a Fourth of July barbecue in Texas. . .is mine.

I watch, gutted, as the sign I lovingly designed shudders, and the wooden rectangle that says "Bevin's Boutique" falls to the ground with a crash.

Clark pushes past me, wand at the ready, already chanting something. He tries his very best, but nothing he does puts out the flames. I almost tell him not to bother. Demon fire's hard to quench, and that's clearly what's at work. Neither of the buildings on either side of my shop have been so much as scorched. Only my store is melting like candles on an octogenarian's birthday cake.

The thing is, if I tell him to throw in the towel, it's the same as telling them I know why it's burning, and I can't do that. I realize, in this moment, that the second I tell them what's going on, my friends will do what good friends do best. They'll rally around me. They'll fight back. They'll support me, no matter what it costs them.

And it's precisely because I love them that I can't let that happen.

"Oh, no," I say, releasing a bit of the horror that's currently crouching deep inside my heart. "How could this have happened?"

"Did you leave a candle burning?" Izaak asks.

"Or maybe one of your little beasties got loose," Minerva says. "Don't you often have things in there, like my flame lizard?"

"Oh!" I have to find a way through to the back. "Harriet!"

"Was she in her pen?" Clark asks.

Before I can answer, the building starts to collapse. It's quickly very clear that nothing has survived, certainly not my poor, sweet chicken who lived on the back porch.

At least I shipped those sink gremlins out earlier, but I feel sick about poor, sweet Harriet.

Being the friends that they are, Roxana shows up almost immediately. Xander shows up moments later, and they all take turns throwing arms around me and commiserating and wiping my tears and hugging me until the building finally burns down to the ground. I should have sent them away. The Demon Council will surely have someone watching, and they're going to be taking notes of anyone who's around, but I can't send them away.

Or they'll know for sure that something is up.

I'm going to have to distance myself from them over the next few days, or there's no way they won't get dragged under with me.

"Oh, Bevin," Roxana says. "I can't believe this happened. You don't think it's connected to. . ." She swallows and grimaces. "To my family in some way, do you?"

"Because it's a fire?" I shake my head. "No way. Everyone was excited about my connection to you, but it wasn't significant enough that anyone from your family would be angry—or Ragar either. He'd definitely have gone after Clark or Minerva or the guys first."

She frowns, but doesn't press.

After I talk to the fire department, who are honestly baffled about why the fire didn't spread, and the police, who ask me a lot of questions about who might have a grudge against me, I force a yawn. It must be convincing, because Roxana, and then Minerva, and then Xander, Clark, and Izaak all yawn afterward. Which makes me yawn again for real.

"It's like we're doing a bad version of the wave," Minerva says, right before she yawns for the second time.

"You should all go to bed," I say.

"But you live over your shop," Minerva reminds me. "You have to come with us, obviously."

"Oh, no!" I practically shout. "I wasn't staying at my place anyway."

"Huh?" Clark glances at Minerva and they both make disbelieving eyes.

"It's no imposition," Minerva says. "You can have the sofa, or you can sleep in with me."

I throw my hands up. "I was actually in the process of remodeling my—" I cough, thanking Gabriel once again that I can lie, now. "My bathroom. I was redoing the toilet."

"The toilet?" Xander lifts his eyebrows. "Not the tile, or the tub, but the toilet?"

"It squeaked," I say. "Every single time I flushed a poop, it would squeak. I was worried it was going to back up and flood the shop." Good heavens, this lie gets worse and worse. Maybe if I'd practiced a little more as a kid, like a normal person, I'd be better at this.

But somehow, miraculously, my friends are all big enough dupes that they seem to buy it.

"So, then, where are you staying?" Roxana tilts her head, like nothing I'm saying is making sense.

I need to come up with something good. "My sister's place," I blurt out. Because normal people stay with their sisters, right? Even if I avoid mine like the bubonic plague, maybe they won't remember that.

"You can't stand her," Minerva says.

What is she, an elephant? "I've been trying to mend fences."

"Trying to what?" Izaak asks.

"Fix things with her," Roxana says. "Even I know that phrase, and I've spent my life in a tower."

"Well excuse me for being a stick in the mud," Izaak says.

"Nope, still not right," Xander says. "We'll learn some new clichés later, okay?"

"Fine," Izaak says. "But I think this may be why I get weird looks at work. We should probably work on more of them."

"Don't worry about me," I say, before anyone else can start pressing for details.

"Of course we're worried about you," Clark says. "In fact, none of us will be able to sleep until we make sure you're okay. I, for one, am going to insist on staying with you until you reach your sister's place."

By the angel's knees, they must be kidding. "That's really not—"

"Me too," Minerva says.

"And me," Xander says.

"Well if everyone's going," Izaak says.

"For the love of all that's winged," I say. "Just go home. I'll be just fine."

But they won't budge. And Roxana hails us an SUV cab that's even large enough for everyone to fit.

Fabulous.

I really hope that the guy in all black lurking behind the 24-hour deli isn't demon-spawn. He's paying a suspicious amount of attention to us as we get into the SUV.

"Where to?" the driver asks.

And I realize I have no idea where Soki lives. Probably in a pasteboard box behind the closest tattoo parlor. Or maybe a highrise she pays for by selling tortured kittens. Who knows?

Only, I have to tell them something. I didn't say I was *supposed* to stay there. I said I am *staying* there. As if I already have.

I whip out my phone and pretend to be searching for

the address I've saved. "I always take the subway," I mumble.

The driver's already annoyed. Someone behind us is honking, but that's just New York City.

WHERE DO YOU LIVE? I text.

To my utter and complete shock, she actually starts responding right away. Maybe I can get dropped off, wave to my friends, and not even let Soki know I'm there.

WHO DIS?

I should have known she'd be difficult. She doesn't even have my number saved? Really?

BEVIN. WHAT'S YOUR ADDRESS?

I DON'T WANT A HOLIDAY CARD.

THIS IS NOT ABOUT A HOLIDAY CARD, YOU F— I accidentally send it. Fat thumbs.

WOW, YOU'RE UPTIGHT. EVEN MORE THAN USUAL. EVERYTHING OKAY? NOT THAT I CARE.

She is texting me back. I should just be giddy about that. MY SHOP BURNED DOWN. NEED TO SEE YOU.

THANK GOSH. COLLECT INSURANCE AND GET A REAL JOB.

She's such a freaking delight. GOOD TIP. ADDRESS?

I'M WORKING. THE JUICY PLUM.

I close my eyes and try not to shudder. What the heck kind of place is The Juicy Plum? I don't even want to know. But I pull it up on my map anyway, because even Clark is about to fail at calming our driver down.

The guy behind us has taken to honking nonstop. It's really charming.

I rattle off the address without even thinking, and finally we're off. Hopefully if they just see Soki's face, they'll let me go. And hopefully The Juicy Plum isn't a brothel. Or something worse.

When the driver stops, I brace myself and look around. Thankfully, it appears to be a restaurant. I hope. I hop out and practically slam the door in Roxana's shocked face.

"Hey!" She taps on the window from inside. "What are you doing?"

"I'm here. Thanks for delivering me."

The door pops open right away. "You almost cut off my arm," Roxana says. "We came all this way—we may as well wave at your sister, especially if you're making up with her."

"Right." I scrunch my nose. "Of course."

"Is the food there any good?" Clark points at The Juicy Plum. "I never had dinner."

"Oh, me either," Izaak says. "I'm starving."

"I could get food," Minerva says. "I need to get to work soon and I'm pretty hungry."

"That's not a good idea," I say. "It's been condemned."

"It seems like a lot of people are in there," Clark says. "I wonder if they know."

"Bevin," a voice calls. "You actually came."

Soki's smoking in front of The Juicy Plum, a billowing cloud of smoke enveloping her head.

"She doesn't actually look much like you," Roxana whispers. "Are you sure you're twins."

"Not all twins are identical," I say, always a little annoyed when people ask that. "Well, thanks for bringing me."

"I am starving," Izaak says. "If this place isn't good, maybe we should grab dinner somewhere else."

"You sure you don't want food or company?" Minerva asks.

"For sure." I wave them off, my panic rising as Soki walks our way.

Luckily, the car pulls away just as she reaches me. "You came all the way out here. Hurry up and tell me what you want."

"Are you a waitress?" I ask.

Soki shakes her head. "I make grill marks and stuff."

"You're a chef?" I can hardly believe what she's saying.

"I said I make grill marks," she says. "I'm sleeping with the chef. Sometimes. And I come when I want and make things look fancier. Then I take whatever I want from the till."

She steals it? I almost don't want to know. "That sounds—"

"What do you want?"

"Nothing," I say. "I just needed my friends to leave me alone, so I told them I'm staying with you."

Her eyebrows both lift. "Why aren't you staying at your place?"

"It burned down," I say. "I said that."

"Your magical friends couldn't stop one little fire?"

I shrug, already turning to leave.

"It was demon-fire, wasn't it?" She would be an expert. That's one of her talents. "You turned them down." She sounds incredulous about it.

"I don't want to join the Demon Guild," I say. "So I said no."

"You're an idiot."

"Right back at you."

"You can't opt out," she says.

"I never opted in."

"But you descended," she says. "Just swear their little oath. It's not like it's a big deal. They're demon-spawn, not the boy scouts. You just promise to do whatever the greater demons ask if they ever make it to Earth, and you promise to help that happen in any way you can. That's it. Easy peasy. Hardly any extra work at all."

"I don't *want* to obey demons, and I don't want to help them come to Earth."

She shakes her head. "How are you how you are?"

"Excuse me?"

"They won't stop."

"Stop what?"

"They'll take away every single thing you have, and they'll ruin everything you care about until you swear the oath. You don't have a choice."

"The akero—"

"Forget the Angel Council. They don't contradict the Demon Council, and they certainly won't protect demon-spawn, no matter what their laws may say. Trust me on this one."

I happen to think she's wrong. And she's given me an idea. "If I petition for their help, they have to give it. I bet the Demon Council won't touch me then."

"You're a bigger idiot than I thought." She drops the butt of her cigarette on the ground and stomps on it. "They will take everything away from you, and it'll be your fault when they do."

"I'll hate them if they do that—surely that can't be their plan."

Her smile is wicked. "How can you know so little

about your own kind? Hate is as important to us as love is to your little angel-followers."

Angel *followers*? "They can't want their members to hate them."

"They don't care. Eventually you'll get that, but by then, you'll wish you'd figured it out sooner."

She turns and walks away.

While I walk to the closest hotel, I call my insurance company. They insist that I cancelled my policy yesterday.

"Why would I do that?" I ask. "I just paid the premium two months ago. I had ten months left."

"We'll send you the refund on your premium," the woman says. "But there's nothing I can do about the policy. It was definitely canceled."

Soki was right about one thing—they really must not care whether I hate them.

14

MINERVA

Bevin's the reason I feel the way I do about demon-spawn. I'd like to think that, even if I hadn't met her, I'd be fighting for justice and fair treatment, but I'm not so sure.

And now, once again, she's being abused because of prejudice.

"They should have to provide you a recording of you canceling," I say. "This is outrageous."

"It's just how it is," she says, more dejected than I've ever seen her. "Please just let it go."

"You come in here and order a black gloffee and then you casually mention that your bigoted insurance company has canceled your policy and won't pay a dime for that burned down building right out there. And you want me to do nothing? Have you met me before? My name's Minerva. I fight for justice everywhere. Every night. Even during the day sometimes."

She shrugs. "It's my building, and it was my policy, and it's up to me whether I fight it."

"What will you do, then?" I ask. "Your shop is your house and your job and, well, it's everything."

"I know." She sounds wrung out. "I guess I'll go back to the mobile pop-up shop on weekends."

"You're going to live in a van again?" I can't believe what she's saying.

"Can't you just let it go?" She sounds weary.

"If you're tired, I get it. Come stay with me and let me fight for you." My spellcraft may suck thanks to my human half, but I can pitch a fit with the best of them. "I can picket, and I can—"

"No." She stands up. "I don't want any of that. Actually, I've been wondering if I need some time away."

"Time *away*?" Her words are a bucket of sea water over my head. "Away from. . .me? From New York?" Does she not like me, now that I can't be a guardian? "I'm not giving up on helping demon-spawn," I say. "It's just that I doubt I'll ever make guardian, so I need to find a new way to—"

"Minerva." Her voice is a whip.

It stings, and I feel like the hurt is right there in my tone. "What?"

"Not everything is about you. I'm going to sell that land and move out of the city for a while. I'm sure I'll be back, but for now, I think I need this."

"It's my fault." Roxana must have come in while we were fighting, but she looks stricken.

"It's no one's fault." A vein in Bevin's head is standing out, like she's trying very hard not to explode. "I just need to get away. Please respect that."

Roxana looks as distraught as I am. "But we can help. We want to help."

"Oh, right!" She was just telling me the other day how much she can charge now for her seances. "Think about how many new customers you have because people know Roxana's your friend. You can do the seances at our place, and if she went on social media and—"

"No." Bevin shakes her head. "I'm going to meet with a real estate agent about selling the land. Please don't bring this up again." She marches out of Grand Central Gloffee like she's heading for her own funeral.

"We should do it anyway," I say.

"Are you sure?" Roxana's brow is furrowed. "She seemed pretty positive that—"

"Bevin hates when attention is drawn to her, but trust me. She's just feeling sorry for herself and doesn't want to impose."

"I've seen a few trailers for Izaak's movie," Roxana says. "If the two of us together offered to, I don't know, pose for photos, maybe? We could possibly make some money that way."

She's brilliant. "I'll look into this right away. That's a great plan. Let me talk to Izaak and—"

"Why are you wearing a dress?" Roxana blinks. "Shouldn't you be ready for work?"

"I'm off today." I spin around. "I'm meeting Ricky in twenty minutes."

Roxana whistles. "Ooh, this is so exciting."

My voice can probably only be heard by dogs when I squeal. "I know."

Giggles flies through the open door and careens into the sofa next to me.

Roxana laughs. "I think she thought you were injured or in danger, judging by that noise you made. I don't blame her."

Gavin's clearly not excited about a pigeon being inside his shop—he comes after her with a broom.

"Wait," I say. "She's my familiar."

He freezes. "Your what?"

"My familiar," I say for the first time in public. I suppose that once I accepted that I was half-human, I stopped worrying as much what people thought. "Her name is Giggles."

"Is she housebroken, then?" he frowns. "Because I hate pigeons. They're stupid, they smell, and they're ugly. Plus, they carry diseases."

"I don't know about houses," Roxana says. "But she's definitely not cafe broken." She looks pointedly at the sofa, a half-smile on her lips.

Giggles has left a present for Gavin. She fluffs up and takes off, turning her rotund body sideways to glide through the door over a very shocked wizard's head.

"She is *not* allowed in here," Gavin says. "If you let her in again, you're not welcome here either. Am I clear?"

I sigh. "Crystal."

"Good. Now use some kind of spell or something to clean this up." He waves his hands theatrically. "Or I'll make good on that threat early."

I'm fairly sure that if he knew about my parentage and my spell success rate, he wouldn't be suggesting that I use a spell for it. But about ten minutes of scrubbing and ten dollars of his paper towels later, you can *barely* tell that Giggles was ever there. Plus, his sofa wasn't accidentally set on fire, turned a different color, or suddenly caused to be crawling with spiders by a faulty spell.

I decide it's probably good enough.

"If he gets really crabby, can you charm my way out of it?"

Roxana giggles. "Probably."

"Okay, then I'm heading out to meet Ricky. Wish me luck."

"You don't need it—you're a catch. Don't forget that."

Sometimes I think my friends are delusional, but I appreciate their support all the same.

"He asked you out," she reminds me. I'm not sure how she knew I needed to hear it, but I really did. "He's had a crush on you for a while, so it's actually a *good* thing that you can't be a guardian. The world isn't ending —your new life is just starting. And it's going to be great. Don't apologize for who you are."

"How are you so smart all of a sudden?"

She shrugs. "I guess I've had a few good friends teach me some things."

When I finally leave to meet Ricky, Giggles fluttering along beside me, swooping and cooing, I'm in an even better mood than I expected. Bevin may think she's on her own, but we'll show her that's not true.

"Wow, you always looked pretty good in uniform, but you look amazing in a dress." Ricky isn't on the bench we discussed. He's on the sidewalk a block closer, walking toward me. "I figured you'd be at that gloffee shop by your place, so when I arrived early, I just started walking toward it."

I narrow my eyes. "How'd you know where I live?"

He tilts his head. "We answered that call for your friend—what was her name? The blonde?"

Bevin. Duh. I catch him up on what happened to her yesterday. "I think she's just worried she'll be a burden.

We're going to set up something to raise funds for her to build a new shop."

"That's a great idea," Ricky says. "And actually, there's a big celebration for small magical businesses in Central Park this weekend. You should just pay for a stand and put up signs. I bet you'd have plenty of people who'd stop for a photo while they're walking around."

"You're brilliant," I say.

"Just wait until you see my dating game," he says.

"What does that mean?"

He glances at the tree on the sidewalk next to me. Giggles is perched there. "I was planning on taking you somewhere nice, but then I thought, they'd probably be upset if you brought a pigeon inside. So instead, I got us a table outside at the Sonic Boom."

It's the hottest magical burger joint in town, and I hear that people routinely wait for over an hour to get in. "You got us a table?"

He shrugs. "I may have saved the owner's kid from a level four demon-spawn last week. He said he'd get me in, and I told him not to feel obligated. Then I called today and told him I'd changed my mind."

"Connections." I point at him. "I like it." When I drop my hand and start to move again, now that I know what direction we're headed, he reaches out and slides his large hand over mine.

Our fingers interlace and my heart expands in my chest.

"Oh."

"Bad oh?" he asks. "Or good oh?"

That fluttering is definitely a good thing. "Not bad."

"Then I'll take it." He squeezes my hand, and we

walk along, taking in the sights and sounds of New York City as we move along.

First a man with a briefcase nearly body checks Ricky.

Then a woman talking to her plant walks past. By the time she moves beyond us, she's yelling. "No. It's not my fault. You said you wanted more sun."

And as we approach the scaffolding on 43rd street, a man who's hanging upside down like an opossum from the lowest crossbar falls and lands on his head.

Ricky releases my hand and rushes toward him.

But Giggles is faster. She lights next to him on the ground and pecks him on the nose.

Sparks fly—the man swears and takes a swipe at her —and then he sits up, arms akimbo. "What was that?"

Giggles is already winging her way up to the bar the man just fell from. She lands ungracefully and fluffs her feathers.

"That bird attacked me," the man shouts. "It spat sparks at my face."

There were definitely sparks, but there's no way they came from my Giggles. She's harmless.

There's a pool of blood on the ground where the man was lying, and at first I'm worried it's his, but there's not a scratch on him.

"Are you alright, sir?" Ricky offers his arm.

"Fine." He points. "Just get that crazy bird away from me."

I call Giggles, and she flies to my arm. "Right away."

As we move farther from the strange, rude man, I can't help asking. "Didn't you think he was hurt?"

"There really were sparks," Ricky says at the same

time. "It was strange all around, but I didn't sense a spell. Did you?"

Clark talks about sensing spells, but I've never been able to. I just feel a strange sort of vibration whenever there's any kind of energy surge. Spells, a shifter changing forms, Roxana using her charm. I definitely felt something, but I can't tell whether it was an official spell. "Not particularly."

"Well, I'm just glad he's alright. If he'd been injured, that might have ruined the night."

Giggles coos as if she agrees. I reach out and pet her feathers. Again, when I drop my hand to my side, Ricky takes it.

This time, I don't bother looking around for the exciting people and sounds of New York City. I just enjoy holding Ricky's hand. Half a block later—so, far too soon—we see the line for the Sonic Boom.

True to Ricky's word, they're expecting us. We walk past a line that runs around the block and step right into the restaurant, the hostess waving us through the back door and onto a cute, sheltered patio. Fireflies float up and down, wobbling gently back and forth but not leaving their stations to provide low light as the sun sets. Vampires in 1950s clothing literally skate to the various tables taking people's orders.

"Don't vampires usually insist on dangerous and violent jobs?" I ask. "How did they manage to convince them to wait tables?"

"The way I heard it, the Sublime Chancellor lost a bet to the owner," Ricky says. "But no one has been able to discover what the bet was about."

"So these aren't weak or unemployable vampires?" I eye our waiter as he sidles up.

"Welcome to Sonic Boom." He looks bored. "May I take your order?"

"We just sat down," Ricky says. "Give us a minute?"

He arches one eyebrow in irritation, but he ambles off unthreateningly.

"They're rumored to be trained guards for the Sublime Chancellor himself," Ricky says. "I guess there's no way to know without asking, and I have a feeling that question won't go over well if it's a true story."

"I guess not," I say.

Giggles is waiting just outside—perched on the fence surrounding the patio. She's watching the floating fireflies intently. Ricky notices her and waves her over.

I hold up my hand to forestall her. She's gotten a lot better about listening to me. Usually. "No one else has a pet," I say. "Are you sure it's fine?"

"I told the owner that my girlfriend's familiar is a bird, and he said it was totally welcome."

My brain freezes when I hear the word *girlfriend*.

As if he can decode my thoughts, Ricky clears his throat. "It seemed easier than saying it was a girl I had a crush on and was taking on a first date. I hope that's okay."

"Oh, sure, that's what I figured," I lie. "Totally fine." Giggles takes advantage of my distraction and flutters over, landing next to me. She ducks her head under my hand, cooing the entire time.

"You're lucky your familiar likes you," he says. "I had a ferret when I was a kid, and it was constantly biting me."

"Wait, familiars can dislike their owners?"

Ricky takes a sip of his water. "I think that's more common than not, actually. My brother's bobcat would take dumps on his bed whenever he ticked it off. It happened a lot.”

“You’re kidding. I thought the bond meant they had to like you.”

“Not at all,” he says. “It means they have to submit to your commands, but the second they’re done with that, they’ll find a way to show you if they didn’t want to be bonded to you.”

The waiter shows up again, and since we still haven’t even glanced at the menu, Ricky tries to send him away.

“Wait,” I say. “I’m starving. Let’s just order whatever is your most popular thing from the menu.”

“You both want the same thing?” He looks singularly unimpressed.

Before I’ve even glanced at Ricky, we both say, “Yes.”

Then we laugh.

“First date?” The vampire’s disgust irritates me. His long nose and haughty eyes are very nicely formed—but he’s sour enough he’d almost put me off my meal. Hopefully he’ll drop it and run.

Ricky wraps an arm around my shoulders. “One year anniversary. We’re just still this happy.”

“How fabulous for you.”

Giggles grunts, and her head bobs, and I realize she’s not responding to our conversation—which I’ve now come to expect—because she’s practically hypnotized by the lightning bugs. And then she darts out and *eats one*. She tilts her head up and wiggles her head and neck around. I can literally *see* it sliding down into her belly. Apparently magical light shines, even through a bird.

“Whoa.” The vampire splutters. “Make her spit it out.”

“Can they do that?” I ask.

Ricky shrugs.

"Giggles," I say. "No. Bad bird. Spit that magical firefly out. You can't eat the decorations."

She chirps, which is a sound I've never heard her make, and eats a *second* firefly.

"Is she stupid?" the vampire asks. "Why am I even asking. She's a pigeon."

Giggles fluffs up and coughs—expelling a firefly right at our waiter. It sails through the air, spinning round and round, and explodes all over his very neat, perfectly pressed white shirt and tie.

Covering him in glowing goo.

Giggles shakes her backside and sits down next to my silverware. Then she hiccups. And of course, she's still glowing.

"She did spit one out," Ricky says.

"Freak." The waiter practically sprints away from us, as if he's not sure what other awful things we might do.

"That guy's terrible." Ricky leans down, closer to Giggles. "Nice work, Madam."

I squirm. "You're not worried we might get kicked out?"

"If we are?" He shrugs. "I'm fine with non-magical burgers, and at those places, your pigeon won't get in trouble for eating a bug."

I laugh.

"And in a year," Ricky says, making my heart flutter again, "let's come back here. If that guy's still around, we can buy him a slice of cake or something and thank him for helping our first date be memorable."

I laugh. "I doubt he eats cake. People who eat cake are happier than he is."

"We should get cake then," Ricky says. "This is the happiest I've been in a while."

Giggles coos. She stands up, like she might be hungry, and I glare. She sits back down.

Thank goodness.

"You know, a pigeon may not be a traditional choice, but I think it was smart. Most people won't expect it, and they'll say things in front of her that they wouldn't say around something more obvious. Have you figured out how to mirror with her yet?"

"Mirror?" I ask.

Ricky frowns. "It's Familiars 101. If your familiar actually likes you, they're often open to mirroring. It's where you slide into her consciousness to see what she's seeing. You hadn't heard of it?"

"I never took a class on familiars, because I could never bond one before. I didn't understand why then, but every attempt I made was a disaster. In fact, I didn't pick Giggles. I tried to bond a flame lizard and failed miserably. Then the next morning, when I woke up. . ." I point. "Giggles."

Ricky's suddenly so still it makes me nervous. "You didn't *try* to bond her?"

I shake my head.

"Would you say that *she* chose *you*?"

I swallow. "I mean, I'm not sure." But the way he's asking has me all kinds of nervous. Why didn't I insist that Clark find me some books on this or something? I think he took the class, so at a baseline, he must have his old textbook somewhere. Although, now that I'm thinking about it, he never wanted a familiar. He thought about a monkey, but when he even got close to the ones available at school, they attacked him. It sort of put him off the whole idea.

"What does it mean if she did?"

Ricky shrugs. "It's not supposed to be possible. You can only bond a familiar intentionally, and you both have to be touching during the spell or it won't work. If you never touched her. . ."

"I was trying my best to touch the flame lizard when it busted through my window and out into the night. It nearly burned my apartment down."

"Are you sure you weren't drunk? Maybe you grabbed a pigeon by mistake and you don't remember."

"I almost never drink, and I hadn't had a drop that night. I was too intent on making sure things went off perfectly."

He rubs his hand along the scruff on his chin, making a scritching sound I quite like. "Huh. Well, maybe it's different with half-humans? I'm not sure. But I would have sworn that—"

Our food arrives then, two burgers, the plates piled high with fries. They look pretty normal. As soon as the grumpy vampire's gone, I ask, "What exactly do people love about this place? Maybe we should have asked before we ordered instead of letting Mr. Grumpy choose for us."

Ricky shrugs, dragging a French fry through a pile of catsup and tossing it into his mouth. And then he closes his eyes and sighs.

I copy him, and the second the fry hits my mouth, I get it.

It tastes like watching the Yankees play in the spring. Like watermelon at the first swimming party of the summer. Like the first time my crush smiled at me in high school.

"What did they do to these fries?" I ask, almost moaning in delight.

"Toadstool oil," Ricky says. "It must be. I've heard of it, but I've never actually tasted it."

"This owner must be a really good gambler," I say.

"How do you figure?"

"He won a bet with the Sublime Chancellor for his waiters, and he serves fries made with toadstool oil?" I shake my head. "What kind of bet did he have to win to get access to that much?"

"Or maybe he's got a friend on the Angel Council."

They say toadstools only grow in places where the akero have slept. To have access to regular toadstool oil, he'd need to know someone on the council for sure. I can't even imagine what something like that costs. "Thanks for bringing me here. My friends will never believe it."

"I'm glad you're having fun," he says.

Afterward, we go for a walk and happen to pass by Central Park where they're setting up for tomorrow's festival. I do my best to get us a table, but they say they're all sold out.

It takes Ricky less than five minutes to sweet talk the same woman who turned me down flat into giving us one. "I swear," I say. "Your smile should be licensed."

"Excuse me?" he asks.

"As a deadly weapon," I say. "I've thought that for years."

"I guess I must really like you," he says. "Because that corny line actually made me smile even bigger."

That makes two of us.

❧ 15 ❧

IZAAK

Playing a villain is everything I hoped it wouldn't be.

The director loves me and tells me every single day that I'm just perfect for this role. He also cringes when he sees me round a corner.

The other actors joke and laugh and chat with each other comfortably. Until I show up.

But I needed a job, and my parents were getting more and more vocal about bringing me back home. This will hopefully get them off my back. Plus, with Xander struggling, I really didn't want to add any stress to his life. I made this decision after a lot of thought, and I don't regret it. I do wish it hadn't come to this.

So when my mom texts and asks me whether I can come home for dinner tomorrow, I make the stupid mistake of telling her that I'm filming. The flurry of messages that follow can't be helped. A simple web search would show the promos the movie producer has been releasing, and my name and headshots have been released far and wide, so there's no point in lying.

Everyone knows.

And now 'everyone' includes my mom. I'm not surprised when she calls. I answer to keep her from just showing up on set. It's a closed set, and no one really knows the exact location, but my mom kills people for a living. I wouldn't put it past her to do whatever it took to find out where I am. It's easier to ask for a short break and head off the killing spree at the pass.

"Mom."

"Izaak Alexander, what's this I hear about you playing a villain?"

I sigh. "It's an amazing role, Mom."

"You left home to make people smile. You wanted to live a different life than the one fate dealt to you."

"And I am," I say. "How many vampire actors—"

"Quit this nonsense already and come home right now. The fact that you're compromising on the one thing you really wanted means it's not working."

"Mom, look, the thing is—"

"I've already heard the thing, and now I don't believe your nonsense anymore. You will come home by tomorrow night, or I'll come looking for you, and I'll bring my soup ladle."

I flinch when I hear that—the soup ladle was always what she used when we'd been *bad*. She never got it out unless she had blown past angry and was approaching rabid. If she pulled the soup ladle out of its spot in the giant mug? You were toast.

"Mom."

"What?" I can practically hear her lips pursing and her eyebrow inching upward.

"I'm in my twenties, nearing thirty. You can't come to the city with a *soup ladle* and spank me. You just can't."

"If you keep telling me what I can't do, I guess we'll find out if it's true."

"They're paying me really well, Mom, and it's good exposure. I won't be playing a villain forever, and—"

"Or you will. There's no way to know."

"It may be harder for me to get the kind of role I want after I play this one well," I say. "But it was already hard. Certainly being well-known won't make it harder for me to get auditions."

"Mhmm."

My mom can say a whole paragraph with a single mhmm. Our pastor growing up would turn white as a sheet when she said mhmm. Our trash men would sprint down the street, skipping a dozen loaded cans on their way after a single mhmm.

"When the movie comes out—"

"I'm coming out there this week," she says. "When the movie comes out? Boy, please."

"But—"

"If you don't want me to bring that ladle, you better smile when you see me, and you better say, 'thanks for coming, Mama.'"

"Yes ma'am."

The second I hang up, I practically race to my director's side. "Are we close to being done with my scenes?"

His mouth drops open. "We just started last week."

"I know, but are we close?"

He stammers a bit before saying, "I mean, we can be."

And I realize that without meaning to, I've scared him. He's not saying that because we were actually close. He can sense the unhappiness of my innate predator and he's reacting. Like a horse rolling its eyes until only the whites are visible. Or a deer flicking its tail straight up in the air. Or a dog squatting and peeing on the floor.

"It's fine if we aren't close," I say. "I was just checking."

He swallows slowly. "When do you need to be done?"

Oh, come on. He's making it too easy. "The sooner the better." I mean, I feel bad, but if the damage is already done. . .

"Did I mention how happy we are with your performance? Early screen tests are showing that people really buy your delivery. One of the writers was very worried that the villain wouldn't be convincing or scary enough to pull this off, but you really manage it. And the way the others react to you—it's so authentic looking."

I grit my teeth and lie. "I'm so pleased to hear it."

"I think, since we only have that one last big scene, we can do that today and tomorrow."

"Perfect," I say. "That would be absolutely amazing."

It makes for some long days, but they seem to like those. I suppose the set and the equipment and the salaries for the tech people are expensive, so running fewer days, even if they're long, helps keep them on budget. I may not really understand it, but as long as we finish before the soup ladle arrives. . .

The next day feels like the worst yet. True to the director's word, though, we manage to wrap the final scene by the end of the day. My shoulders hurt, my head is throbbing, and my feet have started to chafe in the stupid boots they've been making me wear, but no one has seen or heard from my mother, so—

"Izaak Alexander." My blood runs cold, and I finally have a little insight into how everyone on set must feel when they see me.

"Oh. Hey, Mom." I force the words out. "How neat that you found us."

Her smile is staggering, as usual. "I couldn't miss my baby acting in a real feature film."

"Let's go get something to eat," I say. "Your timing is good. We just finished."

"Is anything open this late?" she asks.

"It's New York City," I say. "There's always something open."

"But I want to meet your friends," she insists.

And that's how we wind up walking from one room to the next, forcing smiles and ignoring my castmates' flinches and shivers.

"They hate you," she says the second we leave.

"They don't hate me," I say. "I've kept my distance, and they're a close-knit group."

"They're practically glued together, in comparison to how they act around you."

"I'm a vampire, Mom, and it's an all human cast. What did you expect? They don't know who or what I am, and they don't understand how I make them feel. They're acting exactly the way they should, and it's the reason everyone always wants to cast me as a villain."

"They should cower," she says. "But you shouldn't be trying to be their friend. They're your *food*."

"Please," I say. "We barely need any blood at all, and we can get more than enough thanks to the Red Cross and all their blood drives."

"That *was* a stroke of genius by the Supreme Chancellor—the blood drive initiative. As if humans really need that many blood transfusions." Her laugh is nice to hear—warm and welcoming, like summer rain. "But sweetheart, I'm not here to lecture you. I'm not even here to make you feel bad."

"Then why did you come?" I fold my arms and wait.

"You're an adult now," she says. "And I thought you'd fail at this thing and come home. But now you're doing things you didn't even want to do, and I can't understand why you won't just come home and be who you were always meant to be."

"You're my mom, and I love you." I sigh. "But you don't get to decide what I'm meant to be, or how I have to live. I'm sorry that upsets you, but it's still true."

"Are you really saying that you're happy here?" She puts her hands on her hips. "You're happy surrounded by humans who are terrified of you?"

I shrug.

"Living with a *werewolf?*" She says the word like she'd say *criminal*. "And across the hall from a filthy wizard?"

She's a witch, but I don't bother pointing that out. Women's rights aren't such a big issue with vampires— the women have always been as powerful as the men. It's just that my mom doesn't care enough to keep straight who lives across the hall.

"What kind of girl will you marry, do you think, if you spend all your time consorting with all those misfits?"

"I'm a misfit," I say. "You may not see it, but I don't fit in with you or with my siblings or with the other vampires you always flung at me. I never have. I want things you don't want, and I do things you don't do."

"But—"

"My roommate needs me right now," I say. "He may be fraying, and he's looking for a mate—"

"He may be fraying?" This time, she's the deer with its tail straight up in the air. She's the human female with a mace can, ready to spray me in the face. "You have to come home, Izaak. No more silliness and protests—that's not safe."

"He's perfectly safe around me, Mom. Trust me. I'm not leaving him, or the others either. They're my friends. Soup ladle or not, I'm not coming home."

Mom blinks, and for the first time in my life, she looks at me with respect. "Well, I'll give you this much— you seem to know what you want for once."

And I realize that she's right.

I may be doing a job I didn't want. And I may be forcing myself into a position I didn't want to be in—it may wind up typecasting me as a bad guy forever. But I'm doing it eyes wide open, and I'm here for my best friend, even when my mom's threatening to disown me over it.

Maybe I really have found a place.

When I get home, Minerva's pacing in the hallway. "Finally."

I glance both directions, wondering if she's talking to someone other than me. "Finally?"

"You took forever to get home. Are you always filming this late?"

"I took my mom out for pizza," I say. "I didn't realize we had plans. It might help next time if you told me when we did." I can't help my smirk.

She throws her hands up in the air. "Bevin's insurance claims she canceled her policy, and while I was out with Ricky—"

"You finally went out with him?" I ball my hand into a fist and pump it in the air. "How was it?"

"It was great," she says, clearly brushing me off. "But while we were out, we had an idea."

"'We' being you and Ricky?" I still can't tell whether she's avoiding the date thing, or if she's just fixated. Minerva gets like this, focusing on something to the point of ignoring the rest of her life. But sometimes it's a defense mechanism. "The date really did go well?"

"Yes." She huffs. "It was rainbows and moonbeams and sunshine."

"How could it be sunshine *and* moonbeams? I don't think they can coexist."

"Izaak Alexander!"

"That's not the first time someone has last-named me today," I say. "It doesn't work as well the second time, plus compared to my mom, you're like a fluffy little bunny."

"I booked us a booth at the park tomorrow," Minerva says, rushing to get it out. "And I need you and Roxana to come and let people pay you to pose for photos."

"Huh?" It's like she's speaking gibberish. "A booth?"

"Bevin needs money to build a new shop," she says. "She's talking about moving away and selling that land and not even living here anymore."

If my mom had gotten her way, I'd have left. If Xander finds a mate, her pack may insist he stay there. And now Bevin's leaving? What's going on? It's like fate is trying to yank us apart.

Fate can suck a lemon. That just makes me more determined to hold tight. "No way."

"No way, you won't do it?"

"No, I'm saying she can't leave. And I'm not leaving to move back in with my parents, either."

"Exactly," she says. "That's the spirit. So you'll do it?"

"Of course," I say.

The next morning—only four hours after I finally lie down—when Xander's shaking me awake, I'm way less energized about making money for Bevin.

"Need sleep," I mumble.

"Minerva knew you'd be like this," Xander says. "But you have to wake up. I've got a Red Bull, right here."

I duck under a pillow. "Not strong enough."

"Clark charmed it. We need you, buddy."

"Later. A few more hours."

"The sun isn't going away," he says. "And you're not going to be less tired in a few hours."

"I can't do it," I say. "Tell Minnie I'm sorry."

"Minnie?" Xander laughs. "Why *haven't* we ever called Minerva that? It's hilarious."

"Shut up," I grumble.

Then the sheets are yanked off, so I curl into a ball. The television's turned on full volume, so I cover my ears. And finally, the window shades are thrown wide open. The full force of the sun beats against me. I mumble, "The sun just makes me *more* sleepy, idiot."

"Dang it." He closes the blinds. "Look, Minerva said you stood up to your mom yesterday. Channel some of that energy and get up."

"Just a few more hours." I throw my arms over my face. It's not much, but it helps. The sun made me twice as bleary as before.

"I found a pack," Xander says. "I didn't want to tell you, but confessing seems like it may be the only way to wake you up."

I bolt upright, the fog lifting, but a pounding starting at the base of my skull. "What?"

"The good news is that I'm not fraying, so there's that."

"You're not fraying? Or you won't be if you join this pack?"

He shrugs. "What's the difference? It's always been a risk, and this will eliminate it. I'll be safe, and I won't hurt anyone else." Then he mutters, "You'll all be safe."

"You never would have hurt us," I say. I really believe that's true. I never had any fear around him.

"Well, it turns out, this pack thinks I'm an alpha. They say the erratic things I've been doing are tied to that, not the fray."

"That's good news," I say. "Plus, how cool that you're an alpha!"

He shakes his head. "Not really. The pack's a mess, and they want me to step in and fix it. That's not really a Xander thing, if you catch my drift. I don't make things better."

"I think you do." I yawn. "You got me up."

"I've had years of practice at that," he says. "More often than not, I fail, if you recall."

I think back on the years we've been roommates—the failed auditions, the pep talks he's given me, the way his faith in me never wavered.

And that's when I realize there's a note of sadness in his face. "What aren't you telling me?"

"The pack isn't close."

"They'll let you join?"

He nods.

"How far away are they? Are we talking Yonkers? Jersey?"

He sighs. "Farther. I can't just drive back and forth. I'd have to move there."

"Oh." It's all I can manage to say. I know I should be happy—giddy, really. We were worried he might be *put down*, and now we have a pack that will welcome him into it. That's always been his goal. It's really the best-case scenario.

But it also means he's leaving.

I fought off my mother. We're raising money to keep Bevin here. But it's not like I can tell Xander to skip this —it's his life's dream. A dream he knew he had no hope of ever fulfilling because fate blows.

As his friend, I have to tell him how great it is. But it still stings. "I'm so happy for you, man." But a single tear rolls down my face. I swipe it away.

"You are?" His forehead wrinkles and his eyebrows rise. "You look a little sad."

"I'm, like, so super duper happy right now." More stupid tears roll down my cheeks. "I'm as happy as when I got a bowl of Lucky Charms as a kid that was almost all marshmallows." And now I'm sobbing like a baby. "I'm as happy as I am on Christmas morning."

"Me too."

I finally focus in on his face enough that I notice— he's crying, too.

He hugs me then, and I slap my arms around him and against his back. "I'm just so happy."

"Me too," he says. "Me too."

It takes us a few minutes to work through how happy we are, but eventually I get showered, chug a few charmed Red Bulls, and jog out the door. Xander hails a cab, but by then the girls have come down. The cab only has room for three.

"You guys go ahead," I say. "I'll grab the next one."

"Are you sure?" Minerva asks. "Because if we all wait,

I'm worried they won't hold our table, but if we leave, I'm worried you'll go back up to sleep."

I wave. "I'm fine, I swear. Go."

And while I wait, something occurs to me. I'm delighted that Xander found a pack, but I'm struggling to believe that his dad never knew he was an alpha. It seems like something a father would know. Last year, when he came by the apartment, Xander used my phone to text him.

I saved his number.

My finger hovers over the contact for a full thirty seconds, cabs passing me like mosquitos on a hot summer night. In the end, I can't shake my suspicion. I hit talk. It rings and rings, and just when I think it's about to roll over to voicemail. . .

"Hello?"

"Mr. Binnigas?" I ask.

"Speaking."

"I'm Izaak, your son's roommate."

"Ah. Yes. The black vampire." He chuckles. Not sure why it's funny, but for some reason, people find it humorous.

"That's me." I mean, my entire family's black, and they're all vampires. But I don't bother saying that. It's really not the point.

"Is Xander alright?"

"Actually, that's why I'm calling. We've been worried he might be fraying."

"Fraying?" He snorts. "No way."

"Why 'no way'?" I ask. "He was acting—"

"Why do you think I came out to visit last year?" he asks.

"Uh, to see your son?"

Xander's dad sighs. "He doesn't want to see me, kid, and I don't exactly blame him. I haven't given him the easiest life."

"But someone told us something strange recently, and I was wondering if it could possibly be true—"

"He's an alpha?" his dad asks.

I almost choke.

"And let me guess. Some janky old pack wants him to come lead them. They don't even care that he's half-human."

I have no idea how he could know that. But I guess he did know Xander was an alpha—so there goes my hope that's not true.

"They haven't brought him in yet," he says. "But you're calling because the idea of losing him has you all upset."

His dad's a psychic. He must be. "Actually—"

"It's fine, kid. I'll come talk to him." And then he hangs up.

I wish I knew whether calling him was a huge mistake or a stroke of brilliance. It probably won't be long before I find out, one way or another.

XANDER

One million dollars.

When I was a kid, that was the amount people threw around as an example of extreme wealth. If someone had one million dollars, they had made it. I thought that if I *ever* had a million dollars, I'd be able to buy anything I wanted. I'd be able to have anything *anyone* wanted. And I'd be the *SHIZ WHIZ.*

Unfortunately, I actually used that phrase. A lot. So much that my mother threatened to scrub my mouth with flea bath if I didn't stop. Flea bath tastes *so* much worse than bar soap that there's no comparison.

But now, as an adult, I'm staring at a table that's decorated like a PTA fundraiser—Minerva has clearly gone insane—and has a large pasteboard monstrosity with the goal for our 'save the shop' drive posted at the top in bright, shining letters: one million dollars. She's spelled them to actually glow. I swear, for someone who has trouble making freeze spells work, she sometimes has strokes of actual brilliance.

"It's really going to cost a million dollars?" I can't help looking at the sad glass jar on the corner of the table. I added ten dollars to it a few minutes ago, because when it was empty it looked even more pathetic.

"Oh, are we adding to it ourselves?" Izaak frowns. "I mean, I haven't been paid yet."

"I'm not even employed right now," Roxana says. And then she pointedly adds a twenty-dollar bill while eyeing Izaak.

Her dad does own half of Long Island, but I don't bother pointing that out. I'm pretty sure she's still sponging off Minerva and that daddy hasn't even sent her credit cards. At least she's generous with her friends' money. Since Izaak has been sponging off me for years, I'm not sure whether to be proud or embarrassed that he's so cheap.

"This thing opens in a few minutes," Minerva says, "and we are going to shoot right up toward that goal. I just know it."

"Or we're going to look like greedy, insane idiots and everyone will laugh at me." Roxana shrugs. "Either way, at least we'll be able to tell Bevin that we tried."

When the gates swing open and people begin to filter through, it really looks like it's going to be the greedy, insane idiots one. Sometimes I hate my wolfy hearing.

"A million dollars?" Some woman snickers. "What idiot thinks a new store costs that?"

"Shouldn't she take out a loan from the bank like a normal person? I mean, it sucks it burned down and all, but..."

"Didn't she have insurance? What an idiot."

A few people drop spare change in it, like it's a tip jar at a fast food place. One guy tries to flick his cigarette butt in, but Roxana stops him. "Excuse me, sir, but this is a donations jar. It's not for trash."

He freezes, his eyes moving up her body slowly, and I tense up, ready to punch him in the nose if he says something horrible. "You're actually Roxana Goldenscales."

He smells like mothballs and cigarette ash. What kind of magical being is he?

"I thought the sign up front was fake, but if you're really her, I want a photo." He points at the jar. "How much?"

Roxana's lips flatten. "Fifty dollars."

"Actually, it's only twenty," Minerva amends.

"Ah, ah, ah." Roxana flicks the sign off the table, ignoring Minerva's shriek. "You treated the jar like trash. For you? It's fifty." She taps her foot.

"Can I put my arm around you?" The mothball guy's eyes gleam distastefully.

Her lip curls. "For a hundred."

"Done." He whips the money out so fast that Minerva practically can't catch it.

I'm stuck taking the photo—and he gets exactly one. No more, no less.

"Hey," he says. "My eyes are half closed."

"Looks more authentic that way," I say.

He grumbles about it, but he doesn't push. I wonder how long it'll be before that's up on every social media account he has.

Before it's even had time to hit the net, a flock of women rush over. "Wait, are you really Roxana Goldenscales?"

"Is it true that with a strand of your hair, I can bind the man I love to me forever?"

Roxana snorts and opens her mouth to say how absurd that is, I assume, but Minerva stops her. "One hair is two hundred dollars."

"Twenty dollars for a photo?" The girl asks. "Or can I get both for two hundred?"

"Sure, I can throw in a photo," Minerva says. "But just you." She waves her hand. "Not all of them."

"Duh," the girl says.

"Whoa," Roxana says. "My hair—"

Minerva presses a finger to her mouth. "Hush."

And just like that, the money starts to pile up. Izaak looks less than pleased. No one seems to care that he's even there—until a group of men dressed in all black stop by the table. "Is Izaak Alexander really here?"

He perks up. "Yes. I am!"

They start jostling one another, smiling and whispering. "I knew it."

"It's twenty dollars for a photo, and—"

"What about a kiss?" the tallest one asks. "How much is that?"

Izaak's mouth dangles open.

"Excuse me?" Minerva asks.

"I mean, they have kissing booths," the man says. "It's not that strange a question."

"For your. . .girlfriend?" Izaak asks.

The man sighs. "I guess not."

I can't help my snort.

Izaak glares at me. But he takes half a dozen photos —the men are all part of a group called Villains First, and they promise to text their entire group and notify them that Izaak Alexander is present, in the flesh.

Although, they seem a bit disappointed he's not wearing all black.

And he's bummed that they're excited specifically that he's a villain.

"This is exactly what I never wanted," he says. "I feel like such a fraud."

"You never wanted fans to show up?" I ask. "You never wanted men who want you because you're so freaking foxy?"

Izaak scrunches his nose. "I mean, I guess it's flattering."

Roxana pats his back. "Of course it is. Men like me, women like me. I welcome all of the good energy."

"Okay." His smile still looks a little unhinged.

I don't point out that his crazy smile's perfect for a villain. He'd be glaring immediately thereafter.

For the next hour, about ten people show up for Roxana for every one person who comes to see Izaak, but it's better than before. Almost every one of the ones who come for Izaak are wearing black, but they seem perfectly happy to shell out money for a photo and his autograph. Two more people ask for a kiss, and both are women. He doesn't kiss either of them, of course. It's a good thing, because if word got out that Roxana's table was selling kisses, there might be a stampede.

But at least it seems to really perk him up that some girls are asking, too.

"Hey guys," I say in the next lull. "It's almost lunchtime. I can go get sandwiches if you're hungry."

"Yes!" Izaak says. "I want two."

I know better than to ask whether he wants two kinds of meat or two full sandwiches. It's always two full sandwiches—Izaak means business when it comes to food. "How about you?"

Before they can answer, Clark strolls up, wearing an over-the-shoulder bag.

"Hey, you can't cut the line," a woman shouts.

"I'm not," he says. "I'm with them—their friend. Relax."

"What's that?" Minerva asks.

"A spelled pouch," he says. "Didn't you say I should make a deposit? It took me like an hour to prep this little baby."

"Oh." Minerva claps. "I should count all this out."

Plenty of people transferred money through phone apps, but lots of people still brought cash. Clark helpfully throws up a bubble of privacy so that it's not obvious that she's counting out money.

"What are we up to?" Roxana asks.

It's only been two hours, but it would be nice to have some encouraging amount. Like eighty thousand. Maybe?

"Eleven thousand," Minerva says brightly.

"What about the apps?" I ask.

She frowns. "That's with the cash of four thousand two hundred, and the app transfers."

"Oh." Roxana looks a little depressed. She bumps the large pasteboard with her toe. "Is there even a tick on that for eleven thousand?"

Minerva blinks. "Not really, but we're getting there. Let's not get discouraged. That's a lot of money."

"I'm going to go get some sandwiches," I say again. "Minerva? Roxana?"

Roxana waves her hand. "Sure. Whatever."

"Anything," Minerva says. "But none of that gluten-free bread. Without gluten, bread tastes like crackers."

"Sure, sure." I turn to leave. "Clark?"

"Did you need help carrying the sandwiches?"

I roll my eyes. "No, dummy. I'm asking if you want one."

"Oh." He shakes his head. "I just ate on my way here."

"Okay—be back soon."

It takes me longer than I expected it would to navigate my way out of the extravaganza, making sure they stamp my hand before I leave so I don't have to pay to reenter. It only occurs to me then that they may not allow outside food. But Izaak's favorite sandwich shop is right around the corner. I guess I can text Clark if they won't let me in and ask him to come out and spell the bag to look like something else.

It's really too bad that wolves don't have magic.

Alphas do.

Which brings me back to thinking about the offer Jewel made. Would I really want to be alpha of my own pack? It may be a mess, but I bet we could turn that around. I'd have wolves who were bonded to me—for life, as I understand it. They'd share power with me, and I could use it to protect them. The way no one ever protected me.

I'd be lying if I said the idea didn't appeal to me.

But the thought of leaving my friends? It makes me sick to my stomach. They need me, clearly. Izaak's a mess, Clark is his own worst enemy, Minerva's been flailing ever since she learned about her adoption, and Bevin's life literally just went up in flames. And even though she's relatively new to the group, the thought of ditching Roxana might make me the most uncomfortable. I'd rather not think about why.

How can I even consider abandoning them?

I have to wait in line for longer than usual, but I finally manage to place the order. I'm standing in another line waiting for it to be made, wondering if I should have ordered Clark something anyway, because he's totally the kind of guy who will say he doesn't want anything and then eat your entire sandwich, one begged bite at a time, when someone says my name.

"Xander." The voice is rough—and for some reason, I'm positive it's a wolf. That's always bad in the city. It's either the Manhattan pack, who I'm actively trying to avoid, or a rival, who won't be nice to me for my affiliation, however loose.

I turn slowly, bracing myself for whoever's here and whatever they're going to demand that I do.

But it's not a New York wolf at all.

It's someone way less likely to turn up.

My dad.

"It *is* you," he says.

"You just happened to want a sandwich?" I frown. This *is* the place I brought him the last time he came into town. Over a year ago.

"You still come here."

"Please tell me you haven't been sitting in here, waiting for me to show up." He has a phone. He has my number.

As if he could read my mind, he says, "I wasn't sure you'd take my call."

By the hair of the first dog. "You really were just sitting in here?"

"Since we opened," the man making my sandwiches

says. "And we serve breakfast sandwiches now, so it's been a while."

I am so confused. "What are you doing here?"

"Your buddy called me."

Who? Clark? I'm going to kill him.

"The vampire."

He is *so* not getting those two sandwiches. "Why would he call you?"

Luckily, my sandwich order's ready. I snatch it out of the poor man's hands and stomp out.

As if that might convince my dad to buzz off. Did Izaak tell him I'm fraying? And even if he did, how could Dad think he could help—days and days after I discovered the issue? If I hadn't been smart about how I handled things, I'd already have been killed by Lo Ren. A lot of good my dad has ever done me—he's always at least a day late and more than a thousand dollars short.

"Xander, slow down."

"Why?" I spin around, my hands clenched tightly on the bags. "What are you going to do? Tell me that everything's going to be okay? You've never cared before—don't bother starting now."

His face is ruggedly handsome in a way mine never has been. I clearly take after my mom's side. I'm far too pretty for a wolf, sadly. But right now, he just looks resigned. "I've always cared."

I roll my eyes and start walking again.

His words practically hit me in the back, he says them so loudly. "But caring isn't helpful, not to a young alpha."

I freeze. *An alpha.* He says it so casually, like he's always known. It must have been Izaak who told him. But *why* would he share that with my dad? Did he think

Dad would be able to tell whether it's true? My arms are shaking when I turn back around. "Don't."

"Don't what?"

"Act like you knew."

Dad shrugs. "I did know. I've waited for years for you to find out."

I shake my head. "You would have told me if you knew." I'm flooded with rage. "You *should have* told me, if you really knew. What kind of father would keep something like that from his child?"

"I figured you did know, deep down. Why else would you go to the strongest alpha in the state and ask him to keep you in check?"

"What does that mean?" I practically roar. "I learned nothing in school. I was too busy taking beating after beating. Everyone hated me. They all mocked me and attacked me and ran me down. I ran and hid among the normies, and you didn't think I'd want to know that I was an *alpha* all along?"

"Look, you had bonded your friends, so I figured you already knew."

"I had bonded. . .what?" What garbage is he saying? "Who do you think I bonded?"

"Your wizard friend and his sister. You moved in across the hall from her. And your vampire buddy, and that weird demon girl."

I'm shaking my head so much now that it's hard for me to see his face clearly. I hold out my hand, my index finger pointing at him, the sandwich bag swinging underneath. "No. I can't have bonded them. They're not wolves."

"I wouldn't have believed it either, but you have. I've seen the bonds, when you're upset, when you're agitated.

They calm you down. They keep you safe. They're the reason you've never frayed."

"But they can't possibly ever accept the bonds," I say. *"Because they aren't wolves."*

"I know that as well as you do," Dad says. "It's why I'd never have wanted this for you, but I did my best to surround you with wolves—"

"You sent me to a normie school," I say. "The only friend I had there was Clark."

"That was an inadvertent—"

"He's never drop-kicked me into any bad situations. He's never looked the other way while people beat me up. And he's never ignored my calls because he thought it might toughen me up. I'd say he's a better dad than you ever were."

My dad swallows slowly. "I may have made some miscalculations. Perhaps I should have helped you more or offered more support. But we don't grow stronger by relying on others."

"I think you might be wrong there. We are stronger precisely because we can rely on others."

"Semantics," my dad says. "The point is this. You have a wolf pack that wants you to be their alpha. They're actual wolves, and you could close that bond. You could have what you've always needed: a family that accepts and loves you. You'd be safe, and strong, and cared for."

I realize that he's right.

"Your friends may stand beside you, and they may want to keep you safe, but they can't. There's no way they can close that pack loop—you can't ever really be their alpha like you need to be."

"Why did you let me stay here, bonded but not really bonded, if you knew?"

He shrugs. "I figured it was the best you'd be able to find. At least you weren't fraying, and you had a connection *to* a pack if you needed it. Plus, who knew? Maybe you'd actually wind up being able to sever the bonds with your friends and join Lo Ren's. Alphas like him have had other alphas serve them before. There used to be huge packs like that—each new alpha serving the stronger one, but bonded to wolves below him or her."

"Isn't that illegal now?" I ask.

Dad shrugs. "Laws come and go."

"I'm touched that you came all this way," I say, surprised as I say it that I mean it. "But I don't need your help." Especially not now that he's told me the stuff I didn't know, like that I've bonded my friends. "You can go."

"I will," he says. "But promise me this. At least *consider* releasing your friends. It's not just better for you. There's a reason that we keep to our own kind. We aren't made to be friends with people who aren't like us. It's too hard—for everyone. If you really care about them, you'll let them go."

Is he right? I'm not quite sure. I know Roxana's happier now than she was at home. She's the friend I've known the least time, and yet she's the one that I can't even seem to consider releasing. Then there's Clark—my first real friend. And Izaak, my closest friend. Minerva, the closest thing I'll ever have to a sister. And zany Bevin, who can and will literally say anything. But who broke her own vows to help the newest one of us.

Can I really walk away from them? Are we really

better off with our own kind? Have we just been hurting ourselves?

When I walk up to the table where all but Bevin are gathered, trying to help the one of us who's hurting, I struggle to believe my father. What I see in front of me is *good*, not *bad*. Even if he's right, even if I somehow managed to bond these people, even if it was only partway, that's good too, isn't it?

And somehow, in the time I was gone to get sandwiches, we've reached a hundred thousand dollars. "Whoa," I say. "What happened?"

"Howard Hues came by." Minerva looks effervescently giddy. "He offered to donate fifty grand if Roxana would let him film a little clip with her for his channel."

Roxana shakes her head. "It helps that it's a charitable endeavor. I kind of hate that he's using it to drive traffic to his newest movie, which I am certainly not starring in."

"It was brilliant, though," Minerva says. "We should have charged more. The movie is about a queen who can tame dragons."

"It's a little derivative," Clark says.

"You're just jealous you're not making something like that," Minerva says.

Clark's sideways smile confirms it.

There's a line around the corner now, but I insist that Roxana and Izaak stop to eat something before taking any more photos. When I hand them the food, I try my hardest to sense whether there's some kind of connection between us.

"Um, dude." Izaak glances left and right and drops his voice. "If you need to fart, go over there." He tosses his head.

"What?"

"You're making that weird face you make before you level our family room."

By the angel's wing. "I am not making that fa—I don't make a face."

"Okay," Izaak says. "Whatever."

"I'm not about to—just forget it."

"If you say so. There's just a lot of people here, and I'm not taking the fall for you this time."

Roxana cocks her head. "Taking the fall for him? What are you talking about?"

I splutter. "Nothing. He's not talking at all."

The corner of her mouth quirks. "If you say so."

"I do." I can feel the heat rising in my face.

"It's cool fam," Izaak says. "Don't get too upset. Wouldn't want you to go furry in front of all these people."

"I don't do that," I say. "I never go furry when I shouldn't."

"Is that what this is about?" Roxana says. "I hear it happens to all wolves."

"That's a lie," I say. "It doesn't happen to me."

"Are we talking about shifting?" Minerva asks. "Because it almost sounds like—"

"Okay, I'm going to open the line up again," Clark says. "Let's watch our mouths."

Roxana may be the most elegant and gorgeous woman in this entire park, but boy can she shove an entire sandwich in her mouth when she's in a hurry.

I can't decide whether I'm horrified or in awe. Maybe a bit of both.

"Alright." She wipes her mouth on a napkin and reapplies her lipstick. "Ready."

Izaak, Clark, and I are all just staring at her.

"What?"

Izaak shakes himself, and I wind up doing the same. So what if I look like a dog? Sometimes you've gotta do what you gotta do. The charm is strong with her, which is probably why our line just keeps growing. The cash jar's nearly full again when Minerva calls for a temporary halt to count. Clark seals us in a privacy bubble.

"I can take this to deposit it," Clark says. "But while I'm gone—"

"Clark Lucent, you open that bubble right this second."

That voice sounds disturbingly like Bevin. I say, "I thought we agreed not to tell her—"

"Don't even try to pretend you don't hear me, Xander. I know you're in there."

"Your privacy bubbles suck, Clark," I say. "You need to work on those."

"Dozens of people have shared your video with me on social media. If you want something to be a secret, maybe don't make it so *public*!"

Right. Should've thought of that, what with Howard Hues taking videos. Bevin may not be that connected, but her *name* is on the booth, and with her having run a secondhand magic shop for years, people do know her.

"Let me in." Something whams against the bubble.

Clark straightens. "What was that?"

"I think she's using her power," Roxana says.

"I thought it was the energy of static cling," Clark says. "But that was much more than that."

"She's mad," I say. "Maybe it grows when wet."

"Let me—"

Clark must have done something, because she pops right through. The sound of loud jeering and yelling also manages to squeeze through. Sounds like cutting the line wasn't a popular move on her part.

Once she's in, she straightens up and brushes her patchwork sweater off. There are sticks in her hair.

"Are you alright, Bev?" Roxana asks. "You look like you've been on a nature walk with a super hot warlock."

"Hey, why a warlock?" Izaak asks. "Why not a hot vampire?"

"They're too classy to roll around in the—"

"I wasn't on a walk," Bevin says. "You've got the entire block behind the entrance backed up with your 'photos with Roxana Goldenscales.'"

"And with Izaak Alexander," Izaak says. "I bet a lot of the people are—"

"Yes, yes, I saw a few goths there for you, too." Bevin waves her arm. "But what are you guys doing in there? This is not okay."

"But we've raised a hundred and twenty-five thousand dollars," Minerva says. "Almost."

A hundred and eighteen. Trust her to round up to a weird number. "Yeah," I say, "why are you so angry?"

Bevin opens her mouth, and then she closes it again. Then she opens it, only to snap it shut.

"What's going on?" Clark asks. "I thought you'd be happy."

"Do you really want to leave?" Roxana asks. "We thought it was because of the money." She looks sad—really sad.

"You didn't set your place on fire yourself, did you?" Izaak asks in a whisper. "I mean, that would be—"

"No!" Bevin's shoulders droop and her bottom lip wobbles. "The Demon Council did, when I refused to join their guild."

None of us know what to say to that.

Finally, Minerva opens her mouth. "Why did you refuse?"

Bevin's hands fly to her hips. "Are you kidding? They're evil. They try and prepare the way for actual demons to come to Earth. They steal. They lie. They kill. They're the worst beings on Earth."

"But you are a demon-spawn," Minerva says.

And Bevin's face falls. "But I'm not like that."

Minerva yanks her close for a hug. "I know that. Of course I do. That's why we're helping you."

Bevin sighs and leans into the hug. But when she pulls away, she says, "But this is why you *can't* do this. Because now they know exactly who you are, and next time, instead of burning down my shop, they'll hurt one of you."

"Not all of us are easy to hurt," Roxana says.

"But you are," Bevin says.

I think about how Roxana incinerated those wolves. We haven't really talked about it since, and I don't think she's told anyone else. But even without that taboo topic being broached, her dad's powerful enough that I doubt anyone would want to cross her.

"I am," Roxana says. "But my family is terrifying. There's some safety in that." She steps closer to Bevin and takes her hand. "And I'm not afraid of the Demon Council. Tell them I said that if they mess with you, they can 'bring it.' I'm not afraid of those bullies."

Bevin laughs. "I'm definitely not saying any of that."

"I'm not afraid either," Clark says. "I lost my job last week. What else are they going to do? They may have powers, but I cast a pretty mean spell. And did you hear? I actually fought a full-on dragona and didn't die."

I notice he doesn't say that he won, but that he didn't die. That's a true enough characterization from what I hear. It's not nearly as sexy, though. Clark needs to learn how to brand himself better.

"We're a hard to kill group of friends," Izaak says.

But if we're looking at the group, Izaak and Bevin are the weak links. And maybe the half-human Minerva.

"The point, Bev, is that we get to pick whether we're afraid. And we're not. We're here for you," I say.

But even as I'm saying the encouraging words, I'm wondering if what my dad said was true. Bevin's suffering because of us. I'm suffering because they can't accept my bond. And Clark and Minerva should be surrounded by other mages. None of us are better off because of our strange group of friends.

And that may be my answer.

Sometimes it hurts to do the right thing, but it's still the only thing a good person can really do.

CLARK

I knew that Roxana was a celebrity.

Of course I did. People have posters with her on the front of them. They sing songs about her. She's the United States of America's golden dragon princess. She's a really big deal.

But I didn't really understand what that meant until today.

By the time the festival ends at ten p.m., there are still thousands of people lined up around the city, all of them chanting. They want to see her. They want to touch her. And they're willing to pay a lot of money to do it.

When they finally get close, most of them look dumbfounded. They can't string two words together. They gibber and hiccup and stammer.

And at the very end of the night, as if he knew all along exactly how this would go down, her 'boyfriend' shows up with an entire contingent of combat mages to save her from the adoring fans. Lionel Sol stands at the front of his small army in a black suit with a golden tie that's patterned like scales—like he's proclaiming that she's his to anyone with a camera.

I hate that she smiles when she sees it.

But if he hadn't shown up, I'm not at all sure we'd have gotten away in one piece. She might have been stuck here all night, or she'd have been forced to call her dad to have a dragon show up and give her a ride. I know she'd be worried that if she asked for dragona help, she'd never get her life back.

Lionel, on the other hand, makes it even more of an *event* with the way he handles it. He casts a voice augmentation spell with the flick of his wrist. "Fine magical citizens of New York City. It does me good to see you out in such large numbers. I'll be sure to report to the akero, when next I'm summoned to attend them, that you're all alive and well and working hard in New York City."

They cheer, just like he's the one they came to see.

"As you know, Roxana Goldenscales is a very likable and generous-hearted individual."

More cheers.

Xander hisses in my ear. "What are the normies hearing right now?"

"There aren't many humans close enough to hear. The gloffee everyone has drunk will make this entire place smell bad, probably like body odor. But the ones in listening distance are hearing a local concert—probably a bad one. The festival organizers saw to it that the fliers they posted had a good spell on them too. It wouldn't look like something a human would want to attend."

"It's so strange," Xander says. "I wonder what we'd do without the mages."

"Don't mention his indispensability to him," I say, glaring at Lionel. "His head will swell up so large that he'll look like a blimp."

"Can it really get bigger?"

"—darling girlfriend would stay all night if she could, because she truly loves you all. But even she needs beauty rest, believe it or not."

Some jeers, but mostly more cheers.

"And since the event is officially over, we're going to have to call it a night."

Now there *is* some booing.

"But I've brought four magical mead casks, and they'll provide a lovely amber mead shot through with exuberance for the next two hours. So please, come have a drink on the Illuminae tonight, and raise a glass to the illustrious, the luminous, the vibrant Roxana Goldenscales."

Many people cheer for her, but almost as many are clearly cheering for him.

"We love you, Lionel."

"I'll have your tiny warlocks, Lionel!"

The cheers get more and more ridiculous every time.

"And one more thing," he continues. "I know many of you were moved by her purpose in being here today. Well, I'm here to tell you that my own father was so impressed that she wanted to help her dear friend, the demon-spawn Bevin Bahar, that he's decided to make up the difference between what they needed, and what they raised. The Illuminae are donating more than seven hundred thousand dollars!"

Now the cheers are jubilant.

And I want to stab him in the eye. I hate that he can waltz in, wave his magic wand, and just fix everything. I hate that he's here, throwing magical mead and money around like that's what it means to be a man.

Mostly, though, I hate that I know he was making out with another woman a few nights ago, and Roxana doesn't even know it. Even if I didn't need a job, and even if I didn't hate him, I still think showing Roxana the photos his dad gave me is probably the right thing to do.

I can't really be angry that he's donating the money to Bevin's new shop. That's a pretty awesome thing to do, even if it didn't cost him a dime, and even though he and his dad will probably never even notice it's gone. Plus, they're probably using this to get some positive press. I can practically see the headlines now. "Benevolent mage puts his money where his mouth is: not all demon-spawn are bad." He must be up for reelection soon.

I hate politicians.

I seriously consider, now that he's done with his speech, throwing up a privacy bubble—or not—and confronting him with the photos in my bag, right in front of Roxana.

But if I'm going to share them with her anyway, I may as well do it in the way Lionel's dad wants me to. I'd be an idiot not to get a great job out of this. Besides, the only way I can even compare to Lionel is if I have a decent job. If today taught me anything, it's that Roxana is a bigger deal than I realized.

Someone like her won't want an unemployed magical research mage. I need to up my game, and if I use Lionel's own father to do it, even better.

"Hey, Clark," Minerva says. "Any chance you can drop all this stuff off at home?"

Ricky has shown up. That means she's wanting to go out and celebrate what we've accomplished, and she doesn't want to lug all her table decorations home. But knowing Minerva, she's not willing to just toss all her little knick-knacks and doodads in the trash, either. I think about turning her down, because why should I have to take all that stuff I didn't think we needed in the first place back to her apartment so she can party?

But then I realize that it gives me the perfect reason to be in Roxana's room. Or at least, right by it.

"Sure," I say. "Happy to help."

It's a little harder to remind myself that I'm doing what needs to be done when Lionel gathers Roxana up under his arm and whisks her away. Knowing that everyone is out partying while I have to head back to the apartment with their stuff is a little depressing.

But I need to get this done, the sooner, the better.

Once I start packing things up, I begin to wonder how Minerva ever got all this to fit in the bag she brought. But eventually I manage to wrangle it all in, and then I lug it all the way home. My back hurts, and my feet are aching, but I get it done. I dump all the stuff on the kitchen table, but then I realize that Minerva will freak out if she comes home to this mess.

So I diligently do what I've done since she was born. I ignore how tired I am, and I lend a hand by putting all the decor in her storage closet, the jar back on the counter, the spatulas and implements safely and neatly back in their formerly missing place. That's what makes me a better option than Lionel. I may not be powerful or rich or super eloquent, but I do the little things that no one wants to do. I make their lives easier without insisting on credit for it.

And then I pick up my bag and pull out the photos.

Lionel's face is clear—it's definitely him. And the woman is stunning. He wasn't slumming it. She's elegant, and she's holding a wand in one of the photos. She's a magical person, and they look close.

Very close in a few of them, with Lionel's hand in a place it most certainly should not be while he's dating Roxana. And he's kissing her much more intimately than he would if it were just a friendly greeting in another. I think about waiting and confronting her, but I don't really want to get mixed in with all this nastiness. Better if she thinks it's anonymous.

Actually, I could send it to the press.

They'd eat him alive—they all love Roxana.

But I don't want to embarrass her, and that certainly would. It's better if she's the only one who knows. Surely Lionel's own dad wouldn't release it to the media. He wants their relationship to end, just as I do. No, leaving it on her bed for her to find is the right move.

I'm just closing her door when Xander walks in.

"Oh." I swallow and think of what Roxana had with her. The only thing I recall seeing all day was hand lotion. "I had a, um, the hand lotion that was Roxana's. I just thought I'd—"

"What did you really put in there?" he asks, one eyebrow arched.

"Hand lotion," I say. "Like I said."

Xander holds something up—lavender hand lotion. So clearly, he knows that's not what I had. What are the odds he'd have found that?

"So, the thing is—"

"You like her," he says. "And you hate Lionel."

I blink. "Yes. That's right."

"And you would do anything to break them up."

My mouth dangles open.

"I feel the same way," Xander says.

"Wait." I practically choke. "You *like* her?"

"Let's just say that I really dislike Lionel, and if she liked me, well, I wouldn't kick her out for eating dog biscuits in bed."

"Eww." I can't help my lip curl. "Do you really like dog biscuits?"

He shrugs. "Have you ever tried them? They're way cheaper than Triscuits."

I shake off that disturbing image. "But you don't really think that Roxana and *you* would be—"

"Why?" he asks. "Because I'm a werewolf?" He glares at me. "Or because I'm half-human, like your sister?"

"No, it's not that." This has gotten ugly in a hurry.

"You don't own her," he says.

"I mean, I know that. Obviously."

"And leaving bad things about Lionel on her bed isn't a very cool thing to do. You should talk to her about it—"

I hate that he's right, but I can't very well defend myself by telling him that if I do it the way Lionel's dad wanted, I get a new job out of it. Plus, I'm pretty sure it was Lionel's dad who got me fired in the first place, so it's really only fair that I get the new job.

"There's actually something I wanted to talk to you about," Xander says.

"If it's about Roxana, it may not even matter which of us likes her," I hedge. I'd really rather not have this conversation. Because I absolutely adore Xander, but if

I'm not good enough for her, he's like *way* not good enough. A half-human wolf who may be fraying? Someone who'll never have a pack and comes with so much baggage it couldn't fit into a 747? I mean. . .

"It's not about Roxana." He walks further into the room, sets the lotion on the counter and sighs. "It's actually about what happened this week. See, you're a mage, and you have more schooling than anyone else I know, so—"

"I haven't studied the fray much," I say. "But I did take a class where—"

"Clark," he says. "For once in your life, just listen."

That feels a little unfair. I'm a great listener. I fold my arms to show that I'm ready. "Fine. Talk."

"My dad says I'm an alpha, and I found a pack that wants me to be *their* alpha. Only, it's far away."

That would have wrecked me a year ago. Even a week ago. But if he really does like Roxana—I mentally slap myself. This isn't who I am. I don't push friends away because they may like the same girl as me. "Xander, are you serious?"

He nods.

"I mean, that's awesome you found a pack that wants you—I know you've always wanted that. But moving? Leaving New York?" I sink into the corner of the sofa, grateful for once that it's so plush. "I can't even imagine you not being here."

He perches on the chair next to me, his arms braced and his entire body taut with stress. "I know. And there's something else you should know, too. I was hoping you'd know something about it, actually."

And then the front door opens and Roxana bursts inside. "Phew. I thought I'd never escape." She drops her purse on the counter and breezes in, flipping her heels off and flinging them halfway across the room.

One of them hits the side of the sofa. She glances that direction, and her jaw drops. "Oh. What are you two doing here? I figured Bevin might be here, but I didn't expect either of you."

❧ 18 ❧

ROXANA

It's been a really strange week.

First, I thought I had a crush on Xander—goofy, joke-cracking, wolfy Xander. That same day, I burned up seven wolves like kindling, gone in the blink of an eye. Mom still thinks it's a hoot that they're suing us. I really hope they don't have video footage, because I have no idea how the world will react to that. If I wasn't hallucinating, if it really happened, then I'm pretty sure every single dragona the world over will freaking freak out.

I was ready to end things with Lionel. He was all up in my face starting fights he didn't finish, and then he was just gone. Gone. Gone. Gone. He shows up at my place out of the blue to demand a date, acting like he's the akero's gift to me. . . I'd made up my mind to dump him on our date tomorrow.

But Lionel really came through today. He not only extricated us elegantly, without any unhappiness, he also snapped his fingers and made the whole endeavor a success. He funded the rest of Bevin's shop, even if it was a bit self-serving, and didn't press me for more time and attention after an exhausting day.

When he dropped me on the curb, he hopped out of the stretch limousine and walked me to the door. When I pressed the code and passed through the door, his hand slammed up above my head on the doorframe and he *leaned* toward me slowly, his mouth slightly open, his eyes intent on mine.

"I'm dropping you here because I know you had a long day. That was an amazing thing you did for your friend. I'm proud of you. But I do hope you'll still make time for me tomorrow."

I could barely breathe.

His eyes dropped to my lips and stayed there. "I dream about you, you know. Before, every night in my head was beach parties and ski trips. But now, every single time I sleep, it's the same. A flash of golden scales and a long, gorgeous leg with a slit up the side of a black skirt." His eyes rose to mine again. "Have anything like that?"

"I'm not sure if I should wear it even if I do."

"Oh, you should." He half-smiled then. "You definitely should." He leaned a little farther down and brushed a kiss against my mouth.

Fire flared up when he did, my whole body tingling. His breath against mine felt almost explosive, and I swayed a bit.

But when he backed away, I held my ground. I remembered who I am and what I want, and I don't think it's Lionel. Or at least, I'm pretty sure. Even so, I was still touching my lips with my fingers when I walked into my apartment. . .and saw Xander and Clark chatting in the family room.

"Oh. What are you two doing here? I figured Bevin might be here, but I didn't expect you."

"Bevin's coming?" Xander asks. "I thought she was staying with her sister."

"Apparently that was just another lie she told," I say. "The demon-spawn who never used to lie at all." My nervousness at Lionel and them being here and the whole day—no, the last few days—bubbles out of me and I laugh.

"But she was lying to keep us from being in the crosshairs of the Demon Guild," Clark says. "At least it was for a good reason."

"We ruined that," I say. "We're all doomed, now."

Xander stands. "Do you really think that?"

I shrug. "I mean, I hope not."

"I'm just across the hall," Xander says.

"Actually, I'm happy to stay here," Clark offers. "It might be a good idea to have a high-level mage here, just in case."

"Oh," Xander says. "Did you say Lionel was coming? I didn't realize." He's smirking, but Clark doesn't seem to love the joke.

"I'll be fine," I say. "Honestly, I'm not really that spooked."

"The Demon Guild is a big deal," Clark says. "Better safe than sorry."

"Still, I can handle it. Plus Minerva will be back soon, and the actual demon-spawn they're recruiting will be here any time, too. She just needed to do a little shopping for some essentials."

"So, a divining rod, several ridiculously loud sweaters, and a hat that's covered with fake fruit?" Xander asks.

I laugh, but for a moment, I wonder if that's actually the kind of thing she went out to get. "I was thinking a toothbrush, but knowing Bevin, probably."

"Don't forget a purse that's knit from conflict-free yarn, and has the heads of several creepy dolls somehow incorporated into it," Clark says.

"But for real, guys," I say. "I'm exhausted, and I'll sleep better knowing I'm not inconveniencing anyone. With a vampire and a werewolf across the hall, I'm sure I'll be just fine." I put a hand on Clark's shoulder. "You can go."

He acts like he doesn't want to, but finally, he stands up and walks out, glancing back at Xander several times pointedly first. Meanwhile, Xander's rummaging around in the fridge, but I can't bear the thought of a conversation about the fireball I created, so I duck into my room without another word.

I change into my pink, zebra-striped pajamas and my fluffy pink slippers, and I flop onto my bed, landing on something stiff and hard. Ugh. What is it?

Photos, as it turns out. Of Lionel.

And some woman.

A very beautiful woman, whom he clearly likes quite a lot. And based on the date stamped on the bottom right, they were taken the day before he popped back up in New York City.

Now I know what he had to 'take care of.' I want to chuck them in the trash. I want to forget all about it. It's not like I *really* liked him, or like I even knew what I thought.

But it still hurts.

I can't tell if I'm heartbroken or if it's just my pride, but I hate the feeling. I text Lionel without another thought.

COME BACK.

He texts right away. OOH. OKAY. BE THERE IN FIVE.

On a whim, I throw on the black dress I have that slits high, nearly to my backside. I swipe on some red lipstick, slide my feet into five-inch black pumps, and march out of my room.

Xander's holding a pint of ice cream and staring at me like he just saw an elephant wearing a kimono. He drops his spoon, and it clatters on the floor.

"I need to see someone."

And then something occurs to me. He and Clark were here when I arrived. They were inside the apartment and could easily have walked into my room. Without saying a single word, I pivot on my heel and duck back into my room. Then I emerge, brandishing the stack of lurid photos. "Did you leave these for me? Did you drop them on my bed like a terrorist?"

He's bending over to pick up his discarded spoon, but this time, he drops the entire carton of ice cream, too. Then he shakes his head soundlessly. "What is it?"

"They're photos of Lionel. Did you really not know?"

He blinks.

"Did Clark leave them, then?"

He shrugs.

My hand clenches on the bottom of the photos, crinkling them. "I am not amused. In fact, I'm livid."

"You look like you're going to a night club," Xander says. "You might want to grab a jacket. If you go out dressed like that, you're bound to cause a car accident. Or a heart attack. Or both."

"I hope I do," I snap. "I jolly well hope that I do cause a heart attack." I snatch my purse off the end table and march to the door.

Xander picks up the ice cream, tosses the spoon and the carton in the sink, and follows me out. "Wait, are you sure you should go out? Where are you going? What are you going to do? Do you know who the woman is?" He's craning his neck to see the photos, which convinces me it wasn't him more effectively than anything else he could have done or said.

"I don't know her," I say. "But I certainly know the guy, and he's going to be here in two minutes."

"Oh." He licks his lips. "Did you want me to come down with you?"

I shake my head. "Oh, no. I'm plenty ticked. I can deal with it myself."

"He's actually a high-level mage," he says. "I'm not trying to be patronizing, but are you sure?"

I squeeze Xander's arm, which is surprisingly beefy. "I'm sure. Thank you for caring enough to be willing to face off against him."

"I'm going to stay in the lobby. Shout if you need me."

I actually feel better knowing that—not that I think I need the muscle. But knowing that I have someone who will let me do things the way I want, but will stay on standby in case things go sideways? It means a lot.

It allows me to march out the door with my head held high and my dignity intact. Cars do slow down as they drive past, some people shouting and waving, others cat-calling. It makes me think even more about the photos in my hand. Lionel Sol told the world he was my boyfriend, and then he flew off to who knows where and did this kind of thing with some woman.

What kind of person does that?

And what will people think when they see photos like this? They'll think I'm a loser. That I can't even hold his attention. I'll become a joke—the same way I felt with Ragar. He was a caveman, and now I'm beginning to think that Lionel may be even worse.

The limo pulls up on the curb, and Lionel pops out like a daisy in early spring, a smile on his cheery face. "This is the exact dress from my dream." His eyes are practically smoldering.

"Is it?" I purr just a little. I've never tried it before, but I've practically been raised on my mother doing it.

"How did you know?" His breathing is shallow and quick.

"You did say you wanted a slit." I run my hand up my thigh, separating the fabric farther, and carefully slide my leg forward.

His breathing hitches. His eyes follow my hand and then freeze.

"Aren't you coming over?"

He nods and starts walking. But when he gets close, I press my hand outward, my fingers flattening against his chest. And then I shove my other hand at him, pressing the stack of photos against him, too. "Oh. Whoops. I almost forgot to mention."

His eyes whip upward and lock on mine.

"I'm dumping you, effective immediately."

I drop the pictures and pivot.

But his hand snakes out and grabs my wrist. "Whoa. What's going on?"

The wind picks up just then, and the photos he never even bothered trying to grab are picked up by a big gust and begin to spin away.

I wrench my arm out of his and stumble backward. Stupid high heels make it harder, but I manage. "Your *reason* is currently blowing away."

He looks away from me long enough to see what I mean, and his wand practically appears out of nowhere. He must keep it in his sleeve. "*Revenite*," he snaps.

And the photographs reverse direction, flying right back toward him. He pops his wrist out and they sail into it.

He is definitely a high-level mage. He didn't even think about that first. His expression's annoyed and confused and very, very put out when he finally looks down at the photographs.

It's actually quite satisfying to watch the blood drain from his face.

"I trust that clears things up?"

"We weren't really together." His voice is tight. Higher than usual, too.

"Excuse me?"

"I said we were to help you that night," he explains. "But you and I weren't really together. I left when I did so I could figure out what I wanted. My dad wasn't very pleased at how I handled that whole situation, as it turns out."

I can imagine he wasn't.

"Don't do me any favors," I say. "Tell dear old dad that we're through, and let that be that."

He shakes his head. "But then I couldn't stop thinking about you. I dreamt about you. That part was true."

I shrug. "Clearly not so much that you had eyes for no one else."

"Are you really jealous?" Lionel looks shocked. "You?" He waves the photos at me. "Sure, Genevieve is beautiful, but she's nothing compared to you."

That is nice to hear, but ultimately irrelevant. "Lionel, you told the world we were dating. . .and then rushed off to do who knows what with this Genevieve woman. Doesn't that tell you something?"

"It's my dad's oldest friend's daughter. He's been pushing me to marry her for years. I've known her since we were kids. But we never—this is awkward. We'd never given it a shot. And Dad said he'd make things horrible with you, unless I at least *tried* to see if something was there. Apparently it was for her benefit, but every time I closed my eyes, all I could see was you."

"Uh-huh. It looks like it."

"It's true, I swear." He looks earnest, at least. Then his eyebrows shoot up. "I'd take a truth spell and tell you the same thing. Ask Clark to come cast one."

I roll my eyes. "It's bad enough that Xander has seen these."

"My dad must've taken them," he says. "It had to be him. Gen's dad's villa is spelled and warded up the yin yang."

I arch one eyebrow.

"You know what I mean."

"So you're saying that your father set you up?" I think it through. "He told you that the only way he'd support you is if you—" I clear my throat. "Kissed this woman."

"Genevieve Torchier, yes."

"All the while, he planned to document you doing it,

and then show the images to me to make sure I dumped you?"

"If you knew my father at all, you'd see that's exactly what he set up."

My dad would totally do the same thing. He wouldn't even blink, and he'd be proud of it if he got caught. I huff. "But you know your father, and you fell for it."

He shrugs. "I wanted to make sure that I didn't like her either. It would have been way easier for me if I did."

I purse my lips. "I'm going to be brutally honest with you."

"Do."

"You're a terrible fit for me. There's a reason your dad hates us dating. My dad's also not keen. My people need me."

"To make little baby dragons." He shrugs. "That's not news to me."

"And I haven't been dreaming about you. I don't trust you, and I'm not sure whether I even like you. One minute I want to kiss you, and the next I want to slap your face."

"Those don't sound so different." His lips curl into a full smile. "And for the record, that's how I feel about myself most of the time."

"You want to kiss yourself?"

"I mean, have you seen me? I'm not half bad." He leans against the light pole. "At least consider what you've got in front of you. I'm not bad to look at."

I can't argue with that.

"I'm rich as sin."

Also true.

"My dad's powerful, and so am I. Politically, but also magically."

I've seen evidence of that myself.

"And in my entire life, I've never liked the same woman for more than a week, but we're going on three with you, and I can't think about anyone else. That must have some significance, right?"

"Was there ever a woman you didn't *get* within that week?"

He frowns.

"It could simply be the chase," I say. "And if so—"

"Then as soon as you're caught, I'll lose interest."

I expected him to argue with me, but he doesn't bother.

"That could be true," he says. "But if that's the case, then we'll know quickly. At least I won't drag things out. And you could just as easily lose interest in me. You said you don't know how you feel. So if we're comparing, I'm the one taking the bigger risk."

That's not untrue.

"How about this? Whatever we do, let's not give my dad what he wants. Trust me on this, he does *not* need to get what he wants any more than he already does."

"But I'm not really your girlfriend. Not yet, anyway."

"Which makes it pretty silly for you to be dumping me over these." He waves the images.

"Nevertheless," I say, "I don't want embarrassing photos cropping up in the media."

"Ditto," he says. "So for now, fidelity?"

I laugh.

"Or at least, don't get caught, and tell the other person if we decide we're done."

"This sounds a lot like a real relationship," I say. "And that makes me a little nervous."

"Do you really want to date someone who doesn't

make you nervous?" Lionel smiles his wicked smile again. "Speaking of. You *are* already in that fabulous dress. Any chance you want to go out and—"

I roll my eyes. "Not a chance, loverboy."

"Eh, can't fault a guy for trying."

BEVIN

The first time I realized that I was different than most kids, I was four years old.

Mom was sick of dealing with us, and she drove to some fast food place, bought a small order of French fries and a chocolate shake, and dumped us in the play place while she dipped each French fry slowly, one at a time, into the chocolate shake.

Meanwhile, we were supposed to play in a pit with plastic balls that smelled like pee.

Pass.

The only relatively interesting thing to do in that playground was the slide. Only, this one girl kept climbing up it the wrong way.

"Hey, can you slide down?" I asked.

Nothing. She just kept climbing up, blocking us from the one fun thing available.

"Kid," my sister Soki said, "stop doing that."

She stuck out her tongue.

Soki slid down anyway, knocking her on her still-diapered-at-four-backside, and then grabbed a handful of pee-steeped balls and started chucking them at her head for good measure.

The only reason I didn't join was that the mother showed up too fast. She wailed and pointed fingers and shouted and complained and when our mother shouted back, we got tossed out of the place on our ears.

That's when Mom explained that our natural impulses were almost sure to be wrong. We both thought that sounded crazy, but when Soki disappeared a year later, Mom really took her time drilling it into me. Whatever I *want* to do is surely bad. Whatever behavior sounds onerous and boring? That's probably the right one.

Mom was sad so often that I would have done most anything to make her smile. So even though it was hard, even though I was full of rage and fury, I did my best to ignore everything I wanted and do what Jesus wanted me to do instead.

After having it drilled into me how dark and deep and evil I was for every day of my early life, I'm quite sure of one thing: I should not be here. If there is any place on this earth that I do not belong, it is here, in the Angel Council's assembly room. I mean, it's not like the akero themselves will be hearing my petition, but the people they meet with once a month, their mouthpieces, will be.

Close enough.

My hands tremble as I fill out the form for my petition.

"Do you need help?" a mellifluous voice asks.

"Who, me?" I turn around to wave the woman away, but then I stop.

She's beautiful, but I'm no stranger to beauty. I'm

living with Roxana Goldenscales, for heaven's sake. But in all my life, I've never seen anyone whose skin glows like she swallowed an LED light.

"Sorry," she says. "I'm in an akero swing."

"Ex—excuse me?"

"I'm guessing you've never met an angel-spawn before." Her smile is soft, almost self-effacing. "There aren't many of us, so most people don't know that we're a little erratic, alternating between being more human and more angelic."

"Angelic?" Do the akero *glow*?

"Something about the difficulty of the angel and human pairing," she says, her smile gentle, "makes for times when I'm quite powerful and almost invincible. And then other times, I'm very mortal and my spells are, well, erratic."

So she's alternately like her human or her akero side? And she never knows which? I've certainly never met an akero before, but I can't even imagine one of them. . . copulating. . . with a human. The whole idea is almost unbelievable to me.

"It's okay for you to ask me questions, if you have any."

"Are there many of you?" I ask. "Angel-spawn?" Because she's right. I've not only never met one, I've never heard of anyone who has. No stories, no jokes, nothing. In fact, I wasn't sure there were any in existence. I thought the mages—descendants of the first angel-human crosses and other humans—were as close as it got. Clark is one quarter angel, assuming his ancestors all intermixed only with other mages. One angel-spawn and one human make a mage.

That means an angel-spawn is twice as powerful as a mage, or at least, I assume it does.

Her eyes are wide and sincere. "As far as we know, I'm currently the only one."

"Oh, wow." I'm staring at the only angel-spawn on Earth?

"You're a demon-spawn," she says.

I almost hate to agree, but I nod.

Her smile doesn't falter, as if the idea doesn't bother her at all. "The demons seek to make children with humans, but the akero are rather disdainful of human existence."

I'd never thought about it that way. At least we aren't dirty secrets that our parents wish had never happened. They're cheering for us. They want us to take down the barrier that protects the earth and let them destroy it, but still, cheering is cheering. The reason I've never heard from my dad is that I don't want to.

It seems like she's ostracized intentionally.

"Is it lonely?" I ask. I've felt lonely most of my life, so that's something I at least understand.

She nods slowly.

"For me, too," I say. "I know there are lots of demon-spawn, but sometimes it feels like I'm the only one who wishes I *wasn't* demon-spawn."

Her smile shifts a bit, and now it looks truly weary. "I have to live here—angel-spawn aren't allowed to leave the watchful care of the akero."

Something about the way she says *watchful care* doesn't sound like she finds it very caring. "You're a prisoner, then?"

"I'm here at the insistence of the akero," she says diplomatically. "They must ensure I never Ascend."

Whoa. I chose not to descend, but she can't pick? They make that decision for her? And then they keep her sequestered so she literally *can't* try to do really good things? Is that even how it works?

"Wouldn't they want you to, like, save people and perform miracles?" I ask. "I mean, if you did. . . Wouldn't it shift the balance for the fight against the akero and the daimoni toward *good*? Wouldn't they want that as badly as the daimoni want another demon?"

She shakes her head. "The balance is what matters. An extra akero would destroy everything, and as the 'good guys,' they accept it."

I think about that as I wait, and I end up waiting for a very long time— nine hours. But finally, it's my turn to make my presentation and ask for their help. I know it's a long shot, but it's the only thing I can think of that might keep my friends safe. Even the Demon Council won't dare go against the akero themselves.

"Bevin Bahar, is it true that you're a demon-spawn?" The tall woman with entirely white hair lifts her face from a file and stares at me baldly, her face utterly unafraid. What would it be like to be so unconcerned about whether I was right or wrong, good or bad?

"I am."

"Your father is Rahab?"

I shrug. "No way to know, I guess, but Mom certainly seemed to think so."

She purses her lips and glances back down at my file. "And you've descended one level. Is that right?"

I nod. "Yes ma'am."

"You may call me Galadrienne."

"Like the elf?" I can hardly believe it.

"The what?"

"There's a famous elf in that human show called *Lord of the Rings*. She was named Galadriel."

She blinks. "But my name is Galadr*ienne*."

"Nevermind," I say. "I don't know what I was thinking." Wow, they have no sense of humor here. Xander would die.

"What are you here to ask of us?"

I start at the beginning, explaining my bizarre situation. After trying not to descend, I did, by accident, while protecting Roxana. "So you see, it wasn't really like I did something bad—I don't *want* to become a daimoni. Not ever."

"But you said you descended after you left the interrogation." Galadrienne frowns.

"Well, that's true," I say. "Lying to the dragona didn't cause it, but when I lied to my friends about lying to the dragona, I descended."

The six other members of the Council begin to murmur. That seems to have set them off.

But I plunge ahead, explaining that I don't want to join the Demon Guild, and that they're trying to force me. "They even burned down my shop, but they're still calling me daily, asking me in the same threatening monotone whether I've changed my mind. It's only a matter of time before they do something worse—kill one of my friends or something."

"You're speaking specifically about the shop your friends have raised money to replace for you, right? And it's also your home?" a short man with shockingly black hair asks. Light seems to disappear when it reaches him. It must be some kind of spell, but it's creepy.

I glance at Galadrienne, and then turn back toward

him. Maybe he's taken over the questioning. "Uh, yes. That one."

"So you're actually not really disadvantaged now, is that right?"

"Well, that's only due to the largesse of a lot of people, most notably my friends who—"

"But the largest single donor was Lionel Sol on behalf of the Illuminae. Is that right?" Galadrienne asks.

I snap my face back toward her. "Uh, yes. That's correct."

"And now you want us to do what exactly?"

I swallow. "I'd like you to defend me against the Demon Council. I want you to tell them they can't force me to join their guild." I may as well ask for everything right up front.

"But you are a demon-spawn." Galadrienne tilts her head. "I don't understand."

"I don't like what they do or what they stand for," I say.

"But you could change that from the inside if you joined them." She steeples her hands. "And in any case, what exactly could we do to prevent your own people from harming you?" She leans a bit closer. "Did you envision us going to war over you?"

I splutter. "Well, no."

"How about this?" Galadrienne asks. "We will give you our blessing in your attempt to stay separate, but if you are forced to join, we will entreat you to improve the association by your existence as a part of it."

"Your blessing?"

She nods and smiles. "We officially bless your efforts."

"Does that mean you're like, announcing to the world that I'm under your protection?"

"Oh no," she says. "Nothing like that."

"Then what does the blessing do?"

She shrugs. "Who can say?"

"You," I say. "Right? Aren't you the one who can say?"

Her smile wobbles a bit, like a painting that's been hung on a single nail that's too small. "I think it's time for the next petitioner."

And I'm escorted out without another word. I'm not sure I've ever been quite so bewildered and befuzzled. "That was probably the nicest tone with which I've ever been shut down in my life."

"They do smile while they cut down your hopes and dreams, don't they?" the angel-spawn woman from before asks.

"What's your name?"

"You can just call me 'angel-spawn,'" she says. "That's what everyone else does."

"I'd rather use your real name," I say. "I'm Bevin, by the way." I hold out my hand.

She takes it in hers, her fingers and hand still glowing softly. "Zintrel," she says. "Daughter of Uriel."

"It was a real pleasure to meet you," I say.

"Would you like to take a little break before you go?" She tosses her head to the right. "There's a staff room where there are some amazing snacks."

I can't quite believe what she's saying. "Is that allowed?"

Her laugh is like the tinkling of bells or the warbling of a river, but her eyes are mischievous. "What will they do? Kick me out?"

"They might kick *me*," I say. "Right in the bottom."

She laughs again. I'd do most anything to hear that sound. "You're a delight."

A delight. After sneering at me, after calling me demon-spawn, after deriding me, the council sent me packing. But this woman, the poor woman who's trapped here lest she unsettle the balance of the earth, she offers me treats and calls me a delight.

"Yes," I say. "I'd like some snacks before I go."

After my first bite, I'm glad I didn't turn them down. It's food like I've never seen before, and it tastes better than anything I've ever had. "If you have to be trapped somewhere, this isn't a terrible place to be," I say. "I mean, these are amazing." I hold up a mushroom. It looks disgusting—all crumbling and speckled.

But it tastes like sunshine and spun snow, covered in sweet cream and the sweetest, best strawberries ever. Without seeds.

"I grow these myself in the garden out back. You should try this." She offers me something that looks like a bean pod.

It looks strange, but I'm too smart to turn it down. It tastes like airy, delightful nachos—but without grease. I feel like I could stay full and satisfied without ever gaining a single pound eating this food. The food she makes herself—and could likely make anywhere. It makes me profoundly sad to think about her being locked up in here, denying the world her light and magic. "I love it," I say. But what I want to do is rage against the people who are keeping her imprisoned. Rage against the system that cages beauty and attacks people for being different.

"You're welcome to take some with you," she says.

"You deserve to leave here with some kind of sunshine. I swear, the akero aren't nearly as nasty as their council."

"Why are they so negative?" I ask.

"In part, it's happened because of the steady stream of people who come here demanding things. I'm not trying to make excuses for them, but it gets exhausting."

"I'm sorry," I say.

"But they should still keep their eyes open to help people like you—good people who just want to do the right thing."

"How can you tell—"

"It's your eyes," she says quietly. "I can always see when someone has no light in their eyes, but yours shine."

That's a hard thing to know about the world, and it's not a gift I'd want. It sounds more like a curse. But still, it gives me hope. If my eyes aren't dark, then maybe even after descending... "Thank you."

"I'm sorry they won't help you keep your friends safe." Her eyes brighten. "You could take some treats to your friends."

"I would love that," I say.

She ducks out to grab a bag for me to take her home-grown veggies and fruits home in, and I notice there are drawers lining all the walls. I can't quite help myself from opening one—even though I know I shouldn't.

It *is* the Angel Council's employee room, after all. How often will I have the chance to snoop? The drawers are full of file folders—manila folders, like you'd find at a law office. And when I look closer, there are names on the top, alphabetized by last name.

I can't help it—I check for my name.

It's not there, of course. But that makes me wonder.

Roxana's not there either. Neither are Xander or Izaak. But Clark is. His file is boring, of course.

It looks like it's only for people with angelic blood.

And right next to Clark's is another folder. One I can't keep from glancing at—a folder that's chock full of papers. Not one or two like Clark's. Not three or four like some of the others. A whole sheath of paper. Dozens and dozens of pages.

When I hear footsteps, I tuck the folder behind my back. My heart's pounding, and I'm absolutely positive that I'll be caught, but I can't help myself. Now that I'm contemplating stealing something, will the light be gone from my eyes? Will Zintrel suddenly hate me? Will she find me despicable?

Maybe the council already knew what kind of person I am.

But the woman staring at me is not glowing. In fact, she's glowering. "Bevin Bahar?" The short woman with spiky grey hair thrusts a bag my direction. "The angel-spawn told me she promised you this." Her lips twist. "I'll give you two minutes to put things in it, and then it's time to get out."

I swallow, snatching the bag from her with my free hand. She doesn't seem to realize I have a folder hidden behind my back. And then she ducks back out. I exhale in relief, and I fill the bag with peas, with mushrooms, and with tiny puff turnovers.

And with Minerva Lucent's file.

I have no idea what it says, but I know I can't walk away from the chance to find out. I hold my breath the entire way out, wondering if theft will cause me to descend. I'm shocked when it doesn't—no one notices, and nothing happens.

Of course, once I'm a block away from the council building, I do.

The same power I felt before, only stronger, shoots through me, stiffening my arms, my legs, and my neck. I fly into the air, my hand still clenched on the neck of the bag containing the folder I stole, and then my body contorts outward, stretching, snapping. And then just as quickly, it's gone. My fingers constrict then, pulsing inward and then tightening outward. My nails lengthen and sharpen, quickly turning into claws.

Just as quickly, they retract and my hands look perfectly normal.

I pick up the bag I dropped and crawl as quickly as I can to the blue mailbox right next to me and slide the bag inside the drop slot. It takes every scrap of energy I have to pull it off, but I do it.

I'm lying in a heap, moaning, when the guardians show up.

Ricky's not with them, and they are not gentle. I ask for Minerva, and then I ask again, and again, and again. Finally, more than an hour later, she finally appears. They're still insisting I explain why I descended, and I'm still refusing.

It's not like I can tell them I stole from the Angel Council. They'd go nuts. And they'd demand to know what I stole, and then that would implicate Minerva.

Bad all around.

"What's going on?" Minerva hisses.

"I can't explain now," I say. "Is there some way you can get them to release me?"

"Right. Of course." She stands up, her eyes blazing. "Why are you still detaining her?"

"You're NYPAD, right?" the tall guardian asks, his mouth flat. "Why are you *her* friend?"

Minerva pokes one finger right into his chest. "How dare you insinuate that I can't be friends with a person simply because they're demon-spawn."

"That woman just descended, and we don't know what her crime was," he practically spits.

"Maybe it wasn't a crime at all," she says. "It takes a *sin* to descend, but plenty of those aren't *crimes,* as you should already know. For the last few thousand years, sodomy has been considered a sin by most major religions. Is it still a crime in New York City?"

The man splutters. "You're saying she's—"

"It's none of your business." Minerva smiles. "Let her go. Article 356 demands it. She's not obligated to confess anything to you."

"What's her demon mark?" he asks. "She *is* obligated to share that."

I pick up my hand and tighten it, claws popping out when I do. "Satisfied?"

The man practically attacks his forms with his pen, but he lets things go. "You'll have to sign her out." He thrusts the forms at her.

"Released into the care of officer Lucent?" She arches her eyebrow. "Done." She signs with a flourish. "Thanks, Officer Backward."

"It's Broward." He scowls.

She ignores him.

"Hey, isn't she Ricky's girlfriend?" another guardian asks.

The cocky jerk backs up rather quickly. "No hard feelings, right?"

Minerva just rolls her eyes.

"It's nice to be dating the baddest guardian on the force, huh?" I ask.

She blushes and helps me up. Once they're all gone, she pins me with a stare. "What on earth is going on?"

"How do you feel about breaking into a post office box?" I ask.

"Not good," she says. "Why?"

"I'm kidding," I lie. It's probably better that she not be the first person to read through the file anyway. "Let's go home, and I'll explain how I said something kind of dumb to the head of the akero council."

"You didn't."

I manage to make up a decent story, but I'm going to need to find Clark, stat. Because if the postal people pick up that mail before I get back in and grab that bag.

. .

☙ 20 ❧

IZAAK

A s the oldest of eleven, I should have been swimming in friends. Only, when my brothers would spar, I would beg them to play hide and seek. When my sisters would practice wrestling holds, I wanted to learn how to play an instrument. Not that I could play—my guitar teacher ran away crying like a little baby whenever I struggled with a new chord.

But the point is, even with ten siblings, I never fit in.

When I answered an ad for a roommate, I could smell that he was a werewolf right away. I almost showed myself out. I'd only spent any time alone with about four wolves in my life, and all of them tried to attack me within minutes.

One of them I got stuck with in a waiting room for an audition attacked me quite literally—fangs bared, hands grabbing and ripping. One of them figuratively— he kicked me right out of a small cafe he was running. And two more practically bit my leg clean off, but they were in the middle of a run in the forest when I bumped into them. I really shouldn't have been there to begin with. It's a long story that involves a duck, a bottle of tequila, and two strange floaties that were stolen from a pool party.

But from the second I met Xander, I could tell he wasn't like the other wolves I'd met. He wasn't like *anyone* I'd ever met. He made a dozen jokes in the first ten minutes, for one thing. I didn't know that he made them when he was nervous yet, so I just thought he was really funny.

He also laughed at *my* jokes, which was rare. Most humans either can't think around me for their innate fear of a predator, or if I turn on the charm, they spend every second they're near me trying to climb me like a rock wall. Not that I'm complaining about that, usually, since I can choose when to turn it on. But it does feel a little. . .rapey, if I'm being honest. I haven't used it in aeons.

I think about what Xander told me—about him being an alpha—and how no one else really knows yet, except Roxana, obviously. And then I wonder—does he *have* to leave? Is there any other solution? I was kind of hoping his dad would turn up and tell him how to fix things. Maybe he could bring that ratchet pack here, for instance. New York is big, right? He could stake out a corner no one wants.

I guess I was hoping his dad would have some kind of idea or inspiration that would get us out of this bind. Like the wrench you keep in your sock drawer for years, only to save the day when the toilet float dies. Sure, it's useless and heavy and takes up space, but when you're in trouble, it saves the day. It would've been really nice if Xander's dad could show up like that for once.

Every time I think about Xander leaving, it makes me want to cry. Okay, fine. I do cry.

Tears are rolling down my face when the door to our apartment opens. I spin in my armchair away from the doorway. "No, I'm not crying."

Xander doesn't say a word.

"Look, I know it's not manly, but we've been friends for a long time, okay? I can't just be *fine* with you leaving. It's not easy for me to make friends. I'm sure you were listening to Bevin and thinking how it's probably for the best if we all, like, disband or whatever."

He still doesn't say anything. I still can't bring myself to turn around and see what he's thinking—he always shows it right on his face.

"But that's wrong, okay? I know you're an alpha, and I know you finally found a pack that wants you, but that means others will want you too. And now that you know that you're not fraying, that means you aren't in a rush. You can keep looking for the *right* fit."

I sound really selfish. My best friend has finally found exactly what he needs—what he's always wanted —and all I want is to keep him here with me. I slump back against the chair, practically boneless.

"Fine, okay? I get it. I hate it, but I get it. You have to go." I wait for him to argue with me. He has to at least put up a fight before he leaves, right? Am I the only one who cares about our friendship?

The very least he could do is offer some kind of plan for us to stay in touch. Like, he can come visit every other week. I'll go out there when he can't. We'll have gloffee. We'll play video games. Being part of a new pack won't ruin *everything*, right? I leap out of my chair and spin around, ready to force him to at least pretend to make a plan.

And someone with slitted cat eyes and smallish, curved black horns sprouting out from just in front of his receding hairline hits me in the head with a baseball bat.

I always thought, if the fight found me, I'd be ready for it.

But I'm definitely not ready for this.

My ears are ringing. My body isn't working right. My head feels like a cracked egg. And in that moment, I realize that I'm about to die. I can't move. I can't even seem to make a sound. The demon-spawn standing above me must have been sent by the Demon Council.

To kill the weak link—that's me. I've always been the weak one.

Even the dragon who can't shift is more powerful than I am. The witch whose spells misfire. The half-wolf. That's why they came here first—take out one leg and the chair will topple. I'll be the reason our little group of magical misfits disbands. My death will wreck it for everyone else.

Fury and rage and seething anger flood my body in this moment—useless, helpless, but still there. Why is it me? Why am I the one whom others can target? But somehow, when I pull on that feeling, power floods into me. Churning, twisting power that I don't understand.

Where's the raw energy coming from?

I don't know, and that scares me.

But when the horned demon-spawn's face hovers above mine, his slitted eyes studying my face, I decide that I don't care. I seize that magical force and I use it to shove up to my feet, grabbing the discarded bat as I do.

"You picked the wrong vampire to hit," I say, as I swing it wide and hard at his head.

I'm still shaking when, ten minutes later, Xander bursts through the front door. He looks weak and shaky but also agitated.

"Are you alright, Izaak? I felt something, something strange." He lifts his nose and sniffs, as if unsure whether he likes or hates what he smells. "Ew, what's that smell?"

"Did you know that a head explodes kind of like a melon when you hit it with a bat?"

Xander's eyes widen and his head swivels to the far wall, which is covered with gore. "You're saying that it's someone's *brains* that I'm smelling right now?"

"Oh, no," I say. "Definitely not."

"Thank goodness." He closes his eyes. "What is that, then?"

"Oh, those are definitely brains. It's just not what you're smelling." I point at the pile of vomit I've been too weak and shaky to clean up. "The whole melon thing made me really, really sick."

Xander groans. "I should have recognized the smell of a crawfish po boy." He makes a retching sound. "Add one more thing to the list of foods I'll never eat again."

"They only have them a few weeks a year, you know, so you won't be missing much."

"Yeah, and I thought that timeframe started in January." It's so Xander to be talking about this right now, with a dead body in the room.

"Farms make it possible to get them early," I helpfully share.

"Oh my gosh, stop talking about shellfish. What the heck happened?"

"Turns out, Bevin was right that they'd come after us."

"But I felt, like, a pull of power." Xander's brow furrows. "Did you get hurt?"

A pull of power? I let his words sink in for a moment. "You *felt* a pull of power?" I tilt my very tired head sideways.

He gulps then and looks down at his shoes. "Or, you know, like a crazy premonition thing—some other thing that you might believe."

"Xander."

He sighs, but he finally meets my eye. "My dad said he knew I was an alpha, and I couldn't be fraying." He winces. "Because I apparently bonded all of you guys some time ago."

It takes me a minute to process what he's saying. "But we're not wolves."

"Wait, are you sure?" he asks.

I look at my hands, focusing really hard. "I don't *think* so."

Xander rolls his eyes. "I know you're not."

"Oh."

"But apparently, I did it anyway. You guys can't officially accept the bond, but I guess you can pull power from me anyway."

"Are you okay? I'm sorry—I didn't know what I was doing. I was about to die."

"My head feels like someone drilled a nail through it," he says, "but otherwise I'm fine."

"Wow—he hit me in the head with a bat, too. I'm just thinking about that. I wonder if my head actually cracked open like his before I stole your energy, or whatever."

"Let's hope not," he says. "I feel like that would not be good, even if they're back in your head now."

"Probably not," I agree.

"I think I need to tell—"

The door flings open. "Tell us what?" Bevin asks. But then she takes in the room and the disgusting contents. She slaps her hand over her nose, too.

"I'm sorry," I say. "I'll clean it up—I just figured cleaning up the brains would be the higher priority, and I haven't felt good enough to even do that yet."

Clark steps through the door, already whipping his wand out. *"Emundare hic locus."*

And just like that, the mop flies up into the air, the trash bags too, with chunks of all kinds of disgusting things floating into them.

"Can we go outside?" Xander asks. "Because if not—"

A chunk of pink stuff floats in front of his face and his skin shifts very decidedly toward chartreuse.

"Yep." I grab his arm. "Let's go."

We barely reach the hallway before Xander's clutching his stomach and dry heaving.

"Dude, be a man," Bevin says. "You must've seen brains before."

"Never that up-close," he says. "And never in my family room."

"What was that?" Clark asks.

"A demon-spawn attacked Izaak," Xander says. "He defended himself, and things got real."

"Really dead," I say. "But it was him or me, so I'm going to say this one deserves a pass."

"Oh, right," Clark says. "You've never killed anyone." He pats my head. "Your mom's going to be so proud."

"We are definitely not telling her," I say. "She'll bundle me home within the hour."

"Please," Xander says. "Plenty of us have killed people. It's nothing special." He sounds a little sick when he says it, but I realize that it's true. The paranormal world is a dangerous one.

"I have," Clark says. "There was this demon-spawn attack in college, and—"

"I mean, I have too," Xander says. "But I'm a shredder, so it's kind of my job."

"I haven't!" Bevin hops up and down and throws up her hand for a high five.

I can't believe this is happening. "Yay," I force the word out. "You're not a murderer. . . like me."

"Oh." She stops jumping. "I know it's my fault you had to do that. I'm really sorry."

It's like watching a marionette's strings be cut. "Bev, I didn't mean it like that. You didn't do anything wrong."

"But it *is* my fault." A bag slides off her shoulder and hits the ground and some kind of bean spills out.

"What's that?" It looks disgusting.

"Oh." Her eyes light up.

"Please tell me you didn't have me commit a felony for a bag full of beans," Clark says. "Because if so, that's a violation of our friendship."

She reaches into the bag. "Not just beans. There're mushrooms, too!"

He's going to strangle her—right in front of us.

"We should call the Demon Council," Xander says. "We need to clear the air."

Bevin swallows slowly. "About that."

"What?" I panic a little bit. "As someone who just killed a demon-spawn they sent, I think we should have a plan in place before we invite them over."

"It may be too late for that," Bevin says.

"Excuse me?"

From the stairwell, there's a strange scraping sound. "About that," a deep voice says, "I believe she's referring to our presence. Now that she's descended twice, she can sense others like her." He smiles at Bevin in a disturbingly paternal way, his three-piece suit impossibly dated and somehow still elegant. "You're really coming right along. I'm so proud of your progress." He climbs the last few steps, barely using the cane he's carrying. His silvery hair almost floats around his head, shifting between other colors I can't quite identify as the shadowy light in the hall changes.

"Screw you," Bevin says.

"Feisty," he says. "I love it. Coming along, indeed."

Demon-spawn really are whack. And this guy is strange to look at—at once old and young, in control and raging.

"This is Aquarius Silvertongue," Bevin says. "And I think it's fair to say he speaks for the Demon Council."

"Then please," Clark says. "Come inside." He points at Minerva's front door.

"Do you think that's wise?" Xander asks, at the same time as I say, "I'm coming too."

"The whole gang is here," Aquarius says. "How delightful. I've brought a few friends along as well." He gestures and a nightmarish creature that looks like a walking octopus slither-flops up behind him.

"What the heck is that?" I ask.

Its tentacles flip over backward, revealing a hideous

head with a dinner plate-sized round mouth full of teeth. It hisses, and I want to cry.

I stumble backward and bump into Clark, who has just done the same.

"This is Horatius—they like to eat most anything, and they don't like being othered, so please use they when referring to them."

"I'll keep that in mind," I say. "Maybe we can find them a tin of biscuits or something. They look hungry."

"This is my partner, Violette Cassiopeia." Aquarius shifts and out of nowhere, a woman springs into being. "She possesses the ability to conceal herself." His bemused smile is also proud, like he owns her in some way.

The fact that he acts the same way about Bevin makes me furious. And it's super gross.

"A pleasure to meet you all." Her body sparkles and shimmers, as if stars are somehow pulsing beneath her skin. Her black hair provides a startling contrast, and her bright purple eyes look as close to the images I've seen of the akero as anyone else I've ever met. "It pains me to notify you that tonight is your final petition from the guild to join us." She stares pointedly at Bevin. "I hadn't expected that we'd wind up here, down to the wire, so to speak."

"Why don't you all come inside," Xander says. And then he opens Minerva's door and gestures.

"You never invite a demon-spawn in," Clark hisses.

"Too late now," Xander says. "Let's go."

To my surprise, the octopus thing, the gorgeous lady, and the silver-headed man all waltz right through the door. I know it's warded and cross-warded with things that keep out anyone who means harm—I'm surprised that even with an invite, they could enter.

Then again, they don't mean Bevin harm, as long as she agrees to join them.

And swear a few horrible oaths, I'm sure.

"Xander?" Minerva's voice floats over from the direction of her room. I had no idea she was home across the hall, or I'd have been shouting as loudly as I could earlier.

Although, now that I think about it, I remember that I couldn't get my throat or voice to work after that blow. I must have been in really bad shape before I robbed Xander of his power or whatever.

"Minerva," Xander says. "I've invited a few guests inside to talk about Bevin's position on joining the Demon Guild."

My neighbor and friend ducks out of her room, sets her feet shoulder-width apart, and clenches both her hands. "There's not much talking to be done. They can't force her. We won't allow it." Her eyes flash.

"Easy guys," Bevin says. "I've given it a lot of thought. And I've decided to pledge."

Every face in the entire room goes slack with shock. Even mine, I'm sure.

Roxana has sprinted out from her room, too. "But you said—"

"Why?" Clark asks.

"No way," Xander says.

Minerva's holding her wand. "We will never let—"

"I love you guys," Bevin says. "That's why. Izaak was almost killed—and their deadline hadn't even passed yet. I can't keep letting things that are all my fault cause issues for you." She shoves the bag of beans into Minerva's hands. "Keep this for me, okay?"

"You're not going anywhere," Aquarius says with a smile. "You can continue to live your life as you did before. Your friends can still be your friends, if they so choose."

"Sure, sure, devil man," Bevin says.

"It's viceroy to you," he says, but he's clearly enjoying this.

"Whatever you say, Viceroy Devil." Bevin may be acquiescing, but she's still the same Bevin.

Maybe it really won't matter.

The sick feeling in my stomach doesn't believe it, but I can hope.

"Do we need to leave?" Bevin asks.

"Our ceremony isn't long, and it's not a secret," Aquarius says. "First you need to kneel before us."

"I'll tell you what to say," Violette says.

"Goodie." Bevin glares up at her, but it's not the usual Bevin. She almost looks like she wants to hate her, but doesn't quite.

"First, state your name and your marks and powers," Violette demands.

"My name is Bevin Bahar, and I have the marks of a forked red tail and retractable claws. I have the power of static cling and an unknown second power."

"Unknown?" Violette tilts her head, but she looks pleased for some reason. "It hasn't yet manifested?"

Bevin shakes her head.

Aquarius rubs his hands together. "The longer it takes, the better. Stronger powers sometimes have to be *encouraged* to appear." He steps closer. "Before the oaths, perhaps we start the bond itself."

"The what?" Xander asks.

"The bond," Aquarius says. "It's not unlike the wolf bond, in fact, but it's much more unique. Only demons can siphon energy from it, for example, not us demon-spawn. But it creates the link to them." He pulls a chalice from a pouch hanging off his belt. "You'll need to drink a little blood—we are demon-spawn, after all." Before I can even react, he whips out a knife and slices a gash on his arm.

I've never been keen on demon-spawn, but the smell of this particular one's blood is like kettle corn in the crisp autumn air. I shift closer without even meaning to.

Violette shoves me. "Back off, bloodsucker. It's not meant for your kind."

"You could be a little more creative with your insults," I say.

"Keep away. You're lucky we're even letting you stay alive." She turns back toward the chalice, which is now full of delicious-smelling demon-spawn blood.

"I'm a level five demon-spawn," Aquarius says. "This should create quite a strong bond." He hands it to Bevin.

Her hand retreats at first, but then she grits her teeth and takes it. "I have to drink all this?"

Aquarius nods. "A few drops would probably be fine, but tradition says you down it all."

She lifts the chalice to her lips, her grimace deepening. Before she's even had a drop, she makes a choking sound.

"It's over quick," Violette says, as if she too struggled with this.

"Thanks." I can't tell whether she's being sarcastic or not. But then she presses the cup to her mouth and tips it back again.

I can't tell whether she actually drinks any, or whether the second it hits her mouth, the blood explodes. The cup's blown from Bevin's hand, and blood spatters all over Minerva's apartment.

Boy, she is going to be pissed about that. Once I spilled a cup of grape juice and her eyes popped out like a frog being squeezed by a teenage boy.

"No," Aquarius says. "How can this be?"

"What?" Bevin's hand is smoking where blood hit it. Her entire body is glowing with golden light.

"You're already bonded." He frowns. "But you can't be—" And then his head swivels to take in Xander.

Who is also glowing.

This is not going to be good.

"You can't be bonded for the daimoni, because somehow this wolf has already bonded you." Aquarius glowers. "But you're not a wolf."

Bevin's whole face scrunches up. "What?"

"He's an alpha—this mangy, pathetic, half-wolf is somehow still an alpha," Violette says.

"So that was true," I say.

"What?" Bevin asks again.

"And we just found out I had bonded you guys," Xander says. "It's not like I've been keeping some nefarious secret."

"That's true," I say. "I called his dad, and before that, we had no idea."

"Wait, you knew?" Bevin asks.

"Like, for less than an hour," I say. "We were about to tell everyone when. . ." I gesture at the demon-spawn glaring at us. "The idiot brigade showed up and started threatening you."

"Where is Odeon?" Aquarius asks, as if it's just now

occurring to him. "The demon-spawn we sent to encourage Bevin to swear?"

"About that," I say.

"He's gone," Bevin says. "I disposed of him—and I don't feel bad about it. You sent him to kill a member of *my* pack."

Aquarius rises up, his shoulders squaring, his eyes snapping, and his hair fluffing out as if it's charged with electricity. "You can not *be* part of a pack. It's not possible. He's a wolf—you're a demon-spawn."

"Well, I'm also a person, and we can make choices. I'll never choose to join with the daimoni, but I *choose* to be part of his pack." As she says the words, the entire room floods with light—Xander and Bevin both shining like the sun itself.

And then the light blinks out, and they're back to both softly glowing, like before.

All of us stare, dumbfounded.

Until Violette says, "Alphas are only bonded. . .until they die."

"You can't kill him," I say. "He's our alpha."

"Only hers, vampire," Aquarius says. "There's no way a half-wolf and a level two spawn can withstand us."

"Oh, but that's where you're wrong," I say. "He's also my alpha, by my choice. I'll stand by him today, tomorrow, and forever."

Another enormous flash occurs then, emanating from Xander and then from me.

"And me as well," Minerva says. "He's my alpha, today, tomorrow, and forever."

"And mine," Roxana says. "Xander Binnigas is the alpha I choose today, will follow tomorrow, and that I will serve well as long as he needs me."

"Wait for me," Clark says. "He's my alpha too, and the best one a guy could ever meet. I choose him to be my alpha, whatever that means, for better or worse, in sickness and health."

"Whoa, fam, you're not marrying him," I say.

Clark blushes. "Right, but I choose him today, tomorrow, and forever."

The flash this time is so bright that I can't see a single thing for at least a minute. When my eyes do start working again, the demon-spawn are glaring at us.

"You will regret this decision," Aquarius says. "The Council will never accept it. If you thought we were bad before. . ." He waves his hand and they storm out the door.

Good riddance.

But as I look around the room, Bevin doesn't look upset about their threats before their departure.

She's beaming.

21

MINERVA

I always knew there was something wrong with me.

Clark cast his first spell when he was only five. I still remember it with perfect clarity.

Mom dropped a vase full of water and fresh-cut flowers. It was headed for the floor where it would shatter, ruining the floor, the vase, and Mom's mood, in that order.

Only, it didn't crash. It froze in place a few inches from the ground.

Clark's hand was outstretched, his fingers trembling slightly. He had uttered the word "float" in English—using Latin is a tradition to keep us focused and to prevent accidental spells, but it's not necessary—and it had floated.

Mom was so proud. She told everyone she saw for weeks. She cast spell after spell to preserve those flowers, because letting them finally wither was like letting go of the precious miracle of her talented little angel.

Meanwhile, *I* showed no signs of any kind of magic for the first decade of my life.

I was so late manifesting that Mom and Dad put me in a *Magic for Dummies* class. They didn't call it that, of course. *Basic Spellcraft and Intuitive Casting*, that was the name. It was taught by the most moronic wizard I had ever met.

He was a painter by trade, because he couldn't cast the spells the way most people could. He had a knack for nature magic and used all natural ingredients, which was probably for the best. He kept confusing the water from cleaning his brushes with his glass of ice water, which was at least humorous, even if it wasn't great for his health. But after weeks and weeks of extra classes, still nothing. Mom was worried I was a magical dud—I heard her say that on the phone to one of her friends.

I began to worry about the same thing.

Years later, I had pretty much given up. Mom and Dad held out a little hope still—some of the strongest witches and wizards didn't manifest until quite late—but I was reconciled to the fact that I was a lost cause.

I was fourteen the first time I cast a real spell, and it was a total accident. Mom still insists I'm lying about it when I bring it up, but I know it happened. I got my period three months into my freshman year, and it stained my jeans so badly that I refused to leave the bathroom. I was standing there, staring down at the deep red stains on the crotch of my pants, sobbing.

And then I heard some girls talking.

"Is she gone, then?" I recognized her voice. Her name was Belladonna.

"She didn't come back to class after lunch," Hemlock said.

"Good riddance. Maybe she transferred to human school."

"She's a dud for sure," another girl I couldn't identify said.

Fury flooded into me in that moment—replacing my usual shame and fear.

"I wish you'd all be stuck in a stall, just like me," I muttered. "And that I could be wearing your clean clothing while you bawl your eyes out."

In that moment, the world around me shifted. Then everything began to vibrate. The three girls cried out. . .and suddenly I was standing outside the stall. I was wearing not one, not two, but three pairs of bottoms. A plaid skirt, a pair of jeans, and a pair of leggings.

I darted into the one empty bathroom stall, peeled the skirt and jeans off, and raced to the nurse.

It honestly didn't occur to me until later that those three girls must have been stuck in the stalls—without their pants. I only heard the next day that Hemlock emerged wearing stained jeans that were too short. People mocked her so much that she wound up transferring schools.

My spellcraft wasn't great after that, but at least I could manage some of the basics. And I never told anyone but my mother about the bathroom stall mix-up.

She didn't believe me, so why bother telling anyone else?

But now, standing in my own living room, with three demon-spawn who have vanished and a pulsing bond in the back of my brain tying me to a werewolf, I can't help wondering how many magical things we take as a given, but we don't truly understand.

Sure, I'm half-human, but maybe that's not always bad. I doubt any of those other girls could have place-swapped with me if they'd been fuming in a stall. And that's not the only strange spell I've managed to pull off. Maybe it's *because* my spellcraft is weaker that I'm able to do things no one else thinks are possible.

Maybe my human parent gave me a gift. Maybe it freed me from what mages think is possible.

"You're our alpha," Izaak says. "I still can't believe it."

"It's pretty cool," Bevin says. "How did you find out?"

"That you could accept the bond?" Xander looks like someone zapped him with all the electricity from the entire grid. "I was told you couldn't. That it wasn't possible."

"I'm beginning to think that people are wrong a lot," I say.

Clark laughs. "I've known that for a while."

"What does it mean, though?" Roxana asks. "Do we have to do whatever you say now?"

"Please." Xander shakes his head.

"But isn't that usually how it works?" I ask. "I mean, maybe you won't make us, but you could, right?"

"Try it on me," Izaak says. "Tell me that I. . . have to buy a sandwich and then give it to you."

"I'd be paying for it anyway," Xander says. "Maybe I *should* get a sandwich once in a while."

"I'm serious," Izaak says.

"And so am I," Xander says.

But I realize that we all want to know. What did we just agree to?

"Look," Xander says. "It's irrelevant. You know I would never order any of you around."

"I guess not," Clark says. "But maybe we should come up with some rules."

"I'll grab the paper and a pen." I practically sprint across the floor—this is the part I love most—list making. But I trip on a bag as I move. Mushrooms and pastries roll out of it. "What's this?" I pick up the bag and a folder falls out, papers spreading all over the floor.

Blank pages.

"Um." I hate clutter. Why would someone bring a bag with weird food and blank paper over and just leave it on the floor? Are they trying to torture me? Then I remember that Bevin shoved it into my hands before the demonic crap hit the wall.

"That's the bag Bevin made me steal," Clark says. "What exactly is it?"

"You can't see anything written on that folder?" Bevin asks.

I look at the papers, squinting to try and force myself to focus. "Should I be able to?"

"What about the folder itself?" Bevin asks. "Still nothing?"

I pick it up and stare at it. It looks like a blank manila folder. "Uh, no. Should I be seeing something dire?"

"Not dire," Bevin says. "But it has your name on it."

"My name?" I squint even more. Still nothing.

"What else does it say?" I ask. "Where did you get it from?"

"Maybe that's a sign." Bevin takes it out of my hands and begins gathering the papers into a pile. "Maybe you shouldn't—"

"Oh, no." I snatch them back from her. "If it has my name on it, it's mine. And you better start explaining where you found it, and why you made Clark help you—"

"Not help," he says. "I had to commit a felony to retrieve it from a US Postal Service box."

"Wait." I turn to face Bevin again. "A US Postal Service box?" I lift one eyebrow. "This wouldn't have anything to do with you descending another level, would it?"

Her shoulders slump. "I stole it." She shuffles backward. "From the Angel Council."

"Please tell me you're kidding." Clark glares at her for a moment before he stands up and starts pacing. "And I abetted the theft—unknowingly—but still."

"You're telling me that if you saw a folder that had your sister's name on it, and it was in the angel council's—"

A vein is popping out on Clark's forehead. "I wouldn't steal it!" His face is bright red. "Not from the akero. Have you ever heard of a phone? Snap a few photos, geez."

"Huh, I didn't think of that." Bevin sinks into the edge of the sofa and folds her arms across her chest. "It's not like it was *the akero's* folder. The Council's just a group of people whom they chose to kind of, like, run the boring stuff they don't care about."

"It's only the people the *akero chose?*" Clark's getting more shrill by the second. "Can you hear yourself right now?"

Xander slams his hand down on the kitchen table. "Stop."

They both immediately fall silent. I guess we're seeing firsthand what he can do. He stumbles back then, his eyes widening. "Sorry."

"They needed it," I say. "Now back to these blank pages." I thrust them at Bevin. "Are you saying you can read them?"

She glances at them, and then her eyes flit back up to mine. "Do you care whether I can read them?"

"Of course I do," I practically shout. "The angels have a file on me?"

"They had one on Clark too," I say. "I think they have one on all descendants of the original angel-spawn."

"Mages," Clark says. "They keep files on all mages."

"But why didn't you steal his?" I ask. "Why are we only looking at mine?"

Bevin yawns. "His was a snooze fest, like always. School. Marriage. Divorced. Yada yada."

"But mine isn't boring?" I can't help narrowing my eyes.

"It's longer by a factor of ten or more than anyone else's I saw," Bevin says. "And it has all kinds of things written in it."

"Like what?"

"Can you read a name?" Bevin asks. "Like a name you saw on another file, maybe?"

"Just say it," Izaak says. "If you know something about her, just tell her already."

"I think she's supposed to figure it out herself," Bevin says. "I'll tell her if she can't, but don't you think she would be able to read her own file?"

"But clearly she can't," Clark says.

"And neither can you." Bevin spins around on Clark, shooting to her feet again, her hands falling on her hips. "It probably needs a key, idiot. Did you think of that?"

Clark blinks. "No. I didn't."

"And if I go smashing it open, it might break." She shakes her head. "You two are both terrible mages."

"I'm not." Clark scowls at her. "I'm a high-level one."

Bevin laughs. "At best, you're intermediate."

"Do I really need to yell at you two again?" Xander asks.

"A key." I'm still staring at the pages. "I need a key."

Keys are oddly shaped, usually, with a unique pattern on their teeth that grants entry only to them. Often, if someone needs to use one for something magical, they'll have the key already in their possession, even if they don't know what it's for. It's something that maybe stood out to them, but that made no real sense.

Its purpose only becomes clear when it fits in the lock nothing else could open. Suddenly, the two strange words I've been mulling over for weeks pop into my mind.

My dad's named Holden Lucent. My mother's name is Melina Blitz, now Lucent. But they're not really my parents. They adopted me. The one name I do know for my actual birth father is Mario Leehack.

And it's a strange name.

Human names often are, so I tried not to obsess. Unlike mages, they're not always named after some form of light. Their last names could come from anywhere, really. Their job. The place their ancestors are from. Their style of dress or their quirks and oddities.

But I looked up 'Mario Leehack' and didn't find a single person with that name. Not a single one—not in the United States, and not in other countries, either. Humans have one naming convention in common with us. The parents pass the surname along to their children. So there should at least be *some* Leehacks, but there aren't.

Why is my dad's name so odd?

And then, in front of my eyes, that strange name flashes across the middle of the top sheet of paper.

Mario Leehack, shifting, moving, spelled out in big, bold, black letters.

And then the letters swirl, like if I threw a knife into a cup of beautifully arranged coffee and swiveled it around, ruining the pattern entirely. What once made sense is now only a disarranged blur.

Loimar hackee. Ekelo Mihciar. A dozen other combinations flash in front of my eyes until the letters finally stop rearranging. And they form into a new pair of words.

Words I can't believe at all.

Words that make no sense.

Words that should not be on my file.

"What does it say?" Clark asks. "It looks like you've figured it out. Have you?"

"Yes, what does it say?" Bevin echoes.

The words written across the file Bevin says bears my name are: Michael Akero.

"No," I lie. "It says nothing."

"I think it says your dad's name," Bevin says. "And I think you know exactly who he is."

"What are you talking about?" I ask. "Why would the words written on my file be his name?" I can't quite help laughing for some reason, but it's not a normal laugh. It's high and shrill.

Bevin smiles, a genuine, full-fledged smile. "I met someone at the angel council, you know. She was one of the kindest, one of the best people I have ever met. Her name was Zintrel."

"Zintrel?" Clark's head whips toward me, our eyes locking.

"Do you know someone with that name?" Bevin asks.

"Because if you do, that's even stranger, don't you think?"

"Our aunt is named Zintrel," I say, "but we never get to see her. She did something very bad, so she's been locked up for a long time. Dad missed her a lot."

Bevin walks toward me. "The Zintrel I met had never done anything wrong in her life." She leans closer and whispers, "Other than being born, that is."

"What does that mean?" Xander asks.

"She's angel-spawn," Bevin says. "And unlike us, the akero keep their children locked away, fearing they might Ascend to become full-fledged angels and wreck the precious balance of power between the akero and daimoni."

"And break the universe itself," Clark says. "That's what they teach us in school."

"I think your aunt was an angel-spawn," Bevin says slowly. "And I think you are, too."

"What?" Nothing she's saying makes sense. The Angel Michael, the leader of the akero, definitely can't be my father. She must have seen something different on that paper.

But I did see his name.

It makes no sense.

"What exactly did you see?" Bevin asks again.

"Does it matter?" I ask.

"I think it does," Clark says.

"I want to know," Xander says.

"Me too," Izaak says.

"And me," Roxana says.

"It said Michael Akero," I whisper.

"I think your dad knew what happened to his sister

and thought it was wrong," Bevin says. "I think he decided to prevent the same thing from happening with you. Only redacting who you really are could have kept you safe. That, and letting everyone else believe you're half-human."

What she's saying— "But I'm a magical disaster. That can't be true." Then I start to think of small things —like the bizarre swap that was my first spell. The tingling I feel when I know a spell that doesn't exist will work if only I cast it.

And bonding a familiar who wasn't even in the room.

As if she can read my mind, Giggles lands on my shoulder and coos.

And then she spreads her wings and flaps them, and they flash bright white. For a split second, she's not a pigeon. She's much larger, much brighter, and much more beautiful.

It's about time. The words fly through my head, as if said in a startlingly clear voice.

I swallow, not quite able to believe it.

You should believe it.

I jump, and she flutters off my shoulder.

To think, you wanted to bond that stupid, fire-blowing idiot. He would have wrecked everything.

My jaw drops.

Trust me. You're better off without him.

"Are you alright?" Clark's standing right next to me, and I was so distracted that I didn't notice.

I blink. "I'm fine."

"You're kind of staring at your bird," Roxana says. "Want me to lock it in that cage?"

NEVER AGAIN.

Apparently the cage isn't very well liked.

I hear laughing in my head. *The worst part was*

pretending that I couldn't get out. Like that stupid wire thing could ever have contained me.

"I think you might be right," I say. "I may not be a half-human witch after all."

"Whoa," Roxana says. "Do you really think that the Angel Michael may be your dad?"

I shrug. "Is it really any crazier than everything else that's happened to us this week?"

"Yes," they all say at once.

And I realize. . . they're right. This changes everything.

22

XANDER

No matter what's going on in my life, the streets of New York can always calm me down. There are so many people doing so many things—it never fails to remind me that I'm small in this great big world. I'm a teeny, tiny part of the microcosm of humanity that exists around me.

That might seem depressing to some people, but that perspective has always calmed me down. Nothing that's going on with me can really be *that* bad. It's a small part of a very great whole.

Last night, something that should never have happened—shouldn't have *been able* to happen—did. Five non-wolves accepted my bond, and now I'm their alpha.

I have a pack—the exact one I'd have chosen if I knew I could.

I've longed to have a pack for my entire life, and here I am, living the weirdest version of that dream that anyone could ever have conceived of. Now that I think about it, that's my life to a T. If I wanted an ice cream cone as a kid, I could be sure I'd end up with a home-made popsicle. If I wanted a beach vacation, I'd end up on some kind of pile of sand Mom would move from my backyard sandbox to the two feet in front of my bathtub.

And later, she'd make *me* clean it up.

Nothing in my life ever goes quite like I want.

And here, again, I'm finding that to be true.

Only, for the first time, I'm okay with it. I've never been welcomed by wolves. I've never been accepted as part of what and who they are. I was always *less than*. I was always attacked and belittled and abused. But my friends?

They've always built me up.

So this morning's walk—induced by the panic of realizing that I may have a pack, but I still have no job or plans—is actually helping more than I expected. All these people around me have jobs. They all have work for which they're being paid that has nothing to do with what or who they *are*. It has to do with what they *want to do* and who they *want to be*. And for the first time, it feels like what I want might actually matter.

What is it like to choose an occupation based on your likes and dislikes, instead of your innate instincts, like being a shredder? I've never really thought about it, because that was never an option for me. But now that it is, it feels like the sky is the limit.

"I could be President of the United States of America!" I shout.

"Not likely," a short man next to me mutters.

I can't help my chuckle. He's right, of course. I'm already in my twenties. There are definitely some things that aren't going to happen. But for the most part, I can do and try anything at all.

That doesn't mean that I have any idea what to do or try, but at least I can explore it. Within reason. Like, until my savings run out. It's not like being a werewolf enforcer paid all that well, and poor Izaak hasn't ever contributed much.

Izaak!

He has a real job that's making actual money. Maybe he can pay the rent for a few months. That would be a nice change. A change I probably shouldn't count on. The last time he got a fat paycheck, he came home with a human-sized Statue of Liberty that we now use as a hat rack. He's not exactly the smartest with budgets. Or home decor.

I doubt there will be much left for rent.

And that's when it hits me that the rent is subsidized. . .by a pack I'm no longer affiliated with. I should find a new occupation relatively quickly, assuming I'd prefer not to live on the streets. I'm going to need a job to get a new apartment.

I start running through options in my head. Accountant—but I'd need a special college degree I don't have for that one. Talent manager? Izaak and his friends are always complaining about theirs. On second thought, I'd rather not be someone whom everyone hates. Plus, I'm not sure what they do, exactly, so it would be hard to try and do it.

So far, none of these things sound very promising. I'm tapping a basic career selection search into my phone—there must be a personality quiz or something for this—when someone calls my name.

"Xander Binnigas," he says again, his tone commanding.

My head snaps up, and I spot the speaker immediately.

It's Lo Ren Fang.

And he's pissed.

"Oh, hey man."

"Hey man?" At least a dozen other wolves are standing not-so-casually behind him. Three women, and ten men.

This isn't great.

The most concerning thing is that his mate isn't present. No alpha brings his mate to a fight—they won't risk having their focus split. I really hope that's not why Rylan's not around this morning.

Because I'm alone.

This is looking very, very bad.

"I heard you found a pack who wants you for their alpha," Lo Ren says.

I open my mouth to answer, and then realize I have no idea what to say. It *is* true, but it's not what I'm doing.

"I think Jewel's a desperate idiot, but that's not why I'm here."

"Gee," I say. "I guess this is where I ask why you *are* here?" I point behind him. "Is it for the Best Coffee in New York?" I smirk. "Because they apparently have it."

Lo Ren scowls.

"You know, that look might have more effect on me if I'd ever seen you *not* scowling. You should try smiling sometimes—it could make you scarier when you scowl. It might even lower your blood pressure. They say it's the quiet killer."

"Other wolves complained about your bad jokes," Lo Ren says, "but this is the first time I've heard them."

"Probably because I'm no longer hoping to join your pack," I say. "I don't need you any more."

"About that." Lo Ren gestures and several wolves fan out, clearing the area of bystanders. I wonder if they brought spelled charms. I'd guess the normies who are swearing under their breaths and walking around the other direction are seeing some kind of street construction and a detour sign.

"Yes, benevolent overlord? What about it?" I may sound flippant, but inside I'm freaking out. My brain's doing the equivalent of a tiny dog that's running around in circles, peeing on the floor, and chewing his own tail. In my experience, actually doing any of those things rarely improves the situation, so I'm trying to cover for it with jokes and lots of smirking.

"If you're no longer trying to join my pack, you're no longer allowed to be in Manhattan."

How had I not even considered that he might kick me out?

I knew I had to find a new apartment. Why didn't it occur to me that wolves are territorial? "So, Yonkers?" I ask. "Or like, Jersey? How close is too close?"

"You were never very smart." Cliff spits on the ground next to him. "You should have already been gone."

"I'll give you one day to leave for Waterbury," Lo Ren says. "And that's being generous."

"And what if I say no?" I ask. "Is this where you pretend you think I'm fraying and say you'll have to eliminate me again?"

Lo Ren's frown deepens.

I have a split second to decide how to play this. Now that I'm an alpha, if I clear out, I'll essentially have to tell my friends we need to move. If we stay, I'll be dragging them into this fight. Both of those options are very bad. Both of those things leave them worse off than they were before.

My only way to take care of this without them. . .is to sacrifice myself. Because I'm also the only one who needs a pack bond. They pledged to follow me, but they were all nervous about what it really meant. None of them really wanted me ordering them around, and at the end of the day, that's what it will happen sometimes, even if it's inadvertent.

I won't order them to move, of course, or to fight a two-hundred-wolf pack, but it'll come down to one or the other.

Unless I let them eliminate me.

At least I'll have had a pack during my lifetime. At least I'll have known what it felt like to belong. Surprisingly, I'm at peace with it. Dying to keep my friends safe feels like the right thing to do.

"I hate to say this," I say, "believe me, I really do, but I have no plans of leaving. I didn't actually join Jewel's pack, so I'm going to stay right here."

"But you do have a pack now," Lo Ren says. "I can sense it."

I shrug. "I'm not sure what kind of weird things you can smell, but I swear, I have not bonded a single wolf."

Lo Ren sniffs. "That smells true."

Wolves can often smell lies—perspiration, combined with heart rate and adrenaline, have a certain scent. "It is true."

"Then how—"

"I'm not moving, and I have no wolves following

me," I say. "You can tell I'm not lying, so decide what action you're going to take."

Lo Ren's nostrils flare, and his hands clench.

"I say we kill him," Cliff says. "We should've done it years ago."

Silvie shifts closer to Lo Ren. "But the Oracle—"

Lo Ren waves his hand at her. "No."

"No?"

The Manhattan alpha straightens up, his eyes hardening. "I'm done worrying about that. Cliff's right. We need to just eliminate the threat."

"Do you feel like using the word eliminate makes you sound smarter?" I ask. "Because the word kill actually sounds more bad-a."

"Go," Lo Ren says.

There's no way I can fight a dozen wolves. I'll be ripped to shreds immediately. And apparently no matter how willing I am to sacrifice myself, I'm always holding out hope that there's another way out.

"Wait." I hold up my hand. "You've had me fight the other shredders for years, using your alpha power every time I came close to winning to ensure I always lost. You hid the fact that I'm an alpha from them and from me. And now I'm wondering if maybe the reason you never fought me yourself is that. . .have you been afraid of me all this time? What did this oracle say? Is it something like, I'll kill you and marry your mother? Because I've seen her. She's not half bad."

Lo Ren's scowl finally shifts. Into a look of pure rage.

"In school, I thought the whole Oedipus thing was gross, but now I'm thinking maybe it was misunderstood. She's not *my* mom, after all. Because my mom's normie." I tap my lip. "Oh, wait, speaking of. . .you've been afraid of a halfie all this time? Isn't that kind of pathetic? How does Rylan feel about that?"

The low growl that comes from the base of his throat changes into a full-fledged roar as he shifts on the fly, bounding toward me. I ought to shift. I really ought to change into wolf form to match his. It's harder to reach my throat with the thick fur. I'm better able to match his movements. And the normies will be able to more easily dismiss us as dogs fighting.

But when I pull to shift—nothing happens. Is it because I'm now bonded to non-wolves? What's going on?

It hits me then—I really am about to die.

"Hey, you're one ugly dog," Roxana says behind me. "Has anyone ever told you that?"

Lo Ren pulls up short, his mouth opening, and his tongue lolling out.

"He didn't bond wolves, you idiot," Roxana says. "He bonded a dragon." She throws her hands up as hard and as fast as she can. . .but nothing happens. She does it again, and a few sparks fly away from her, like she struck a flint rock with a rod.

"That was a lot cooler in my head," she mutters.

"*Stupefaciunt*," Clark says, his wand swishing.

Lo Ren freezes in that dopey pose, drool dripping from the side of his mouth. For a single heartbeat, and then one more, none of the other wolves react. But then they all snarl at once and they lunge for us.

"This is a terrible way to start a Saturday morning," Clark says, "for the record."

"Why are you here?" I ask.

"Where else would we be?" Izaak asks, jogging around the corner. He's wheezing so hard, I'm worried he'll asphyxiate and die. "Geez. I should really be in better shape, shouldn't I?"

"*Nolite ube es,*" Minerva says, appearing seconds after Izaak.

The entire area in front of me flashes bright green. . .and then a blob of gelatinous goo appears, capturing the mass of angry wolves inside it.

"What the heck is that?" Clark asks.

"It looks like Jello." Bevin's strolling along like she was headed for the spa or out on a nature walk. "Pretty cool, if you ask me."

"No one asked you," Minerva snaps. "It was supposed to stop them, and it did."

"It sure did," I say. "But what *is* it?"

"Look," she says. "Sometimes I can't help what fabulous things I do. I'm part angel, you know."

Clark starts laughing. "One little revelation, and she's impossible to live with."

"She wasn't exactly easy before," Roxana says.

But about thirty seconds later, the stun spell on Lo Ren wears off, and he straightens. He growls, but makes no move to attack us. He's too busy glancing over his shoulder at his Jello-encased pack.

"How did you know I needed you?" I ask again.

"That pulse you sent," Roxana says. "We figured it was like a bat signal."

"You're lucky Minerva had just made muffins," Izaak says, "or we might not all have been together. Clark's pretty good with directions, or we would not have gotten here so fast."

"You took a cab, didn't you?" I ask.

Lo Ren shifts then, snatching a free Autotrader sheet from a plastic box to cover his important bits.

"Wow, it's not *that* cold," Roxana says. "You should be careful where you change. People won't all be as nice as we are."

Lo Ren's eyes spark, but he chooses to ignore her. It's really the right call. What else is he going to say? We all saw it. "You bonded non-wolves?"

I shrug.

"It's not allowed."

"Funny," I say. "I was told *it's not possible*, but clearly *that's* not true."

"The Wolf Council will kill you for this."

"Will they?" I ask. "Or are you just wishing they would?"

"You can't live here," Lo Ren says. "It's my area."

I tap my lip. "Hmm, let's see. I bet that if I look, the bylaws say a new alpha can't establish a wolf pack in the same geographic location as an existing *wolf* pack. I wonder if they allow a lone wolf." I smile. "Oh, wait. They do! I know, because I already looked it up, before I came here in the first place."

"You have to leave our pack apartment immediately."

"Or how about this?" Roxana steps closer, her eyes darting down toward the newspaper pointedly. "You let us have the apartment, as an apology for attacking us, and then we don't tell everyone in the entire magical community that you have a teensy weensy weenie."

The muscles in Lo Ren's jaw work furiously.

"Or, you know, I could try the magical sparking thing again. The time before last it worked *really* well. I killed seven whole wolves with it, and they were almost as horrible as you."

"Get out of my sight," Lo Ren says.

"So that's a no to the apartment?" Clark asks.

The Jello appears to be melting, and the wolves trapped inside are starting to snarl and snap.

"I think it's a good time to go," Minerva says. "But you think about that apartment thing. Because if we don't hear from you one way or another, we'll assume you're giving it to us and we'll keep quiet. But if you *do* feel the need to take it away. . . Magical people are notoriously cruel. And alphas who see you as weak, well. . ." Minerva shrugs.

"We may not be wolves," Izaak says, "but our bite is still scary." He snaps at the air, and I suppress a laugh.

My friends may not be very scary, but they're mine, and I wouldn't trade my magical misfits for every wolf in America.

*** I hope you loved My Mongrel Pack. The third book will be out summer of 2024. I'm not sure the exact date yet, but it should be up on preorder soon. I'll announce it on FB and in my newsletter as soon as I know! You can sign up for my newsletter (and get a free book!) at www.BridgetEBakerWrites.com

If you enjoyed *My Mongrel Pack* and would like *more*, excellent! You might enjoy my Birthright Series, starting with Displaced, or you might like the Anchored Series, starting with Anchored. Both of those series are complete, so you won't have to wait for any books to be written.

ACKNOWLEDGMENTS

Big thanks to Demetrius Rouse *again*. This poor guy is a champ. He has family and work and life and he still gives so generously of his time to help my book be as good as it can be.

Huge thanks to my son Elijah, who is the biggest fan of this series.

And to my husband who is very patient with my frustrations and grumpiness when I'm behind on a deadline.

My ARC team and my readers are just the biggest cheerleaders and I love you all.

ABOUT THE AUTHOR

Bridget's a lawyer, but does as little legal work as possible. She has five kids and soooo many animals that she loses count.

Horses, dogs, cats, rabbits, and so many chickens. Animals are her great love, after the hubby, the kids, and the books.

She makes cookies waaaaay too often and believes they should be their own food group. In a (possibly misguided) attempt at balancing the scales, she kick-boxes daily. So if you don't like her books, maybe don't tell her in person.

Bridget is active on social media, and has a facebook group she comments in often. (Her husband even gets on there sometimes.) Please feel free to join her there: https://www.facebook.com/groups/750807222376182

The Anchored Series:

Anchored (1)

Adrift (2)

Awoken (3)

Capsized (4)

The Sins of Our Ancestors Series:

Marked (1)

Suppressed (2)

Redeemed (3)

Renounced (4)

Reclaimed (5) a novella!

A stand alone YA romantic suspense:

Already Gone

I also write women's fiction and contemporary romance under B. E. Baker.

The Scarsdale Fosters Series:

Seed Money

Nouveau Riche (2)

Minted (3)

Loaded (4)

The Finding Home Series:

Finding Grace (1)

Finding Faith (2)

Finding Cupid (3)

Finding Spring (4)

Finding Liberty (5)

The Birch Creek Ranch Series:

Children's Picture Book

9 781949 655810